THE IRISH HARPER

THE NORSEWOMEN
BOOK SEVEN

JOHANNA WITTENBERG

SHELLBACK STUDIO

BOOKS BY JOHANNA WITTENBERG

The Norsewomen Series

The Norse Queen

The Falcon Queen

The Raider Bride

The Queen in the Mound

The Queen of Hel

The Queen of War

The Irish Harper

THE IRISH HARPER

THE NORSEWOMEN BOOK 7

JOHANNA WITTENBERG

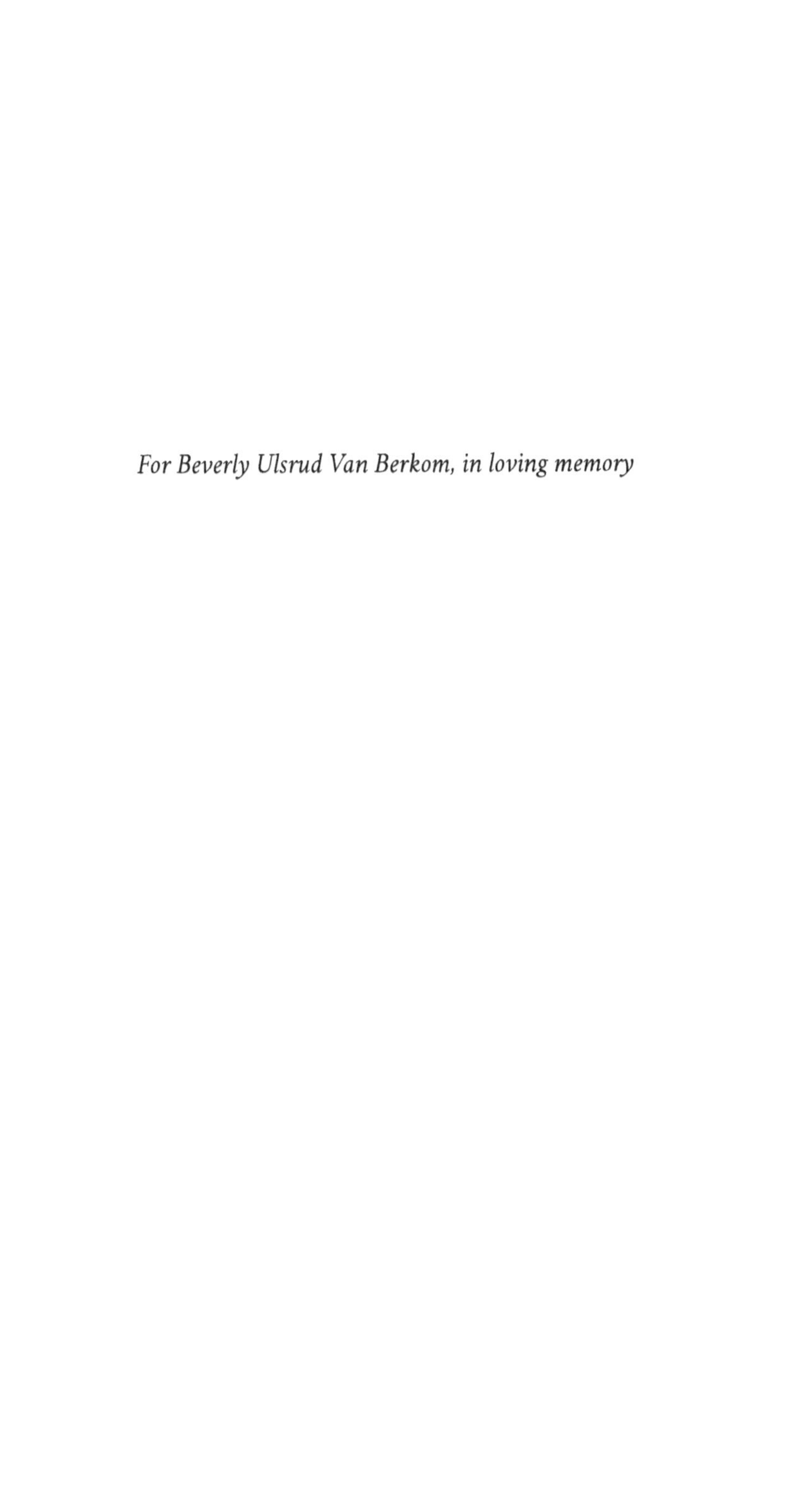

For Beverly Ulsrud Van Berkom, in loving memory

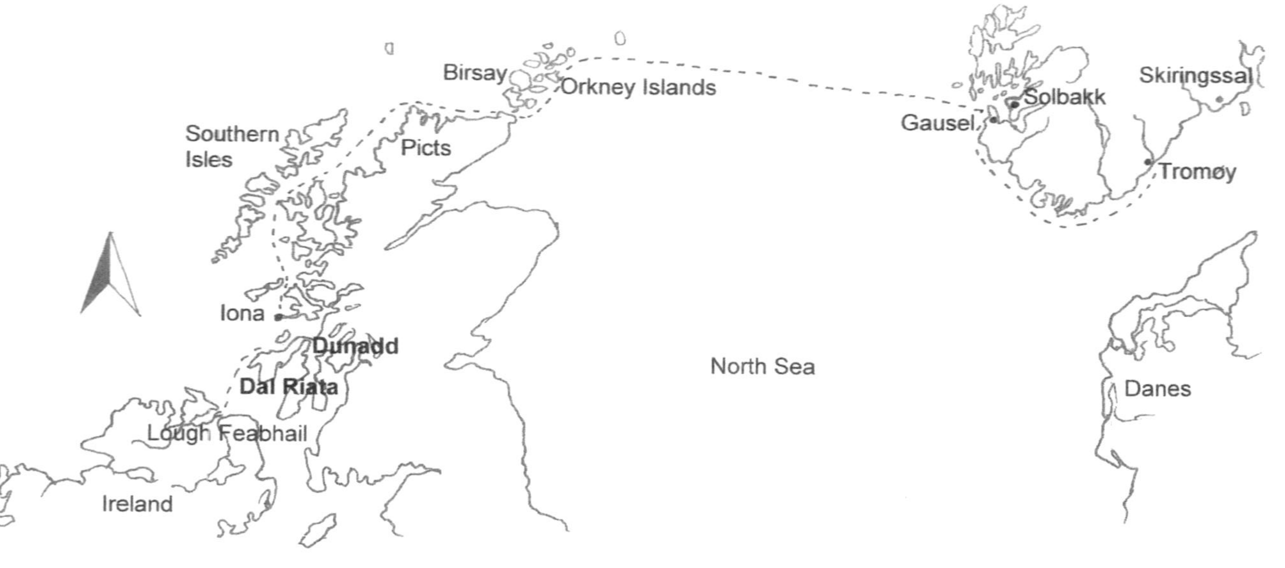

Skiringssal
Tromøy
Solbakk
Gausel
Danes
North Sea
Birsay
Orkney Islands
Picts
Southern Isles
Iona
Dunadd
Dal Riata
Lough Feabhail
Ireland

Atlantic Ocean
North Channel
Lough Súilí
Inish Eoghain
Tullynavin
Binevenagh
Lough Feabhail
Aileach
Dun Ciannacta
River Feabhail
Ireland
Daire Calgaich
Dun Geimhin

CHAPTER 1

Tromøy
August, AD 825

Åsa and Ragnhild surveyed the captured Danish vessels that rested on Tromøy's shore. They had recovered twenty-one ships abandoned by Horik when he fled in defeat. Alfgeir had chosen five of the most seaworthy to replace those he had lost in the battle with the Danish king. Olaf had also accepted seven replacements, some badly damaged. He'd left his second-in-command, Kalv, behind with his wounded húskarlar to sail them back to Skiringssal when both warriors and ships were mended.

Åsa had awarded Ragnhild one of the most seaworthy of the prizes, a karvi about the size of *Raider Bride*, with tholes for thirty oars. Its figurehead was a stag, its antlers pointed and sharp. The hull had sustained only cosmetic damage in the battle. The addition would bring Ragnhild's fleet to six ships, still small but a force to be reckoned with.

"You're very generous," she said to Åsa. "I feel a bit guilty accepting such a rich reward for what little fighting I did. The battle was nearly over when I got here. My crew sustained only minor injuries, and my ships were barely nicked by a few arrows and casting spears."

"I owe you more than I can repay," said Åsa. "You answered my call to war when I needed you most, even though you had a new baby at home."

Ragnhild felt a guilty twinge. She'd been more than happy to escape the restrictions of motherhood and answer Åsa's summons.

Åsa continued to heap on praise. "You arrived in time to turn the tide of battle against Horik. Your appearance was instrumental in forcing him to flee."

"Too bad he escaped."

Åsa sighed. "No doubt he'll cause more trouble for Tromøy once he's recovered."

Ragnhild grinned at the prospect. "I'll come to your aid again, anytime."

"That's what I'm hoping," Åsa said. "I'm sure you're anxious to get home."

Ragnhild nodded, fending off another guilty twinge. Glad as she'd been to answer Åsa's call to war and escape the onus of motherhood, and much as she'd reveled in being back in battle, she missed her husband and their four-month-old son, Herulf. The maternal urge, she thought ruefully. Something she'd never sought, but now it had her in its grips and there was no escape.

She embraced Åsa and turned to *Raider Bride*. Her crew was already aboard, their gear stowed.

"I appreciate you agreeing to take Cian home to Ireland." Åsa nodded toward the Irishman, seated on his sea chest on board *Raider Bride*. "I owe him my life, and Halfdan's as well." Cian had aided Åsa in her escape from Horik, and fought by her side in the sea battle against the Danes.

Åsa believed in paying her debts and had been generous with the Irishman. She'd outfitted him with a sea chest, two new sets of linen tunics and wool breeks, new leather boots, and a quilted, varnished battle jacket. One of Ulf's seaxes hung from its holder at his waist, an axe was tucked in his belt, and she'd given him a spear and a helmet from Tromøy's armory.

"I'm sorry to ask you to leave your child again so soon."

Ragnhild shrugged. "Your debts are mine." The truth was, she was eager to make the voyage to Ireland again. "If this fair weather holds, we'll get him to Ireland before winter. Herulf will be in better hands than mine." Liv, Herulf's fóstra, had several children of her own and knew her way around a baby, unlike Ragnhild, to whom a wailing child was a terror and a mystery. But one she couldn't wait to get back to. "I'll have the entire winter with him." Something she both longed for and dreaded.

Ragnhild turned her attention to assigning crew to the new prize. Three of the ships were commanded by her senior retainers, Thorgeir, Einar, and Svein. Einar's ship, *Eagle's Treasure*, was a captured Danish prize from an earlier battle, an even match for *Raider Bride* with thirty oars. Thorgeir commanded *Raven's Loot*, another Danish prize of similar size.

For this passage to Tromøy, Ragnhild had given charge of a smaller ship, *Sea Wolf*, to Unn, the eldest remaining of four sisters who had long sailed with Ragnhild. Farm-girls all, they'd taken up the shield and sword for a better life.

Sea Wolf had been Unn's first command. At nineteen winters old, she'd sailed around the cape and to Ireland more than once in Ragnhild's fleet. Unn was steady as a rock, and Ragnhild had complete faith in the girl.

Now with an extra ship to crew, Ragnhild conferred with her three húskarlar.

"Svein, you're the best choice to take charge of the newly captured Danish ship. Your expertise is needed for a ship of unknown handling qualities."

"Agreed," said Einar.

That left Svein's ship, *Wave Horse*, without a skipper.

"Do you think Ursa's ready for her first command?" At eighteen, Ursa was the next sister in line and the obvious choice, but Ragnhild felt a little uneasy about it. Unn had proven herself to be level-headed, but Ursa was another matter. She reminded Ragnhild of Helga, the eldest sister, who had been a talented warrior. But Helga's overconfidence had been her downfall. Ragnhild still winced at the memory of the girl's self-assured smile, just before an enemy sword had decapitated her.

Einar stroked his beard. "It's a bit soon, but what choice do we have? It's either her or leave the prize behind. Ursa's a good seaman with steady nerves."

Svein agreed. "*Wave Horse* is an easy ship to handle, and Ursa has sailed on it now for over a year."

Thorgeir nodded. "You were younger than her when you skippered *Raider Bride*."

"Yes, but I had you three on board to keep me out of trouble."

"We didn't succeed, though, did we?" Svein smirked. "We can leave my crew with her—they're experienced enough."

Ragnhild shook away her doubts. "It's settled then. Ursa will skipper *Wave Horse* with its existing crew. The two younger sisters will keep their positions on Einar's and Thorgeir's ships."

Ursa was coiling lines on *Wave Horse*. Ragnhild approached and leaned over the gunnel. "I've decided to give you command of this ship."

Ursa's eyes widened. "Oh, Lady, thank you! I won't let you down!"

"I wish I could send one of the húskarlar with you, but they each have their own ship to captain. I have confidence that you will be cautious, but not timid."

"That I will, Lady. You can count on me."

The other crew members grinned and congratulated Ursa. That was a good sign. She'd need their support.

The crew assignments finalized and orders given, Ragnhild strode to *Raider Bride* and climbed aboard. She took hold of the tiller and turned to wave at Åsa as Tromøy's hands heaved her ships off the beach.

Wave Horse's crew lined up in their places without any direction. Ragnhild felt better, knowing Ursa had experienced sailors to support her. As they fitted their oars and rowed out of the harbor, Ragnhild forced her gaze away from *Wave Horse* and studied Cian at his place on the rowing bench.

The Irishman was about her age and strong enough—slim with wiry muscles. She was happy to note that he pulled his weight on the oar. A few weeks of Tromøy's rich summer diet of pork and barley had begun to fill out his body, overworked and half-starved from three years of slavery to the Danish king Horik. Cian's hair and beard were light brown, his skin pale and freckled, his eyes a shade of gray like the sea on a stormy day. His hands displayed the long hooked fingernails of a harper, something Ragnhild had seen on professional harpers in the halls of Irish lords.

Åsa had heaped rewards upon him, and Ragnhild was bringing him home to Ireland, yet he did not seem overjoyed at having his wishes fulfilled. He never smiled, and there was a wary look about his eyes.

A breeze tickled Ragnhild's cheek, drawing her attention from the Irishman. She wet her finger and held it up to test the strength and direction of the wind. Enough to move the ship and from the right quarter. "Raise sail!" she shouted. Einar's crew were already throwing the ties off the sail on *Eagle's Treasure*, and Svein and Thorgeir were following suit. Ragnhild turned to *Wave Horse*, where Ursa's sailors were scrambling to get their sail unbound. They were doing all right.

Cries filled the air as sails bloomed from the masts of the six ships in succession. It made a pretty sight, and Ragnhild was proud of their skill, even if no one else was around to admire it.

The breeze held steady and enabled them to sail for a few hours, but as the afternoon warmed, the wind petered out. Ragnhild felt the tide's pull on the tiller ease as the current slackened. She signaled her fleet to drop sail and row through slack water, but as soon as she felt the quiver on the steering oar that told her the tide had turned against them, she directed them toward shore. They would just wear themselves out fighting the current, making little headway, if they didn't actually lose ground.

She sought a familiar cove where they'd sheltered before, with a sandy beach big enough to accommodate all six boat crews, near a freshwater spring. While the sailors pitched tents and topped off the water barrels, Ragnhild broke out barrels of good ale, some fresh mutton, and root vegetables Åsa had provided. Each crew built their own fire and dragged up driftwood logs to sit on.

Soapstone cauldrons were hung on tripods over the fires and the mutton set over it to stew with wild garlic, cabbages, and turnips. Her appetite whetted by the sea air and vigorous exercise, Ragnhild's mouth watered at the scent of cooking meat wafting in the air. She passed out flatbread to staunch the crew's hunger while they waited for the stew to be ready.

They broached a barrel of ale, and Cian brought out his harp. Ragnhild had listened to harpers in the halls of kings in Ireland, the status of the best of their kind second only to the kings they served. She recognized this young Irishman's exceptional ability.

Tonight he tuned his harp and gazed thoughtfully into the darkening sky. He struck a chord that sent a shiver down Ragnhild's spine. The talk ceased as Cian plucked his strings and began his tale in a deep, resonant voice. He spoke in fluent Norse, with the accent of the Danes acquired from his three years as Horik's slave, though the melody he played was pure Irish.

"You Norse have your Allfather, Odin," he declared. "The Irish have our own Allfather, the Dagda. He's the chief of the Tuatha Dé Danann, the children of the goddess Dana. We know them as the Fae folk. The Dagda is the wisest and most powerful of them, the forefather of the druids."

As Cian spoke, the power of his voice and the magical vibration of his harp seemed to cast a spell over the rowdy crew. Silence fell, and they listened with rapt attention.

"Like Odin, the Dagda has many names. He possesses three magical treasures…" Here Cian's fingers played a new melody. "A cauldron that can feed an army…" Another tune sounded from the harp. "His mighty staff, a single strike from its head could kill nine men…" Cian struck the lower strings with a deep resonance. "While the touch of its handle can raise the dead." Pure hope emanated from the upper strings.

Cian paused dramatically before plucking the harp again. "But the Dagda's most valued treasure is his cláirseach, Uaithne. With its music, the Dagda commands the seasons and the will of men.

"He plays three magical strains of music. First, the *Geantraí*, the melody of merriment." Cian played a tune that made his listeners tap their feet in time. "Then the *Goiltai*, the melody of sadness, that makes even hardened warriors weep uncontrollably." Cian's playing took on a melancholy air that sobered his audience. "And finally, the *Suantraí*, music that will bring sleep over the listeners." He strummed the harp strings in a soothing tune.

Just as eyes began to blink, Cian's voice smote the air and startled them all awake. "The Tuatha Dé Danaan were at war with the Fomorians, a race of giants hideously deformed by an ancient curse. The Fomorians were evil and violent, the sworn enemies of the Tuatha Dé Danaan. Their king was Balor of the Evil Eye." Cian's discordant notes raised gooseflesh on Ragnhild's arms.

Then he switched to a triumphant tune, his voice like a trumpet. "The Dagda played a *Geantraí* on his harp before his men went into battle, and his music made his warriors fearless and filled them with bloodlust. After the battle, his song revived his men and filled their hearts with glory.

"The Fomorians knew that the Dagda's harp made the Tuatha

Dé Danaan invincible." Cian's melody turned dark and stealthy. "During the battle, a few of them managed to sneak into the Dagda's camp and steal Uaithne. The thieves took refuge in an abandoned ringfort. They hung the Dagda's cláirseach up on the far wall, then settled in to wait for their warband to join them with tales of victory.

"But as their warriors straggled in, they brought news that the Tuatha Dé Danaan had defeated the Fomorians. They consoled themselves with the fact that they had taken one of the Dagda's greatest treasures, and he would not be able to heal his wounded.

"The Fomorians all lay down to sleep, placing their bodies between the harp and the door, so no one could reach it without rousing them."

Cian's voice vibrated with alarm. "When the Dagda returned to camp to find Uaithne missing, he summoned his two greatest allies to help him find his harp. He called Ogma the Artificer, god of poetry, and Lugh of the Long Arm, god of craftsmen, to retrieve Uaithne.

"The three traveled long and hard in search of the thieves. At last they found the ringfort where their enemies hid, and there the Dagda's harp hung on the far wall. Though the Fomorians had lost many warriors in the battle, still the number who lay sleeping between them and the harp was formidable. 'We can't fight them all,' Ogma protested.

"'We don't have to.' The Dagda called to Uaithne. The harp sprang off the wall and flew over the sleeping warriors into his arms.

"But Uaithne made a sound of joy as she was reunited with the Dagda. The Fomorians woke and drew their weapons to attack the three men of the Tuatha Dé Danaan.

"Lugh whispered to the Dagda: 'I think you'd better play your harp!'"

Cian launched into a rollicking tune. "The Dagda plucked the strings in the *Geantraí*, the music of merriment, and the

Fomorians began to laugh uncontrollably. They laughed so hard that the weapons fell from their hands, and their feet began to dance of their own accord. But when the song ended, they snatched up their weapons, and came at the Tuatha Dé Danaan again.

"Ogma whispered to the Dagda: 'I think you'd better play your harp!' The Dagda struck the strings, playing the *Goiltai*, the melody of sadness, which caused the Fomorians to weep so hard they couldn't see." Cian strummed a melancholy tune. "They dropped their weapons and writhed on the ground in uncontrollable misery. But when the music faded, they rose from the ground and took up their spears.

"'I'd better play my harp!' the Dagda murmured. He strummed his cláirseach so softly it could barely be heard. But he brought forth the *Suantraí*, and, though they fought to keep their eyes open, all the Fomorians dropped to the ground, fast asleep." And here Cian played a soothing lullaby.

"The three Tuatha Dé Danaan left their enemies sleeping there, and stole away. No one ever dared to steal the Dagda's harp again."

As Cian struck the last chord on his harp, the Norse sighed. It was rare for them to hear a tale they had not heard before, and the Irishman's melancholy delivery was far different than Thorgeir's bawdy antics. Cian nodded solemnly at their compliments.

Ursa had wandered over from her camp to hear the tale, and Ragnhild watched as she spoke to the Irishman, her eyes glowing with admiration. Cian offered her a fleeting smile, but he still looked like a man with a toothache.

He had reason to be unhappy. His entire family was dead, and Cian had little to look forward to by way of future prospects. But Ragnhild was returning him to a land where his abilities on the harp would be much revered by his countrymen. Åsa had made sure he brought with him the means to return to his schooling and become a master harper. It seemed like a man in his position should be more cheerful.

Darkness had fallen, and the tantalizing scent of cooking meat filled her nostrils. To Ragnhild's relief, Svein proclaimed the stew ready at last. The crews eagerly lined up to fill their wooden bowls and ate with relish. Nobody spoke a word as they shoveled the stew in with their horn spoons.

No sooner had they finished eating and scrubbed out the cauldron, their bowls, and spoons, than the weary sailors bedded down for the night.

Ragnhild snuggled into her hudfat and gazed at the moon that danced on the placid waters of the Skagerrak. Soon she would be home, in Murchad's arms, holding their infant son.

CHAPTER 2

In the morning a freshening breeze sprang up. Einar studied the waves. "We can round the cape with this wind, but we should stay well offshore, away from any hazards."

Worry nipped at Ragnhild. Were Unn and Ursa ready to round the cape in a blow? Unn had brought *Sea Wolf* around it without problems on their way to Tromøy, but that had been with an easy breeze. The seas off the cape could be large and unpredictable, even this time of year.

"Ursa, you should take a reef," Ragnhild said.

The shield-maiden frowned. "Unn isn't taking a reef."

"Unn has more experience than you."

"Barely. I can handle it." Ursa was adamant.

Ragnhild exchanged glances with Einar. He shrugged. Ragnhild mulled over the repercussions of letting the shield-maiden have her way. It was much more dangerous to take a reef in a seaway than to do it now before they departed. Ragnhild put herself in Ursa's place. She would be humiliated to be singled out to take precautions that her sister was not required to.

Ragnhild forced herself to drop her doubts. She had decided to give command of the ship to Ursa; now she had to trust her.

She had to take the risk some time, and there were no others more experienced in the crew. If Einar thought Ursa was ready, it was good enough for Ragnhild.

"All right, but use caution."

"I will," said Ursa. "Thank you, Lady!" The shield-maiden strode proudly to her ship. She vaulted aboard and took her place at the helm, grinning from ear to ear as her crew shoved off.

The sailors clambered aboard, ran out their oars, and rowed out of the protection of the cove into open waters and a brisk breeze. At Ragnhild's signal, sails rose up the masts and caught the wind, sending the ships bounding over the seas. Ragnhild smiled as the spray stung her face, all her doubts forgotten. Every wave brought her closer to home.

By midafternoon the rocky headland of Lindesnes hove into view, the southern tip of land. As the ships emerged from the shelter of the cape into choppy seas, the wind hit them full force, heeling them over. Summer was the time of year to brave the seas off the southern cape, but this wind was right on the edge.

Ragnhild glanced over at Einar on *Eagle's Treasure*. As if he could read her thoughts, he nodded his head toward the sisters' ships. Ragnhild nodded back, relieved that he agreed they were up to the challenge.

Eagle's Treasure surged ahead, and Ragnhild shouted to her crew to trim the sail, squeezing every last bit of speed out of the ship while keeping the rail out of the water.

The wind freshened as they rounded the cape. The tiller quivered in Ragnhild's grip as *Raider Bride* came up on the wave and tried to shake off the steering oar. She considered reefing the sail and decided it wasn't worth the risk. She felt confident in her own ability, but she wondered about Unn and Ursa. Her gaze flicked to Einar and he grinned. Put them to the test. Thorgeir and Svein nodded their agreement.

Ragnhild firmed her grip on the tiller and relaxed, sensing the wind shifts and wave patterns. She had to move with the ship rather than try to control it.

The little fleet stuck together, keeping close to Unn and Ursa. The sisters' eyes were wide, but they were both grinning in exhilaration. Ursa met Ragnhild's gaze and the girl's smile widened.

As they rounded land's end, the full force of the wind hit them across the beam. The ships heeled over abruptly, dipping their rails in the water. Ragnhild sneaked a glance at Unn on *Sea Wolf*. The girl's face blanched white, but she held her little ship steady.

Wave Horse was another matter. The ship was heeled far over, waves crashing aboard the lee side. Ursa had too much sail up. "You need to luff the sail!" Ragnhild shouted.

Ursa shook her head. "We can carry it!"

"No, you can't!" No sooner were the words out of Ragnhild's mouth than a gust hit *Wave Horse* broadside. The rail kissed the waves, and the sail scooped up water, drenching the crew. Ursa's eyes were ringed with white like a frightened horse, but she kept her grip on the tiller. The wind slackened and the ship snapped back up. Ragnhild let out her breath, only to inhale sharply as a huge rogue wave raced down on the ship. Another gust struck broadside along with the wave and *Wave Horse* rolled onto its side. The mast smacked the water. This time the ship did not come back up but lay pinned against the roiling sea by the water-filled sail. Ursa and several other sailors clung to the mast while those on the windward side were flung into the sea.

Einar was first on the scene. His crew dropped sail and he set a few to the oars to maneuver the ship. The húskarl steered alongside the pinned vessel, skirting the downed mast and sail, and held steady while his crew pulled sailors from the water. Once Einar had picked up the swimmers, he shouted to Ursa: "We have to cut away the sail!"

The shield-maiden nodded helplessly. There was no way for her to get to the prow and loose the sail. If she let go of the mast, the seas would rip her from the ship.

Ragnhild's crew had gotten their sail down and maneuvered under oar to the bow of *Wave Horse*.

Einar had given the tiller over to a sailor. Now he stood on *Eagle's Treasure*'s bow, timing the wave. He launched himself and grabbed hold of *Wave Horse*'s figurehead, and swung aboard Ursa's ship. He straddled the prow like a bucking horse, holding on with his thighs as he drew his knife and sawed at the forward sheet. A wooden pole held the corner of the sail, the other end attached to the mast.

Thorgeir brought his ship alongside the mast. One of his sailors leaned over the side to slash the halyard on the masthead, while a shipmate gripped his waist to keep him from going overboard. The top edge of the sail was attached to a yard, which kept the fabric afloat. The sail's coating of a thin layer of tar kept the wool from becoming completely sodden, though it was growing heavier every moment, and the water lapped over its surface.

On the bow, Einar sawed through the forward rope, and Thorgeir's crew member cut the halyard free of the masthead. *Eagle's Treasure*'s helmsman maneuvered alongside, and Einar leaped nimbly aboard.

"Well done," said Ragnhild.

Einar steered his ship away as *Wave Horse* gave a shudder and sluggishly righted itself. Ursa and those crew members who had managed to cling on began to bail with whatever they could get their hands on—buckets, helmets, bare hands.

The sail was still attached by the clew to the ship's leeward side. The huge spread of fabric dragged at the hull, taking control of the ship.

"Cut it!" shouted Ragnhild.

Ursa hesitated, staring at the vast expanse of wool. Ragnhild knew what she was thinking. It was a huge loss. It took three years' labor to weave enough fabric to make a sail.

"We can pull it aboard!" Ursa shouted.

The crew was willing to try. They clambered to the rail and

gripped the stiff, heavy wool and heaved. The ship heeled with the combined weight of their bodies and the wet sail. The wind and swell rolled the hull.

"Too dangerous!" Ragnhild yelled back. "Cut it loose!"

"No, we can get it!" Determined, Ursa and her crew hauled on the sail while the seas sloshed aboard.

"You're going to sink the ship!" Ragnhild cried.

A heavy wave rolled the hull onto its side, spilling the crew into the sea. The sail kept it beam-on to the swell while the heavy seas tossed the disabled ship, threatening to crush the sailors in the water.

"Loki's balls!" Ragnhild steered *Raider Bride* alongside the ship.

Heads popped up in the waves, splashing and gasping for air.

"Pick up as many as you can!" roared Einar, coming along the other side. Thorgeir and Svein jockeyed for position to help, while Unn wisely kept her distance.

The sail kept the ship beam-on to the seas. The hull rolled in the waves, slamming down on the struggling crew. Heads were bashed. Some went under. The mast and yard slapped the waves, threatening to smash the floundering swimmers.

Ragnhild spotted Ursa's dark head bobbing in the waves. She maneuvered *Raider Bride* toward the shield-maiden, who swam to *Wave Horse*'s side. Ursa gripped the railing as it bucked in the seaway. She drew her knife and sawed through the last rope that held the sail to the ship.

Releasing her grip on the rail, Ursa watched in defeat as the heavy, sodden sail sank into the sea, pulling the yard and the pole with it. Full of water, the ship righted itself sluggishly, but Ursa made no move to climb aboard. She bobbed listlessly in the water.

"Ursa, you fool! I'm going to make you wish you'd drowned!" Ragnhild maneuvered *Raider Bride* alongside the shield-maiden.

Cian leaned far over the side until his feet were off the deck, reaching for Ursa. "Hold on to him!" Ragnhild shouted. A crew member grabbed the Irishman's legs as he nearly went over.

Cian groped in the waves, blinded by seawater that bucketed over him. He got hold of Ursa's hand and gripped it hard, but it was apparent he didn't have the strength to pull her up.

"Pull!" Ragnhild shouted. "Pull him in!" Two more burly men grabbed the Irishman's legs and hauled.

He came aboard, dragging Ursa with him. They thumped to the deck in a puddle of seawater.

"Hel take you, girl, when I give you an order, you follow it!" Ragnhild shouted.

She kept all the crews at work, hauling survivors aboard. Ursa roused herself and joined her younger sisters as they pulled the last of the bodies out of the water. They went to work on them, pumping chests to get the water out. The half-drowned sailors sprawled on the deck, vomiting up gallons of seawater.

Without its sail, *Wave Horse* rolled beam-on to the swell. Thorgeir went aboard the disabled ship, taking half a dozen of his crew with him. Ragnhild sent a few sailors from each of the other vessels over. The steering oar was still lashed to its gudgeon, so maneuvering was possible. All of the oars had gone overboard, but the sailors fished enough of them out to give the ship steerage. Some fitted oars and began to row, while others continued bailing. Shepherded by the rest of the fleet, Thorgeir maneuvered the ship into the lee of the headland.

Once safely around the cape, Ragnhild headed northwest, putting the wind behind them. The seas came aft, gently pushing them homeward.

When the wounded were tended to as well as was possible, Ursa slumped to the deck, leaning against the side. She kept her head down, wet strands of hair covering her face. Ragnhild was still too angry to trust herself to speak. She had to cool off before she said a word.

Ragnhild led the little fleet into the nearest cove big enough to hold all of them that was reasonably well protected from every direction. They ran their ships onto the sandy beach and clambered ashore gratefully.

The wounded were brought down with care and laid out on the beach. Amid much groaning and a few screams, Unn and her sisters set broken limbs, bandaged sprains and lacerations, administered salves and herbs. Two of Ursa's crew lay dead, and five more had sustained serious injuries. One had a broken arm, another a concussion. The other three were too battered and bruised to be of any use in ship-handling. Ragnhild's fury roiled.

When the work was done, Ursa sat with her sisters, staring blankly into space. Ragnhild seated herself some distance away. They were all so exhausted that they could barely choke down some dried meat and flatbread.

The three húskarlar sat down beside Ragnhild. Einar cleared his throat and murmured, "Wait until tomorrow to talk to her. Let her think it over tonight."

Ragnhild stared at the fire, rage seething inside her.

Thorgeir said, "It will be a fine line between reprimanding the girl and crushing her spirit."

Svein agreed. "Ursa's crew followed her without question. She's a courageous and valuable leader. We need people like her."

Ragnhild said nothing, struggling for control.

"She tried to save the sail," Einar said. "That was certainly courageous and foolhardy, but she was also trying to salvage as much as she could from her mistake. It's a lucky thing it was the smallest ship. We won't need to take it on the voyage to Ireland, and the lost sail was half the size of the others."

"The women can work on weaving the sailcloth over the winter," said Svein.

"As if they had nothing better to do," said Ragnhild bitterly. She took a deep breath. With one last effort, she fought her anger down. "There are some lengths of wool already woven that we can use. They may be able to get the sail completed by next summer." She was not including herself, of course. Ragnhild was no weaver. She'd scorned any attempts to teach her the art. Fortunately, there were plenty of skilled weavers at Gausel.

Heeding Einar's advice, Ragnhild said nothing to Ursa that night. She laid out her hudfat and crawled in, hoping to be calm enough to speak to the girl in the morning. Justified as her anger was, she had to rise above it and handle the incident to best advantage rather than vent her rage. The húskarlar were right—it would be foolish to destroy a promising commander for one mistake, no matter how serious. Courage went hand in hand with hubris, and it was only luck and her allies that had kept Ragnhild from her own disaster. She wished Murchad were here to advise her, but this was her responsibility.

It dawned on her that she was as angry at herself as she was at Ursa. Her instincts had told her the girl wasn't ready, and she'd ignored them. That would never happen again.

She slept restlessly, waking several times during the night, her mind busy formulating the best approach to Ursa. Some kind of punishment was called for, but tempered with encouragement and support.

By dawn, she knew what to say.

She crawled out of her hudfat and spotted Ursa, leaning against a log, looking miserable. The shield-maiden had obviously not slept. Ragnhild approached and took a seat beside her.

Ursa looked up at her, and Ragnhild glimpsed the self-hatred in the girl's eyes. Tears streaked her face. Her words sounded as angry as Ragnhild had felt. "Arne and Lars are dead, the others injured, the sail lost, and it's my fault."

"Yes, it is." Ragnhild kept her tone gentle.

Ursa's hands trembled as she pushed back her rat's nest of hair. A wave of sympathy surged through Ragnhild. "You were over-confident."

Ursa nodded, the corners of her mouth sagging.

"That happens when you're good at what you do and know it.

It will get knocked out of you, trust me. You have to realize that when you make decisions, it affects those who rely on your judgement. Never disobey an order from me again. Understood?"

Ursa nodded.

Ragnhild laid a hand on her shoulder. "Get your ship ready."

The shield-maiden stared at her in disbelief.

"You have to get back on the horse that bucked you off, the sooner the better. You're short-handed and without a sail. Your crew can't keep up with us. They won't be able to row all the way up the coast to Boknafjord, so you'll put in at Solavika and portage the ship overland to the Hafrsfjord." Ragnhild and Ursa both knew from personal experience that the arduous process of dragging a ship across the land to Gausel was enough punishment to last a lifetime. Once they made it to Hafrsfjord, they had to row across the fjord to the eastern shore, then undertake another, shorter portage overland to Gausel. It was backbreaking labor. But without a sail, there was no other way to get the ship back to Gausel, and it was Ursa's responsibility to do so. It was the perfect punishment and penance. If anything could make her feel she'd atoned for her mistake, this was it.

Ursa rose and strode to her disabled ship, determination evident in the set of her shoulders. She mustered those of her crew who were still fit. Ragnhild spread the injured out among the fleet and assigned experienced sailors from the other ships who had made the portage before to augment *Wave Horse*'s crew. They would have to row all day to reach Solavika, so everyone had to be in top form. Ragnhild wished she could send one of her húskarlar, but they were needed to captain their own ships safely through the tricky waters of the fjords.

The seas were mercifully gentle as the fleet headed north, past the familiar stretches of dunes and sandy beaches of the Jaeren coast, Ragnhild's territory. The ships raised sail to a friendly breeze while *Wave Horse* hugged the coast under oar. To Ursa's credit, she managed enough speed to keep in sight of the fleet.

Around midday they came abreast of the sandy half-moon bay of Solavika. With a wave, Ursa headed for the beach. Ragnhild wished her the blessings of the gods.

The rest of the ships sailed north until a scattering of islands appeared off the coast, signaling home waters. The fleet rounded the headland, and the Boknafjord opened up before them. Prows aligned, they cruised past the island where the unlit war beacon stood on its perch on the cliff.

Once in the fjord's protected waters, the crews dropped sail and took up their oars, threading between the skerries. Unn was wise enough to follow Einar through the treacherous waters.

As they neared Gausel, Ragnhild strained to catch sight of the settlement. Soon the familiar shore materialized, a crowd of people waiting.

Her eyes riveted on Murchad's dark head and wiry form. Beside him stood Liv, Herulf's fóstra, Ragnhild's son in her arms, Liv's own small children clustered around her legs.

The sight of her little family made Ragnhild's chest tighten. As soon as *Raider Bride*'s prow touched shore, Ragnhild shipped the steering oar and hurried to the bow. She sprang down onto the sand beside her husband. Green eyes sparkling, Murchad swept her into his arms and kissed her ardently. Ragnhild let herself absorb her husband's warmth and passion for a moment before turning in his arms to receive Herulf from his nurse.

Ragnhild pressed her nose against the baby's downy head, inhaling his milky scent. A sense of bliss flooded her. She drew the infant between herself and Murchad, and they remained in an embrace. For a moment, Ragnhild was completely content.

Murchad peered over her shoulder. "I'm glad to see you home safe, but isn't a ship missing? Where is *Wave Horse*?"

"Yes, I'll tell you that tale over a cup of ale," said Ragnhild.

Murchad's gaze fell on Cian. "I see you have a new addition to your crew."

Ragnhild turned to the Irishman. "Yes, this is a countryman of yours." Herulf began to squirm, and she tightened her hold on him.

"Greetings," said Murchad, releasing her and holding his hand out in welcome. "I am Murchad mac Maele Duin."

Herulf started to fuss, reaching chubby arms out to Liv. Ragnhild's joy collapsed, and she turned to the fóstra in resignation. She was not maternal material, and her son knew it.

Cian came forward to embrace Murchad. "I know who you are. I am Cian son of Cumuscach of the Ard Ciannachta, and I now take vengeance for my father."

Murchad's eyes widened. Ragnhild glimpsed a flash of steel in Cian's hand. She thrust Herulf into Liv's arms and lunged, but she was a heartbeat too late to stop the blade from plunging into Murchad's chest.

CHAPTER 3

Tromøy

Eyvind sat on a bench, sunlight glinting on his glossy brown hair. He was surrounded by a vast sea of red-and-white checked wool. A section of the heavy sailcloth was stretched taut between his knees, and he wielded a bone needle, meticulously weaving waxed wool thread through the fabric to reinforce a weak spot. He glanced up as Åsa approached, a smile spreading across his tanned face and a sparkle in his glacier-blue eyes.

"How are you feeling?" she asked.

"Much restored, thanks to your healing and your care. I think I'll be well enough to make a late-season voyage."

"I'm so happy for you." Åsa bit back disappointment that he would be departing so soon, without her. She would miss him, and envied him the adventures that awaited him in the distant ports he would visit in his knarr, *Far Traveler*.

"I wish you would come with me," he said.

Åsa stifled the longing that rose in her chest and shook her head. "I wish I could. But it's too soon. Even though we dealt Horik a disabling blow, you know he's still got spies watching the ports, hoping to catch me again and take revenge. I can't risk it. I need to stay on Tromøy for now, looking after my people and reinforcing our defenses."

Taking a seat beside him, she accepted a needle from his case. She threaded it with waxed woolen thread and examined the sail. Finding a worn spot in the fabric, she stretched the length between her knees and tucked it under her feet, then set to work, weaving the thread in and out. The familiar repair soothed her. She and Eyvind worked in companionable silence, while all around them caulking irons rang and saws rasped as crews overhauled Tromøy's fleet after the recent battle with Horik.

A tiny but firm glimmer of hope ignited deep inside. There was much to be done to prepare for any coming threats, but with patience and persistence, Tromøy would be ready. For now, Halfdan was safe with his wolf in Skiringssal, under the watchful eyes of Olaf, Sonja, and Ulf. Åsa missed her son and made the half-day sail to Skiringssal frequently to visit.

The spot mended, Åsa kissed Eyvind on the cheek and rose, ready to face her most difficult task of the day. She climbed the trail to the hall, where the barley was being harvested. In the smithy, hammers rang as weapons and tools were being repaired. With Ulf in Skiringssal, Tromøy had no regular smith, but there was not one among them who could not sharpen a seax or straighten a bent blade.

Åsa entered the bower and found Heid in her usual place. The sorceress blinked in the shaft of daylight that came in through the open door. Though the day was warm, the völva huddled by a brazier, bundled in her shawl.

The harsh light revealed how much the sorceress had aged in recent weeks. Heid had lost even more weight from her slight frame. Deep lines grooved her face; her hair was thin and dry as chaff. Most worrisome of all was the vagueness in her eyes. Her gaze wandered about the room and lit on Åsa without recognition.

Worry pinched Åsa's heart. They'd nearly lost Heid twice. Åsa had gone to retrieve the völva from Hel both times, and the sorceress had only returned reluctantly. Åsa couldn't blame her. Heid's husband and child awaited her in the land of the dead, where the sorceress would be forever young and free of the crippling pain she'd endured for years. The völva had tried to stay with her family, but the Nornir sent her back to Midgaard, decreeing she had to see her mission through to the end. Yet what could the aging völva accomplish in her condition?

Åsa was grateful to have Heid with her in body, if not in mind. Cian had brought the sorceress back from the brink of death with his harp music. The völva lived, but she functioned as if in a waking dream. Åsa existed in a constant state of fear and grief, knowing Heid desired death and would return to Hel the moment she was released from her obligations here. Åsa did everything she could to prepare for the day when she would have to carry on without her mentor.

Vigdis entered the room from the bower hall, carrying a bowl of broth. Three years ago, Heid had selected the apprentice as her successor. Vigdis had accepted the appointment, vowing never to marry, rather to remain by the völva's side, learning the sorceress's art, as long as Heid lived. Vigdis was loyal to her mentor, diligent in her studies, and willing to take on more responsibility, but it would be years before she could fill Heid's shoes, if ever. At twenty-one winters old, Vigdis did not have the völva's innate personal power and self-confidence. Though the apprentice knew all the rituals by heart, Åsa herself was more adept in magic.

The three of them managed to stumble along together, for now. They couldn't spare the völva.

"I don't know what else to do for her," said Åsa, staring down at Heid.

"All we can do is wait, care for her, and hope that time will heal her mind," said Vigdis.

Åsa wished she had not let the Irish harper go. She wondered if repeated sessions of his healing music could have cured Heid completely. Too late now. Cian was on his way to Gausel with Ragnhild and thence to Ireland. After their escape from Horik, Åsa owed the Irishman so much, she hadn't felt she could refuse his request to go home.

"Tomorrow I will fly to Erritsø in Stormrider and see how the land lies."

Vigdis looked at her with concern. "Take care, Lady. If something happens to you, then all is lost."

She nodded, knowing Vigdis's worries were well-founded. Just this spring, spies sent by Horik, the ruthless king of the Danes, had kidnapped Åsa when she sailed to Erritsø with Eyvind, and nearly cost her life as well as several others. Åsa had escaped, thanks to the sacrifice of many and the assistance of Cian, who had been a slave in the Danish hall.

Horik came after her with his war fleet, but Åsa's allies helped her fight him off. Despite his defeat, the Danish king still posed a formidable threat. But Horik's powerful sorceress, Groa, had perished, so Åsa felt secure spying in her falcon's body.

That night, she kissed Eyvind a reluctant goodnight, then retired to the bower, where she prepared carefully for the long flight. She fed Stormrider well on choice tidbits of dove breast, and hooded the falcon on her perch to ensure the bird rested. Then Åsa lay down to sleep.

Her dreams were jumbled and confused, reliving her captivity and battles with Horik and his fearsome sorceress. When dawn came, Åsa woke drenched in sweat. She sat up and tried to reassure herself. She had vanquished her enemies, at least for now. Horik's forces were depleted, if not destroyed. Groa had burned in Horik's hall.

With a sigh of relief, Åsa put her nightmares aside. She sat up and drank water from the jug near her bed. Then she unhooded Stormrider, fed her and untied the bird's jesses.

Åsa lay back down and called the trance down on her, glad to be taking action. Her breathing slowed along with her heart rate, her mind calmed, and she slipped into Stormrider's mind as easily as she put on a gown. The bird's body was familiar as a well-worn garment. She adapted quickly to the fast heartbeat, the raptor's keen vision and enhanced perception.

The peregrine roused and spread her wings. With powerful leg muscles, she launched off the perch, flapping her wings vigorously, until she caught the warm air current that rose toward the ceiling and rode it up to the open gable end. She soared through, out into the morning sky.

THE SKAGERRAK SEA stretched to the horizon. Gray skies emitted a gentle rain that the falcon's feathers shed. By the time she sighted land, Stormrider was tired. On the northernmost end of Jutland, she sought a forest and selected a tall pine to shelter in. Once perched amid the branches, the peregrine tucked her beak under one wing and dozed.

When she woke, she felt more refreshed than she had in days. Being in the falcon's body was pure joy. The bird did not worry about what might happen. The here and now was all there was.

A sense of exhilaration filled her as she took to the skies once more. The clouds had lightened and the rain let up. Stormrider soared south across the flat, low-lying Jutland peninsula. A landscape of peat bogs and forests passed beneath her until she spotted the Little Belt, the body of water on which Horik had built his fortress.

The remains of the Danish fleet lay derelict on the shore. The ships were in a sorry state, with gouged keels and splintered planks from the battle against Åsa and her allies. Horik had barely escaped with his life.

No workmen were in evidence. It appeared that nothing had

been done since the fleet limped home after their attempted invasion of Tromøy. Flying inland over the fields, the falcon spotted people scurrying around the palisade that guarded empty ground.

A rectangle of blackened earth inside the wall was all that was left of Horik's hall after the fire that had started during Åsa's struggle with Horik's völva. The Danish sorceress had been engulfed in flames, while Åsa escaped with Halfdan and his wolf.

The remains of the burned building had been cleared from the foundation and piled in a blackened heap outside the gates. The sound of hammers and axes rang in the air as work proceeded on the Danish king's new hall. Teams of oxen hauled massive tree trunks into the muddy yard, where workmen shaped them with saws and adze. Some would be used as pillars, others roof beams, still others split and planed into planks for the walls.

The new hall was a long way from completion. A team of oxen dragged a plank to smooth the ground where the old hall had stood. Behind them came men with logs, tamping the soil firm. Workers dug postholes and filled them with gravel to provide drainage for the new pillars. From the dimensions of the layout, Horik's new hall would be enormous, even larger than the original. Tromøy's hall was barely an outbuilding by comparison. Even the grandeur of Skiringssal would be eclipsed by this new hall's size.

Landing on a stockade post, Stormrider spotted Horik walking toward a workshop. The Danish king's stride seemed to lack something of his past vigor. He appeared weary as he stooped to enter the building.

The falcon landed on the roof beside the smokehole. Stormrider peered in, then hopped inside and perched on a rafter in the ceiling's dim recesses.

Her keen falcon's vision made out the shapes in the workshop's gloom. The building had been furnished as temporary living quarters, with chests, beds, tables, and stools. A hideous odor like rotting corpses permeated the room.

A young woman sat with her spindle, spinning fine linen thread near the open door, where the light was better and the air fresher. "How long must I live like a barn animal?" The whiny voice belonged to Ingebjorg, Horik's niece. A year or two younger than Åsa, Ingebjorg performed the duties of hostess for her uncle. Åsa met her briefly when she'd been brought before Horik as a captive.

"You ask me this every day, and every day I answer: as long as it takes," Horik growled. "My new hall will be far grander than the old one. It will be worth waiting for."

Ingebjorg huffed. "When are you going to bring Åsa to me? I want to torture her until she begs for death. Too long has my father's murder gone unavenged."

Stormrider's feathers ruffled. Åsa had killed the girl's father, Rorik, in a fair fight, one that he'd started by invading Tromøy. Obviously, that made no difference to Ingebjorg.

Like his dead brother, Horik wanted Tromøy, a foothold across the Skagerrak Sea along the lucrative North Way. Since Åsa had made it clear she would never marry him, he'd decided to take it over her dead body. But Åsa and her allies had soundly beaten the Danish warlord, and driven him back across the sea.

"I can do nothing about that right now," Horik said, impatience grating in his voice. "I lost many warriors and ships in the battle. Until my hall is completed, ships repaired and more built, warriors recruited and trained, you will have to bide your time."

"That will take years!" Ingebjorg protested.

Horik shrugged. "With Harald Klak and the Franks threatening us from the south, and my brothers in the north, I cannot risk going after Åsa right now. She has too many allies. If you want her, you'll have to get her yourself."

"Åsa is protected by her powerful völva," Ingebjorg said. "But I hear the old witch has one foot on the Hel road."

"Well, then, you and Groa should be able to send the old woman on her way." Horik wrinkled his nose. "Speaking of Groa, her potion smells like it's about ready."

Ingebjorg sniffed. "Yes." She wound her thread around the spindle and set it aside. She hurried over to the darkest corner of the makeshift hall, where the foul-smelling brew simmered over a brazier in a pot. Ingebjorg poured a cupful and carried it over to the far corner of the room.

On a pallet against the wall lay a corpselike creature, wrapped in linen.

Shock rippled through Stormrider. Only the open eyes, burning like coals in the light of the brazier, betrayed the fact that Groa the sorceress still lived. Her skin was tanned like shoe leather. Her hair had been scorched away completely, and new grew back in a stark white stubble.

Her fiery eyes seemed to search the rafters. The falcon's heart stuttered and she shrank farther into the shadows.

Just as Stormrider felt sure those penetrating eyes would spot her, Ingebjorg seated herself beside the sorceress with the cup of malodorous brew. Groa cried out in pain as the younger woman lifted her head gently and held the cup to the dry, cracked lips.

"Come, you must regain your strength," Ingebjorg murmured. "I can't get to Åsa without your help. After what she's done to you, I know you want revenge as much as I do. Her and her völva. Together we'll kill them both."

The völva grimaced and sipped the potion with a will.

The falcon knew it was time to leave. She'd learned everything she could for now. In his weakened state, Horik was not likely to attack Tromøy anytime soon. Shocking as it was that Groa had survived, the sorceress had a long recovery ahead before she could become any kind of threat. Despite her malice, Ingebjorg could do little on her own.

Groa stopped drinking the potion. Stormrider froze, but it was too late. The völva's eyes flicked up and caught the falcon with her gaze. Her lips curled in a malicious grin that made the bird's heart beat like a shaman's drum.

"Drink, Groa," Ingebjorg demanded, shoving the cup to her lips.

The peregrine eased her way out of the smokehole and took to the sky, putting a safe distance between herself and her enemies before coming to roost in a tall oak for the night.

CHAPTER 4

Gausel

Ragnhild slammed into Cian, knocking him away from her husband. Thorgeir seized the Irishman while Einar reached out to catch Murchad as he fell.

Ragnhild rushed to her husband, who sagged in Einar's arms. She yanked the knife out of his chest. The tip glistened with blood. As Einar gently lowered Murchad to the ground, she peeled back his cloak to reveal blood spreading across his tunic. Sucking in her breath, she pressed his cloak to staunch the wound.

Murchad flinched. "Gently!" His eyes fluttered open and he grimaced up at her. "I'm alive."

"*A mhuirin*," she cried, sweeping him into an embrace. "Thank the gods."

Murchad winced. "*A chroi*, you saved my life. I saw the warning in your face and turned as he struck. The blade was turned aside by my brooch."

Ragnhild broke the embrace, laying her husband down gently.

She drew her seax and sprang up from her crouch, advancing on Cian. "You're a dead man, whatever your name is."

"Say the word, my lady." Still gripping the Irishman in his burly embrace, Thorgeir held his own seax to the Irishman's throat.

Cian glared defiantly. "Murchad mac Maele Duin, you murdered my father."

"Wait," said Murchad, struggling into a sitting position.

Everyone froze, staring at him.

"We need to find out more. This man seems to believe he has an obligation to claim blood vengeance. That's within his rights under Irish law as well as yours."

Thorgeir shrugged and pressed his blade against Cian's throat. "He failed. He has to die."

"What would you have us do, keep him alive to try again?" Ragnhild demanded.

Murchad tried to stand. Einar pulled him to his feet and steadied him, pressing a cloth to his wound. "I think there's been a misunderstanding." Murchad looked at Cian. "I did not kill your father."

Cian thrust his chin out. "My vengeance is justified by the laws of Ireland, if not this godforsaken place. Maybe you didn't wield the blade, but you ordered his death, and that of my brother as well."

"Who told you that?" Murchad demanded.

"My uncle, Dunchad, told me you had them both killed for my father's betrayal in your battle against Conchobar."

"I'm sure he said that." Sarcasm was thick in Murchad's voice. "But my informants discovered it was your uncle who betrayed me, then tried to blame it on your father. I knew the truth all along. I had no reason to kill your father, or your brother."

Cian stared at him.

Murchad continued. "Think, lad. Who has gained by your

father's death? If your older brother, the tanist, is dead as well, who took your father's place at the head of your clan?"

Cian's face went white as the truth struck him.

Murchad said it for him. "I have proof your uncle is a betrayer and a liar. Isn't it more likely he had your father and brother murdered and laid it at my doorstep, since I was in no position to exonerate myself? It's a very neat package Dunchad has wrapped up."

There was a long silence as everyone grappled with the situation. Ragnhild's fingers twitched on her seax, but she waited.

Cian slumped. "My lord, I have wronged you."

Murchad gave a nod to Thorgeir, who loosened his hold on the Irishman. Cian slipped from Thorgeir's grasp and fell to his knees, head bowed. "Lord Murchad, I offer you my life to do with as you will."

Murchad stepped away from Einar and stood over the Irishman. "I accept your life, Cian mac Cumuscach."

Cian tensed, gaze fixed on the ground.

"Your fate is mine to do with as I wish," Murchad continued. "You have vowed to take vengeance on your father's murderer, and you must fulfill that vow. But Dunchad is also guilty of betraying me, lying to me, falsely accusing me of murder, and defiling my reputation with his lies. I order you to sail for Ireland and avenge your father's murder and your brother's. And you will clear my name of any guilt in their slayings."

Thorgeir sheathed his seax, and Ragnhild's shoulders relaxed. Though she'd been ready to cut the Irishman's throat, a part of her was relieved they wouldn't have to. Despite her suspicions, she'd been impressed by his magical touch on the harp. It would be a shame to waste such ability.

Murchad stared down at Cian and said, "Then, as the last eligible candidate of your line, you will claim your rightful place as head of your clan."

Cian raised his head and stared at Murchad. Ragnhild was surprised to note that his expression was one of dismay, not relief at being alive nor joy at the opportunity to become a chieftain.

Murchad commanded, "You will swear the oath."

Cian swallowed hard. His voice faltered as he spoke. "My lord Murchad mac Maele Duin, I accept your order to take vengeance for the deaths of my father and brother, to clear your name of any wrongdoing, and to take my rightful place as the head of my clan." His voice broke down entirely for a moment. Cian bit his lip, seeming to gather strength, and continued. "This I swear to fulfill, unless the sky falls and crushes me, or the earth opens up and swallows me, or the sea rises and overwhelms me."

The oath rang out with power, and Murchad nodded, satisfied. He held out his hand and raised Cian to his feet.

The Irishman blurted, "Lord Murchad, I do not know how I can fulfill my vow. My uncle has long been a favorite of your cousin, King Niall. I have no army, no followers. I don't know how I can go against him."

Murchad considered. "I will sail to Ireland with you and present your cause to my cousin. And I will commit forces to support you in your enterprise."

Ragnhild was impressed with Cian's oath, but a myriad of practicalities fluttered in her mind. All this was fine drama, but there was much to consider. "Husband, I gave Åsa my oath to bring Cian to Ireland, not to wage war on his uncle. To do so will require us to bring a fleet of ships against him. With fair winds it will take us at least a week to reach Ireland, and a week or more to get home. There are only a few weeks left of decent weather. Once the winter storms set in, we could be forced to overwinter in Ireland. We must depart in the next few days just to make it there and back, leaving little time to fight a war."

Murchad nodded grimly. "If we have to overwinter in Ireland, so be it."

Ragnhild could not believe what she was hearing. She glanced at Herulf, asleep in Liv's arms. She had not bargained on a winter apart from her son. "Why would you fight for this man after he tried to kill you?"

Murchad wheeled on her, green eyes blazing. "Dunchad betrayed me in my war with Conchobar and cost me the high kingship, and blamed his own brother for it. He murdered his brother and his nephew, and falsely accused me for it knowing I could not clear my name. It's likely his lies cost me the kingship of Aileach as well. Cian has an obligation to take vengeance, the same as under your laws. And I cannot let this betrayal and slander stand against my name."

Ragnhild was shocked by the vehemence in her husband's voice. She realized that Murchad's loss meant more to him than he let on. He was always so calm, so restrained. It was easy to forget the passion that burned beneath his highly polished façade. But after losing his bid for the high kingship, then being deposed as king, his reputation was all he had left in his homeland. Here, he was a lord only because he was married to her. She knew it was hard for him to accept.

Murchad looked to her expectantly. She glanced at Herulf, cooing and smiling up at Liv, and a jealous despair gripped her heart. Her son loved his fóstra far more than he did his mother, and why shouldn't he? Even when she was home, Ragnhild avoided the bower as if it were Niflheim and spent most of her time training with her warriors and running the estate. It was Liv's milk that slaked Herulf's hunger, Liv's arms that comforted him, Liv's voice that sang to him. And Herulf was better off for it. Ragnhild was no kind of mother, nor had she ever wished to be.

Suddenly she longed to get away. The prospect of going to sea, with the promise of battle at the end, gave her relief. She'd be doing what she was good at, and she and Murchad would be together. Her husband asked little enough of her—she could grant him what was so important to him.

She took her son from Liv and held him close despite his squirming. Images of her own mother flashed through her mind, sending a crushing sense of loss that squeezed the breath out of her. She'd barely known her mother, who'd died when Ragnhild was very young. She remembered her as sweet, loving, and fair, all that a mother should be. All that Ragnhild was not.

Ragnhild gazed up at her husband, noticing how pale his face was. "Very well. Let's get you to bed."

Murchad nodded his head wearily. Dismissing Cian with a curt nod, he put his arm around her shoulders, and she guided him to their private rooms off the main hall.

Inside, he sagged onto the bed. Ragnhild laid Herulf in his cradle and got a cloth and warm water from the pot by the fire. She carefully stripped off Murchad's tunic and washed the wound. "It's not deep," she said. "You'll be fine in a few days. It's a good thing you have quick reflexes." She laid a clean linen cloth over the wound and wrapped a strip of linen around his chest. She propped him up with pillows and fetched their son.

She unwrapped Herulf from his swaddling and laid him on the bed. They both stared as he kicked his legs and gurgled, luxuriating in the freedom.

Her child was barely four months old. Ragnhild had been gone this past month, and now she must leave him again. Her eyes drank him in, striving to etch his presence on her mind. It was still hard to believe she was a mother, that this boy was hers. She ran her hand down his soft cheek.

"I'm sorry to take you away from him so soon, *a chroi*," said Murchad, watching her.

She shrugged. "It can't be helped. I'm a sea king first; mother comes a distant second. A child never figured in my plans." She turned to her husband. "Liv will take better care of him than I ever could. I can see she cares for him as much as if he were her own." *And he for her.*

Tears were running down her cheeks. She picked up Herulf

and laid him in the cradle that hung suspended from the rafters, within arm's reach of their bed. After kissing her son and tucking him in, she took Murchad into a careful embrace.

CIAN LAY awake on his bench in the great hall, rigid with tension, waiting for a knife in the dark. All around him, Ragnhild's and Murchad's warriors slept. Nobody had spoken to him since the encounter with Murchad, though all eyes watched him as if they expected him to stab someone else. In one short moment, he'd gone from being nearly accepted as one of them, a hero who'd saved Queen Åsa's life, to a pariah. They all probably wanted him dead.

Well, let them come. He had not been prepared to live beyond this day. He'd accepted the fact that when he killed Murchad, the Norse would slay him immediately. Just because Murchad had let him live didn't mean he was safe. If he were in Ireland, a shadow would slip in under cover of darkness, a knife would flash, and that would be the end of Cian.

During those three long years as a slave of that Danish king, Murchad had loomed as a larger-than-life villain in Cian's mind, the man responsible for the murder of his father, his brother, and for selling him to the Danes. Murchad had been the king of the Northern Ui Neil then, an all-powerful man, and Cian had dreamed of sinking his knife into him, never believing it was a dream that could come true.

Like the answer to a prayer the chance had come. Murchad, now a deposed king living among the Norse, had fallen into his path. Cian had taken the chance, believing vengeance had been granted by God.

All a mistake. He'd learned the truth at last. Thank God his knife had not found its home in Murchad's heart.

In a few days, if he lived through this night, they would sail to

Ireland. He'd see his homeland for the first time in three years, a sight he'd given up hope of long ago. He was not looking forward to his return. His family was gone, his training on the harp hopelessly lapsed. There was nothing and no one left for him, everyone dead except for his treacherous uncle.

There was one thing left. He must fulfill his oath and take vengeance for his father's and brother's deaths—or die trying. His thirst for revenge, so carefully nurtured during his time in captivity, had dimmed. It was as if it all burnt itself out on Murchad, and when he discovered his mistake, the fire had been snuffed out. Yet here he was, about to embark on a mission he'd never imagined, with a crew who didn't trust him.

Honor left him no choice.

He must kill Dunchad and avenge his kin. Then he must take his uncle's place as head of his clan. Cian's stomach felt hollow. Whether he lived or died, his life as a harper was over. He was the only eligible person left alive who could serve as chieftain of his clan. He'd never been prepared for this. His elder brother Cináed had been tanist, chosen by their father years ago and elected by the clan, leaving Cian free to pursue the arcane mysteries of music and poetry. But Cináed was dead. It seemed impossible to believe that his invincible older brother was gone forever.

Cian fought the urge to leap off the bench and flee into the night. He could never survive on his own here among the Norse. He'd be killed or enslaved in no time. In Ireland, where he knew the country and the language, he could slip away given half a chance. There he could make his way as a wandering harper without home or family. The Irish valued musicians and poets and would open their homes to him.

Dismay laid a cold hand on his heart. He didn't deserve to live. His father and brother were dead—why should he be alive? If he didn't try to take vengeance for their murders and take responsibility for his clan, what meaning did his life have? He would be haunted by failure for the rest of his days.

He set his jaw and turned his face to the wall, his back tensed, waiting for the blade of a vengeful Norseman.

The night passed in a gray trance of memories and regrets. He woke from his restless slumber, more dismayed than relieved to find he was still alive. He hoisted himself out of bed and joined a chattering, cheerful group at breakfast in the yard.

Cian helped himself to small beer and barley porridge, then took his seat on the bench, listening to the crew talk. They ignored him, consumed by plans for the voyage to Ireland.

"I wonder if we'll be stopping at Tullynavin again. Lord Aed nearly worked us to death when we were his prisoners."

"Now that Lord Murchad has made peace with his cousin the king, we'll be welcome wherever he takes us."

"I can't believe Murchad made up with Niall after he deposed him and took his place as king."

"Lord Murchad is happier here, with us and our lady."

"Those priests didn't like Lord Murchad choosing Lady Ragnhild over the kingship."

"Lord Murchad knows when he's well off. He's as good as a king here, or at least a jarl."

"Those priests hated us."

"They liked us better after we saved the monastery from the Danes."

"Except that Blathmac on Iona. He had no gratitude."

"That one wants to be a martyr for his White Christ." This comment was met with scornful laughter.

They spoke as if Cian weren't there, though he caught several glancing at him out of the corner of their eyes. He sighed. This voyage would be difficult enough without cold shoulders from his shipmates.

After breakfast, Murchad called Cian aside. He escorted him into the hall, where Ragnhild presided on her high seat, her three húskarlar gathered around her.

Murchad motioned Cian to a nearby bench, then took his

place beside Ragnhild. "Lad, we need to strategize. You must tell me everything you know about your uncle's stronghold: the construction, layout, size, defenses; how many men your uncle might have; what the surrounding terrain is like. Is there any place suitable to launch an attack?"

Cian closed his eyes, conjuring up the image of his father's fortress. A wave of grief swept over him, but he was determined to achieve his goal. "The hall is large—as big as this one—but of course it's round. It can house over one hundred warriors, officials, servants, and others of my uncle's court. The fortress differs from the usual Irish holding where many smaller structures are enclosed inside a defensive wall. My father's hall is one enormous building, with the palisade forming the outer walls. A broad thatched roof covers the entire yard, right down to the outer palisade. The fort is surrounded by a ditch as deep as two men's height. The only access is by a land bridge, wide enough for two men to walk abreast."

Murchad stroked his moustache. "Difficult to attack. Is there a souterrain?"

Cian nodded. "Yes, of course, there is a tunnel that leads out of the cold stores into the forest, though it has not been used in years. My brother and I used to play in it." He choked, remembering himself and Cináed as boys, exploring the dark depths of the ancient tunnel. The dank passage had been filled with cobwebs and rodents and probably ghosts, but Cináed had no fear. He'd led his younger brother boldly into the darkness. The thought of that courage, gone from the earth, made Cian's throat tighten.

Murchad waited while Cian recovered himself, then went on, "Would you be able to locate the entrance to it?"

Cian nodded, his throat too constricted for speech.

Murchad turned to his wife. "What size force will we bring?"

"Four ships, with thirty-five crew on each ship."

"I will ask Niall for one hundred mounted men and horses for us," Murchad said. "That would give us a force of two hundred and forty or so. We can ride from Aileach to Daire Calgaich, cross the River Feabhail, then on up the east side of Lough Feabhail to the fortress. How long a ride from the monastery to your fortress?"

Cian thought back to his childhood trips. "It's a solid day's ride through thick forest," he ventured. "The road was good last time I passed that way."

"And how soon would your uncle know we were coming?"

"My father had lookouts posted along the road. The forest gives good cover most of the way, but if my uncle maintains the same posts, his men would spot that large a force as soon as we crossed the River Feabhail. The news would reach him well before we arrived."

Murchad nodded. "We'll have to attack as soon as we get there, give your uncle as little time to prepare as possible. But it sounds as if no matter how many fighters we bring, we can't get into the fortress, with a guarded land bridge and a souterrain as the only ways in."

"True. We always felt safe from attack when I was a boy." Cian shuddered. It was treachery from within that had brought his father down.

"How long would the inhabitants be able to hold out against a siege? Is there a fresh water well within the fortress?"

Cian nodded. "Yes, there's a good well. As for food, in addition to the cold stores, there are two granaries within the stronghold. Assuming my uncle keeps them well stocked, as my father did, they could hold out for a long time."

Murchad furrowed his brow. "We will have to find a way to draw your uncle out of his fortress."

Einar said, "We can set fire to the roof. That would bring them out."

Cian stared at Einar, the horror of it dawning. They would burn his boyhood home and most likely kill folk he had grown up with, childhood friends, no matter that they had sworn to a usurper. What choice had they?

Murchad did not seem to notice his distress. "That settles it." He clapped Cian on the shoulder. "You've given me what I need to succeed."

Cian joined the others on the shore where the ships lay, still laden from the voyage home. The crew's sea chests had been left aboard along with weapons from the battle at Tromøy.

Ragnhild selected the four ships for the voyage, leaving the newly captured Danish longship behind, though its crew would sail to Ireland. The fleet had been thinly manned on the return trip due to the addition of the Danish prize, even more after Ursa's losses. For this trip, Ragnhild would take enough sailors to man the oars with about five extra on each ship to provide relief and fill in for any losses.

A cart brought new spears and arrows to replace those expended in the battle against Horik. Shields and axes had remained intact since they had not gotten close enough to the enemy for hand-to-hand fights. Reprovisioning was quickly done, with kegs of ale and fresh water, root vegetables, cabbages, and dried meat laid in to replenish their stores.

Cian found himself constantly glancing off to the west, hoping to see Ursa and her crew hauling *Wave Horse* across the land. He wondered how she fared. It seemed like such an impossible thing to drag a ship across miles of land, but he knew the Norse undertook such ventures all the time. Nothing could stand between them and their desire.

Late in the afternoon his longing was finally fulfilled when he glimpsed a black speck in the distance. Shouts filled the air. "It's them!" Ursa's three sisters took off running to lend a hand. Cian dropped what he was doing and followed them.

They arrived to find Ursa and her crew exhausted, sweaty, filthy, but triumphant. The strongest among them hauled the bow of *Wave Horse* with ropes tied around their chests like a harness. Cian joined Ursa's sisters to fall in beside those who gripped the gunnels and heaved the heavy wooden ship across greased log rollers. As the ship came off the rollers, those following behind picked the logs up and carried them forward, laying them down in front of the ship to provide a continuous log road. It was a laborious process, filled with sweat and toil, but they made progress.

Others arrived, relieving Ursa's crew, but Ursa herself refused to leave her position at the head of the line, insisting on hauling the ship all the way to Gausel's shore. Cian was thankful that it was not one of the big ships.

When *Wave Horse* was finally heaved onto Gausel's shore beside the rest of Ragnhild's fleet, Ursa dropped to the sand, completely spent. Cian hurried to bring her water while the others crowded around, congratulating her and her crew. They had just performed an amazing feat, and their grins of triumph showed they knew it.

The others made way for Cian as he bore a leather water flask to Ursa. They stood back while she drank and the congratulations trailed off. The well-wishers gradually drifted back to work, and Ursa and Cian were left alone.

"I'm sorry," he mumbled, feeling his face heat up. "I seem to have driven the others away."

She smiled at him, and his spirits buoyed. "It's all right. Thank you for the water."

Too tired to say more, Ursa drank from the leather flask. Her chestnut hair was spiked with sweat, her brown eyes half-closed in exhaustion. Food was brought, flatbread and skyr, and she joined her shipmates in eating ravenously. Cian remained silent, glad to be beside her. Once they were fed, Ursa and the crew of

Wave Horse staggered to their quarters to wash and sleep. Cian returned to work, but his tasks seemed so much easier with Ursa back, safe and sound.

But that night Cian found it impossible to sleep. In a few days he would return to his childhood home, and destroy it.

CHAPTER 5

The next day, Cian found himself assigned to *Raider Bride*, no doubt so that Murchad and Ragnhild could keep a watchful eye on him. Ursa was also in their crew, perhaps to receive further training from Ragnhild. Whatever the reason, Cian was glad that he would have one person who'd been friendly to him on board for the journey. Of course, once she found out what he'd done, that would probably change.

After Ragnhild made her choices, her húskarlar, Einar, Thorgeir, and Svein, picked their crews. There would be no untested captains on this cruise.

By evening the fleet was completely outfitted and supplied, ready to depart in the morning. When everyone retired to the great hall for the farewell feast, Cian sat in a corner by himself. He did not bring out his harp, nor did anyone ask him to play. Thorgeir entertained the crowd with an uproarious tale of Loki and the jotun shield-maiden, Skadi. The hall echoed with laughter, but though Cian understood the story well enough, he did not join the others.

Someone else was alone—Ursa. She came over and took a seat by him. "I heard about what you did," she said.

Cian did not know what to say.

"You were brave, trying to avenge your father and brother."

"But I was wrong. Everyone hates me."

"What you did had honor and courage. Give them time. They'll come around."

"You were brave, too," Cian ventured.

Ursa's smile faded. "My 'bravery' caused the death of two good men. They were little more than boys. Five others were injured, and I lost the sail."

"But you've learned your lesson, and made amends by hauling your ship back overland."

"I wasn't the only one who had to suffer through that portage, nor the only one who will weave the new sail. And I'm not the one who lost my life."

Cian sighed, unable to refute her points.

Ursa said, "We're outcasts, but at least there's two of us."

THE NEXT MORNING, Cian stood up to his knees in the gentle surf beside his shipmates, holding the gunnels of *Raider Bride* while Ragnhild took Herulf from Liv's arms for one last kiss good-bye. "Be good for your fóstra, son," she admonished in playful tones. Tears glimmered in her eyes as she handed the infant back to his nurse. "Take good care of my boy, as you have done in the past."

Cian wondered how Lady Ragnhild could bear to be parted from her child again so soon. The babe was only a few months old, though he did not make a fuss at being separated from his mother the way most children his age did. He seemed content with his nurse.

Ragnhild turned abruptly and vaulted onto *Raider Bride*, ordering the crew to shove off. Cian heaved with the others until the keel lost its grip on the sand. He scrambled aboard as the ship slid into the water.

He took an oar down from the rack, then seated himself on his sea chest and fitted his oar into the thole. The others ignored him as they took their places, chattering amongst themselves.

Ragnhild gave the orders to deploy the oars and row. She seemed completely immersed in the workings of the ship, and never turned to look back at her son. Cian eyed Lord Murchad, who stood beside his wife as she gave orders while simultaneously handling the steering oar. Murchad stared back at the shore, a hint of longing in his gaze.

Ursa had taken her place across from Cian and met his gaze with a nod and a sparkle in her brown eyes. He gave her a tentative smile. She looked fresh and hearty, fully recovered from her ordeal. Her chestnut hair gleamed in its single thick braid that hung down her back. Her tanned arms rippled with muscle as she plied her oar with ease.

Cian heaved on his oar, falling into the rhythm with the crew. At least this made him feel like he belonged. He dismissed his loneliness and let his thoughts quiet as he became part of the ship itself, skimming across the water that was calm on the surface yet roiling with currents beneath. He was proud to be able to pull his oar in time with the others. It was only recently that he'd regained his strength, thanks to the generous food and vigorous lifestyle of the Norse.

The little fleet stroked their way up the fjord, passing between the flat Jaeren plains on the western shore and rugged highlands to the east. By midmorning they were skirting the western shore, wending through the islands and skerries. The coastline opened up into a broad waterway, and beyond the last island the sea glinted like polished silver. The sight of that huge expanse of water, stretching to the horizon, took Cian's breath away.

A light breeze sprang up from the north, and Ragnhild called them to hoist the sail. Cian racked his oar with the others and joined the heaving line as they hauled the vast rectangle of tar-impregnated wool affixed to the heavy yard up the mast. When the sail was up and drawing, Ragnhild gathered the crew to the helm for a lesson. Cian hung back, unsure of his welcome, but Ursa motioned him to come beside her.

Once they were assembled, Ragnhild spoke. "All of you must learn how to find your way on the whale road, and I will share with you what I know of it."

Excitement stirred in Cian's chest. Though he'd been raised with boats and could handle oars and sails expertly, his experience had been with small coastal craft on rivers and lakes, and fishing boats plying the waters close to shore. He had little knowledge of the open sea. His only voyages out of sight of land had been on the Danish slave ship to Horik's hall. That trip had been a blur of hunger and misery, and he remembered little of it. After he'd been rescued by Åsa, the trip across the Skagerrak to Tromøy had been during pleasant weather, amid the triumphant sailors returning home. That passage had been quick and easy, and he'd given little thought to how they found their way. Ragnhild's offer to share her knowledge stirred his interest.

Ragnhild gestured out to sea. "Though we can't see them yet, the Orkney Islands lie due west of us, about a day's sail. But we can't just aim straight there. The sea currents set us a little to the south, toward the land of the Picts. The Picts don't like us much, and we don't care for them. We don't want to go there. So, to avoid Pictland and reach the islands, we have to steer just a hair to the north.

"But if we make too much northing, we'll miss the Orkneys. There are other islands to the north, the Shetlands and the Faroes, but they are just tiny dots in a vast sea. If we miss the islands, there's nothing out there but open sea for days on end. We'd become hafvilla, lost at sea, sailing until we ran out of water and food."

Her words sent a shiver down Cian's spine. He'd not considered the possibility of getting lost on this vast expanse. Panic rose in his throat.

"I'm going to set our course due west," Ragnhild said. "How do I find my direction without the sunset?" She turned to the stern and pointed. "See those two islets behind us?" Everyone craned their necks to spot the small skerries. Ragnhild worked the steering oar. "See, I'm lining them up, one behind the other." As she maneuvered, Cian watched the two islets align. She worked the steering oar some more. "When they are lined up with each other and the ship's keel is aligned with them, I know the stern is pointing due east. The prow is heading due west, away from the islets."

She directed them to adjust the sail according to her new course. "As long as I can see those two particular rocks, I can use them to maintain my heading. But by nightfall, we'll be out of sight of those islands, and land in every direction. I'll take a bearing on the sunset. After that, we must rely on the stars to find our way."

Cian took some reassurance from Ragnhild's confidence, and fear loosened its grip on his throat. The little fleet was commanded by experienced sailors who had found their way before.

The evening sky's blue deepened, and the crew shared out a meal of small beer, flatbread, and dried meat. Cian found Ursa. She smiled at him and patted the deck beside her, inviting him to sit. They stretched out on deck, leaning against the sides and enjoying the fine weather, the smooth motion of the ship bowling across the sea. The water made a shushing sound as it creamed along the hull.

"Sunset," said Ragnhild. The glowing orb hovered just above the horizon, and Ragnhild aligned the ship's prow with it. Just as the sun slipped below the horizon, she altered course a bit to the south. "The sun only sets due west on the equinox, at the beginning of Harvest Month. Since we are about midway between the summer solstice and the autumn equinox, I'm lining our prow up just a little south of the setting sun." She gestured to the other ships, where Einar, Thorgeir, and Svein all made course changes of their own. "At night, we're on our own. We can't count on being able to see each other until dawn."

As soon as it was dark enough to see the stars, she gave the steering oar over to Murchad and called the crew together again. "Now we are on star-time, not sun-time. We are lucky that this time of year it gets dark enough to see the stars, and tonight there are no clouds or fog. First we need to find the Leading Star."

Murchad leaned over to Cian. "We call it *Réalta Eolais* in Irish." A little spark of excitement jumped in Cian as he recognized the name of the star.

Ragnhild continued. "While the other stars move throughout the night, the Leading Star is always in the north. Our stories say the Leading Star is a jewel on the end of a spike the gods stuck through the nine worlds. That's why it never moves. It's a bright light, though not the brightest. To find it, first we must find Thor's Wagon." Ragnhild pointed out a familiar constellation high in the northwest sky.

Cian recognized it immediately. "*Cam Céachta*, the crooked plow."

"That's right," said Murchad. Cian warmed at the approval in his voice.

Ragnhild pointed at the constellation. "The two stars that form the back of the wagon point directly to the Leading Star. It is always alone." Cian's gaze followed her gesture, and he felt a jolt of triumph as he picked out *Réalta Eolais*, the Leading Star.

"Now I know which way is north," said Ragnhild, "I can see I'm heading west. But how far to the north am I? I can measure the Leading Star's height above the horizon." Ragnhild held her clenched fist at arm's length. "I can determine how high the star is by measuring how many fist-widths above the horizon it is." She laid her other fist on top of it, and, holding the upper fist steady, brought the one beneath it on top, and kept stacking fist upon fist until she reached the star.

"When we leave Gausel, the star is less than six fists above the horizon. I never want it to be more than six fists high. Otherwise, I'm too far north and I could miss the Northern Isles. I'll take a bearing on the Leading Star every change of watch, as long as it's dark enough to see it, to make sure we're on track. Before dawn, three bright stars in a row, Frigg's Distaff, will rise in the east. It should be directly astern. I'll take a bearing on it as well to be sure we're heading west. And when the sun rises, I can double-check our course."

Cian stared in fascination at the starry sky, the Leading Star shining brilliantly among them. Once he'd sighted it, his eyes found the star again easily. Ragnhild pointed out other constellations, naming them for the Norse gods: Fenrir's jaws, Thjiazi's eyes, and Freyja's chariot.

Ragnhild set watches to allow everyone to get some sleep, then relieved Murchad on the helm. Cian laid out his hudfat on the deck beside Ursa. She smiled in welcome, and they lay side by side, gazing up at the starry sky, pointing out the constellations to each other.

Ursa fell silent. When he looked over at her, her eyes were closed. She was fast asleep. He felt bereft, abandoned.

The hiss and gurgle of water flowing past the hull seemed to murmur to him as *Raider Bride* plowed through the waves. He didn't think he'd sleep, but the hard day's work had worn him out, and the ship's rhythmic passage over the seas soothed him.

Cian woke to daylight and the creak of ropes and the groan of timbers as the ship heeled over sharply. He slid across the deck, out of control until he bumped the leeward side. He scrambled out of his hudfat. The wind had strengthened with the dawn and come around to the north, sending *Raider Bride* racing over the waves. Land was nowhere to be seen.

Cian's heart thudded and he clutched the rail, eyeing the

Norse sailors going about their work. All it would take was one shove and he'd be overboard, adrift far from shore. Hafvilla.

But nobody took any notice of him. Cian slowed his breathing, scanning the crew for Ursa. He spotted her adjusting the sail at Ragnhild's direction. She didn't look his way. He leaned against the rail, out of the way, and looked on glumly.

Sailors darted about the slanting decks, taking turns as lookouts, pausing to wash down flatbread and dried meat with a cup of ale, burrowing into their hudfat for a nap in the shelter of the bow. The crew's vigor and enthusiasm was infectious, and soon he found the courage to join in, coiling ropes and bailing the water that seeped in beneath the floorboards. He began to feel more like a member of the crew rather than an unwanted passenger. He shook off his gloom and bent to the work at hand, and before long his fear had dissipated.

He paused to catch his breath, leaning against the windward side. Ursa took the spot beside him. "Are you excited to be returning home?" she asked.

"I never thought to see Ireland again," he blurted. "My close kin are all dead. I have my oath to fulfill, to take vengeance on my uncle for my father's death. Then I must rule in his place."

"You don't sound too happy about that." Ursa's brown eyes held genuine compassion.

"I was never raised to be a chieftain of my clan. That was my brother's role. Our father chose him as his successor, and he was groomed for the position. But now he's dead, and there are no other qualified candidates but me."

"What happened to him?"

Cian shook his head, sneaking a glance at Murchad. "My uncle only told me that he was killed not long after my father. He blamed both murders on Lord Murchad, but now I know it to be a lie."

"I'm sorry," she said.

Cian stared at her, undone by the sympathy in her voice.

"Your harp music is magical," she said, lowering her gaze. "I've never heard anything like it."

The note of reticence in her voice startled him. She was such a powerful, confident woman, afraid of nothing. Yet she seemed shy with him.

"Thank you. I had been training for eight years when I was taken by the Danes. Becoming a harper is all I've ever wanted." The loss was like a stone weighing in his gut.

"Won't you be able to play the harp when you are the ruler of your clan?"

"Many kings and chieftains play the harp. But it's a pastime for them, not the same as being dedicated to the cláirseach. I will not return to school. I will never progress to the higher degrees. Music will become secondary to my position as head of my clan." He could find no words to express the longing that rose up in his soul to follow the music where it took him, to unknown realms, realms forever lost to him.

Yet when his eyes met Ursa's, he glimpsed comprehension glimmering in their warm depths.

IN THE MORNING, Cian woke to the cry of "Land ho!"

He scrambled out of his hudfat and joined the crowd at the rail, staring at the low humps rising from the sea. At first he thought they could have been whale backs, but they didn't move.

"The Orkney Islands," Ragnhild announced, satisfaction in her tone. "We'll give the settlement of Birsay a wide berth. The chieftain is no friend of mine." She exchanged a look with Murchad. "We'll go down the eastern side of the islands. Get ready to man oars."

Cian ate a hasty breakfast of flatbread washed down with small beer, then took his place on his sea chest and fitted his oar in the thole. Ursa shot him a grin as she took her place across from him.

When his stint was up, another sailor came to relieve him on the oar. Cian saw Murchad and a few others on the stern, trolling baited lines. Murchad beckoned him with a welcoming smile, and he joined in. Fishing was something he was good at. He helped haul aboard several haddock and a big salmon. Cian was proud of his expertise in cleaning and gutting the catch, which earned him a few nods of approval.

Raider Bride sailed past the first island in the group. "There are no good anchorages here," Ragnhild explained. "Too exposed to the prevailing winds." They crossed a brief, roiling stretch of water to the next island, where they put in to a shallow bay rimmed with inviting white-sand beaches.

Cian's shoulders unclenched as he helped drop the sail and rowed with the others toward the shore. The ships surged onto the sand with a gentle hiss. The rowers racked their oars and spilled over the side, eager for solid land under their feet after the long passage.

As he started up the beach, Cian stumbled and nearly fell. Murchad grabbed him by the scruff of his neck and righted him. "Steady, lad." Then he hurried after Ragnhild.

Cian swayed on his feet, struggling to find his balance. His stomach churned.

"We've lost our land legs," said Ursa, staggering up alongside him. "Don't worry, it's normal after a rough passage. It will pass eventually. Be glad it doesn't make you vomit, like some."

Many of the crew were experiencing the same phenomenon. They stumbled up the beach, the land shifting and rolling beneath their feet as if they were in a seaway. A few stopped to throw up.

Ragnhild and Murchad showed no effects, nor did Thorgeir, Einar, or Svein. They sat on a driftwood log, watching in amusement as the sailors collapsed in a heap. Everyone perked up when

Ragnhild broke out a keg of ale. They dusted themselves off and set off to gather driftwood. Before long they had a cooking fire lit and roasted their catch on long, green sticks.

By the time they'd eaten a meal of fresh fish and flatbread washed down with ale, Cian had regained his land legs. He brought out his harp hesitantly, hoping his music would be well received after his fall from grace.

He struck up a merry *Geantraí* tune and began to sing a well-known Irish song in a faltering voice. To his surprise, Murchad chimed in with his deep bass. Ragnhild raised her voice, and soon the Norse were singing along in their ludicrous Irish. Cian's heart swelled with the music and the unexpected comradery.

When the song ended, Cian began to strum a lament, the song of a man in love with a Fae woman. Murchad sat down beside him, crooning the woeful tune, while the Norse sailors listened raptly to the heartrending music. Most could not understand the words, but the music told its own tale.

As the song faded, Murchad sighed and laid a hand on Cian's shoulder. "I'm glad I spared you, lad." Then he rose, wandering off to join Ragnhild.

Ursa seated herself beside him. Her eyes gleamed in the fire-light. "How do you make us laugh, then turn around and make us cry, when we don't even know the words?"

Cian carefully stowed his harp in its leather case. "We are schooled to make music that all living creatures respond to. But my skill is paltry. If I had completed my training, my harp could lead armies into battle."

"You have the ability to heal. I saw what you did with the völva. How did you do that?"

"The harp wakes the healing deep inside the patient. I restored the völva enough to bring her back to the land of the living, but she was not really willing. She's half in this world, half in the next. She knows she must remain among us for now, but longs for that other world where her loved ones await her."

"It must be very difficult, to be in neither one world nor the other."

Cian sighed. "It is."

Ursa stared at him, her eyes gleaming in the twilight. Then she got to her feet. "We should get some sleep."

Cian watched the shield-maiden cross the sand. Then he crawled into his hudfat. He lay gazing at the stars for a long time, listening to the gentle lapping of the waves on the sand, dreaming of seeing home for the first time in years.

CHAPTER 6

Tromøy

Stormrider departed the land of the Danes and soared over the Skagerrak to Tromøy. Night was falling when the falcon circled the steading, lit on the bower roof and entered through the smokehole. She glided across the room and landed on the perch beside the bed, releasing her hugr to flow into the inert form that lay there. Åsa did not wake at the transition. Falcon and human slept, side by side.

In the morning, Åsa woke refreshed from her long sleep and turned her attention from things she could do nothing about to those she could, namely, Olvir and Dagny's wedding. Åsa's second-in-command had fallen in love with the young healer while Dagny nursed Olvir back from a battle wound that could easily have killed him.

Åsa had been very happy to give them her blessing as long as they promised to make their new home on Tromøy. She couldn't risk losing either of them and offered them land on which to build their house. The young couple had been thrilled to accept.

Now the modest house was finished and the wedding preparations nearly complete. Vigdis would perform the ceremony the next day since it seemed unlikely Heid would be able to.

Åsa knew Vigdis was nervous, for this was the first time the apprentice had performed a wedding.

"Don't worry," Åsa reassured her. "You know the ceremony backwards and forwards."

Vigdis still looked worried. "If I make a mistake, I could bring ill-luck to their marriage."

"You won't make a mistake." Åsa was adamant. "Now let's go through the ceremony one more time."

At daybreak, Åsa donned her best garments. Handed down from her mother, the gown was a finely woven diamond twill of wool dyed red with madder. Around the neckline, hem, and cuffs, the garment was edged in narrow bands of precious silk, cut in thin strips painstakingly sewn on from fabric Åsa's father had brought back years ago from the East. Brenna combed out her red-gold hair and tamed it into a knot at the back of her head. Lastly, Åsa put on the amber necklace and earrings her mother had left her.

Arrayed in her finery, Åsa left her room and joined Tromøy's women to rouse the bride for her wedding day. They gathered outside the bower, where they gave voice to a vardlokkur to attract the spirits to bless the marriage.

When all the women of the steading were present, Åsa led them inside, still singing. Heid's apprentices were already up and had filled the wooden tub with warm water.

"It's time," said Åsa, gently pulling Dagny from the bed and guiding her to the bath. Dagny stepped into the tub and sat obediently while Brenna washed her hair and scrubbed her skin rosy.

The women helped her from the tub and dried her with a linen towel. Åsa and Brenna dressed the bride in the fine new gown the women had helped her make, of blue, wode-dyed linen embroidered with yellow flowers. Åsa remembered when she had so painstakingly embroidered her own gown for her wedding to Gudrød, her father's murderer. She'd sewn a tiny but lethal blade into a seam of that gown, with which to kill her husband on their wedding night.

Åsa shuddered as that awful day flooded back into her mind, when she'd been forced to wed the man who killed her father and her brother. She shook her head to rid herself of the image. This was the wedding of her two dear friends, who loved each other. A day of joy.

Brenna combed out Dagny's long brown hair, arranging it loose and flowing over her shoulders in an unmarried girl's style for the last time. Crowning her with the gilded bridal headdress, Åsa bestowed her blessing. "May you and Olvir have much happiness, and healthy children."

Taking up the vardlokkur once more, the women escorted the bride-to-be outside, to the sacred grove where hazel rods staked out the sanctuary. Early this morning, Vigdis had blessed the enclosure. Within its hallowed bounds the freemen sworn to Åsa gathered with their families.

Åsa led Dagny through the crowd, who greeted the bride with smiles and well-wishes as she passed. Together they stepped onto the platform where Olvir waited beneath the carved images of the gods. His eyes shone as his gaze fastened on his bride.

Vigdis mounted the platform, dressed in the völva's robes. The apprentice looked pale but resolute. Åsa sent her an encouraging smile.

She squeezed Dagny's trembling hand, and stepped back into the crowd to stand beside Eyvind. Her heart gave a little leap at the sight of him, handsome in a blue tunic that matched his eyes, his hair and beard freshly washed.

Vigdis took her place before the wedding couple and raised her arms, calling down the blessing of the gods. She turned to the altar and picked up a sword that lay there and offered it to Dagny, who took it with her left hand.

Vigdis nodded to Olvir. He held his own sword out to Dagny, hilt first. "Wife, I ask you to take my grandfather's sword into keeping for our firstborn child."

Åsa remembered exchanging swords with Gudrød at their ceremony, and how she'd longed to run him through with the blade.

Dagny took the proffered sword with her right hand and extended the weapon in her left hand to Olvir. "Husband, I give you this sword in return, to keep us safe." Dagny's father was a farmer, from a family without swords, so Åsa had given the girl a good one from the armory.

Having exchanged weapons, the couple turned to the altar. It was an ancient, weathered stone, its top worn smooth from years of use. On it gleamed a massive golden arm ring, passed down in Åsa's family for generations. Within this ring, Vigdis placed two gold finger rings, which Åsa had gifted to the young couple, and intoned a blessing over them. The apprentice picked up one of the rings and placed it on the tip of Olvir's sword. He turned carefully to Dagny, balancing the ring on the flat of his blade, and offered it to her. She took the ring and placed it on her finger. She then held out her sword to receive the other ring from Vigdis.

Åsa remembered how her hands shook so hard when she married Gudrød that the ring fell to the ground, a bad omen. It had certainly boded ill, especially for Gudrød. But Dagny received the ring on her sword without incident and offered it to Olvir. He took it from the blade and placed it on his own finger.

Åsa let out a sigh of relief. "Frigg be with you," she murmured. As Vigdis and the other women surrounded the bride, Dagny turned to Åsa and handed the sword to her for safekeeping.

The onlookers ushered the newlyweds into the hall, to their place of honor. Once the couple was seated, Vigdis brought in the double-handled wedding cup of honey mead. She offered it first to Olvir, who raised it in a toast to Thor. He drank and gave the cup to Dagny, who took the handles and drank to Freyja.

The crowd cheered as Åsa toasted the new couple. Eyvind took her hand, and a bitter wind of regret blew through her. She would never marry him or any other man, never share her sovereignty or the burden of it. Not after Gudrød, not after Rorik or Horik, men who had tried to control her, to take her power by force.

Vigdis approached the couple once more, this time bearing Thor's hammer, Mjölnir. This she laid in Dagny's lap and declared, "May the marriage be blessed with many children." The crowd cheered again. The newlyweds shared the loving cup, and the drinking began in earnest.

The song and laughter swirled in the air like woodsmoke. When the tumult had reached a deafening peak, a delicious aroma wafted into the hall as the cooks carried in platters of pork and venison, baskets of bread, and bowls of root vegetables. The merrymakers quieted appreciatively as the feast was set before them. Little could be heard but the scrape of eating knives on wooden platters as the attendees steadily demolished the food.

Once the platters had been picked clean and the servers had cleared away the wreckage, Åsa raised her horn again. "To the happy couple!" she cried. The feasters banged their cups on the trestle tables.

Åsa signaled the musicians to play. At the sound of harps and pipes, the guests got up to dance. Olvir swept his bride into a lively jig while everyone clapped.

As others took to the floor, Eyvind and Åsa joined them. The dancing went on until everyone had exhausted themselves.

Åsa announced that the time had come to bed the newlyweds. The crowd spilled out of the hall into the yard, cheering.

Laughing and calling out bawdy advice, the women surrounded the bride and steered her to the couple's new house, singing and strewing flowers in her path. They arrived at the threshold, where Olvir waited, surrounded by the men of Tromøy.

The memory of her struggle with Gudrød in Borre's chamber swept over Åsa, when she did her best to kill him while he tried to rape her. They both had failed that awful night.

She pushed her thoughts away and gave Dagny a hug. Vigdis drew the bride forward, kissing her on both cheeks in the goddess's embrace, saying, "May Freyja bless you and make you fruitful." Then she gave Dagny a little push toward Olvir and backed away.

Olvir picked his wife up gently and carried her inside, then set her carefully on her feet. He drew his sword and drove it into the central pillar of the house, where it stuck fast. The company sent up a mighty cheer, shouting lewd suggestions as Olvir firmly closed the door.

Arm in arm, Åsa and Eyvind found their way to her private chamber. They did not speak of the wedding that would never be theirs.

Erritsø

GROA LAY UPON HER BED, summoning her strength. She was determined to take her revenge, as well as the vengeance Ingebjorg demanded. Her frail body was no obstacle. If anything, the agony she'd endured had strengthened her mind and will. Since recovering from burns that should have killed her, she'd spent days confined to her bed, mastering unbearable pain, pain that unbound her hugr from her body. She discovered she no longer needed her poor dead fylgja to travel.

Groa focused on the faint pulsation in her toes. She concentrated on the sensation, drawing it up. Bit by bit she coaxed the vibration up her legs and into her torso until it surged through her body in waves. When her head began to pulse, she released the energy and let it carry her mind out into the air.

Free of her body, she flew across the Skagerrak, swifter than any hawk.

She went first to the hall of the queen, Åsa. To her fury, she found her enemy hale and healthy in the arms of her lover. In spite of all Groa and Horik had thrown at her, the woman had escaped without a scratch. Åsa's steading looked prosperous, bustling with workers and warriors. On the beach lay a fleet of longships. To her consternation, Groa recognized a number of Horik's vessels captured in the last battle. The once-mighty warlord had lost badly to the upstart queen.

The völva sensed the atmosphere surrounding the queen carefully. Åsa's power was strong. Maybe too strong. Groa searched for an easier target. Her lover was one, but he was closely protected by Åsa's power.

In the bower, Groa found the völva Heid, huddled in the bower close to the fire, clutching her shawl around her. Groa probed the woman's energy and recoiled from the force she encountered. The völva appeared weak, but Åsa's sorceress emanated waves of immense, unregulated power. The sorceress's mind wandered aimlessly, blasting the space around her with energy. She had no control over her power. Should Heid ever regain command of her mind, the völva would be a formidable adversary, but for now, she was no threat. Even so, Groa dared not get closer to the furor of magic that erupted from her.

Groa searched fruitlessly for some other weakness on Tromøy. There must be something. Åsa was a great queen, but she was still a human woman. She had a flaw, and Groa would find it.

She remembered the boy. Halfdan, Åsa's son. A child was always a mother's weakness. Where was he?

She sent her spirit high above the island, seeking the boy. She called up everything she remembered about him, his black hair, his personality, but even more, his nascent power. Nothing. He was not there. Not with his mother, nor her völva.

That was not all bad. Here he was protected by his mother and her sorceress. If he were somewhere else, there might be weakness Groa could exploit. She sent her hugr over a broader vista, seeking the boy's essence.

She soared over the landscape, casting a wider and wider net across the countryside, searching for some trace of him.

At last a hint of his essence wafted toward her on the breeze. She followed it like a hound on a scent, over hills and streams. Then the trail grew fainter until it petered out. She paused in the air, casting in all directions, but the boy's hugr had vanished.

Cursing, she headed home.

Then, as she neared the Skagerrak, she caught a new whiff of her quarry on the breeze. She drew closer, scenting the boy's hugr, until Halfdan began to materialize. Then Groa sharpened her senses to discern his location.

She spotted his raven's-wing hair at Skiringssal. He was with Olaf, and his queen, Sonja. Olaf had nearly given his life for the boy, and for Åsa. There was love there.

Love meant weakness.

Groa focused her attention back on Halfdan.

A grizzled blacksmith guarded the boy. Groa carefully sensed the aura of magic around the old craftsman. He had some power, but he was no match for her. The blind wolf who lay by the warmth of the forge twitched in his sleep, emitting a warning growl. That wolf had attacked her, and killed a warrior in defense of the boy. She would have to take care of that threat.

She homed in on Halfdan, sending a shroud of death over him. *May he never grow up to achieve his fate. May Åsa mourn him for the rest of her life.*

Something was wrong. The boy did not respond to her curse. Groa probed the atmosphere around him and was rebuffed by a powerful spell. It reeked of Heid's power, still functioning despite the ruin of its mistress. The völva's spell had taken on a life of its own.

As long as Heid lived, the spell would protect the boy. Possibly even beyond the völva's lifetime.

Groa would have to try another tactic. She hovered above, watching.

CHAPTER 7

Orkney Islands

When they got underway in the morning, Ragnhild directed them into the archipelago, its waters rife with churning tide rips and submerged rocks. *Raider Bride* took the lead, though the four ships remained within hailing distance of each other.

Tova, one of Ursa's younger sisters, stood in the prow, one hand gripping the ship's stem and the other holding a white signal flag. She leaned over the side, peering intently into the depths. When she spotted a hazard, she shouted and pointed the flag at the threat while Ragnhild steered the ship out of harm's way.

The crews were silent in concentration as they threaded their way through the treacherous waters of the Orkneys. The hard-running current flushed the four ships between the islands, allowing the rowers to rest their oars while the helmsmen steered them south through the maelstrom of submerged rocks and riptides. Despite Tova's vigilance, from time to time the hull scraped bottom or the oarsmen had to fend off a rock.

After several intense hours the current gradually eased, and Ragnhild turned the helm over to Murchad. The crew fitted their oars and rowed hard through the slack. Tova kept a close lookout, finding it much easier to navigate the shoals without the current threatening to dash them on the rocks. By evening, the tide had strengthened against them, and they turned into a vast body of sheltered water.

Ragnhild directed the exhausted crews into a cove, where they set anchor for the night and slept on board. The intense focus had left everyone shaky. Half asleep, they gulped down another cold meal of dried meat and flatbread, washed down with water, and set watches for the night. It was a fine evening, and Ragnhild let them sleep on board without the need to raise the awnings.

As she crawled into her hudfat beside Murchad, Ragnhild thought of Herulf. She missed his soft skin and downy hair, and longed to hold him again. She didn't need his favor; she just needed to be able to see him, to touch him, and hear his baby noises. The long winter, with him and Murchad close by, sounded better and better.

Murchad held her tight and, as if he read her thoughts, said, "I miss him too."

Once again she worried how her husband must feel, returning to the home he'd left and the kingship he'd renounced for her sake, to become a stranger in her land, a man whose standing was based on that of his wife. What if they were forced to spend a winter in Ireland? What kind of reception would they get? Murchad was still a lord in Ireland and owned a manmade island fortress on the forest lake in his own right. They would be well housed there, and the idea of spending a winter in Ireland was not all bad, but the thought of going months without seeing Herulf filled her with anxiety. Their son would likely say his first words and take his first steps without his parents to cheer him on.

Yet she knew herself. Huddling in the bower with an infant all winter would drive her mad. She'd be out on skis most of the time, hunting. Herulf was too young even to ride on a sled. How would she make it work?

She sighed. Her oath to Åsa was binding, thank the gods. It did no good to worry about the winter. It would take care of itself, one way or another. She nuzzled Murchad's chest and held him tight, inhaling his scent of brine and leather. He gathered her into a drowsy embrace, and she drifted off to sleep, warm in Murchad's arms.

At first light, Einar floated his buoy, watching for the tide to favor them. As soon as the rope slackened, they raised anchor and fitted their oars once more. This time Einar's ship took the lead, with an experienced crew member on the bow with the signal flags, while Tova rested from the previous day's rigors. Ragnhild relaxed at the helm, enjoying the scenery without the need for constant focus.

Early in the day they rowed through a narrow passage between two headlands. Rounding a cape, the little fleet found themselves once more in the open sea. Ragnhild ordered sails raised and steered south until land hove into sight ahead. She remembered a good harbor that was not far. Coming alongside *Eagle's Treasure*, she conferred with Einar. The húskarl agreed about the location of the anchorage she was thinking of.

Taking the lead, *Raider Bride* veered off and turned west to reach along the distant coast until a headland reared out of the sea. Ragnhild rounded the bluff and headed south again, and soon land was in sight on either side of the ship, just as she remembered. With satisfaction she led the fleet into a sheltered bay.

They drew the ships up on the beach. Ragnhild decided they were isolated enough to let them build a proper fire to cook a pot of barley porridge. They needed a hot meal and an evening's rest. Afterward, the crew lingered around the campfire, sipping their ale in silence, too tired from the day's work and too full of hot food for their usual chatter.

Cian took out his harp once again and tuned it with care. Even though he kept it in its leather case, the sea air was hard on the instrument. Once it was tuned to his satisfaction, he strummed a melody, and Ragnhild recognized the *Suantraí*, a song for deep and healing sleep.

Nobody sang along to the unfamiliar tune, but they all listened, faces rapt. Ragnhild thought it wouldn't be long before they accepted the Irishman back into their fold. She watched Ursa, sitting beside the harper, mesmerized by his music. She was a bold girl, who did not care what others thought. She too would soon regain the respect she had lost. Ursa had all the hallmarks of a leader. Ragnhild hoped she would survive long enough for her abilities to come to fruition.

When Cian strummed the last note, Ursa was asleep beside him. He covered her with his cloak, gazing at her tenderly. There was a budding romance if ever there was one. Perhaps the Irishman would be a good influence.

Ragnhild sought out her husband, already asleep, and crawled into the hudfat, warm from his body heat. The stars glimmered above her, and she fell asleep reveling in her freedom and the adventures that lay before her.

At dawn, the sailors climbed out of their sheepskins to gather around the campfire for steaming bowls of porridge. They struck camp, rolling up their hudfat and washing breakfast pots, wooden cups, and bowls before stowing them on the ships.

The morning was clear with just enough breeze. Sail set and drawing, they followed a southerly course through a gradually narrowing passage. Soon they were threading their way through an archipelago that sheltered them on both sides. The wind died off and the crew plied their oars once more. The currents here were less treacherous than in the Orkneys, and they sighted dolphins, eagles, puffins, and seabirds of all descriptions.

This was the life Ragnhild loved. She would never give it up, even for her chieftainship, even for Herulf. One day, her son would be old enough to go on voyages with her. She imagined him, a young boy, nimble and full of energy, delighting in the sea. No fosterage for him. As soon as he was big enough to safely travel by sea, she'd take him. Until then, she would miss him every summer and be with him through the long Nordic winters.

Late in the day they broke out of the islands into broad ocean swells and hoisted sail to a good northerly breeze, pushing them south across the open water. Murchad scanned the coastline. "There is the sacred Isle of Colm Cille," he said, pointing out the island in the distance. The longing in his voice was palpable.

"I'm sorry, love, you know I'm not welcome there, nor the rest of my people," said Ragnhild. "Father Blathmac would not take kindly to one hundred and forty *finn gaill* descending on his island."

"I know," said Murchad with a sigh.

Ragnhild felt his disappointment. Iona was a place of holy legend, where one of Ireland's great saints, the blessed Saint Colm Cille, had spent his days. There, monks working in a great scriptorium had once produced treasured illuminated manuscripts. The Dane raiders had ravaged the island in recent times, massacring the brethren and destroying the settlement. They took the beautiful books for their bejeweled and gilded covers, never caring about the writing within. The scriptorium had been moved to safety at the monastery of Kells in Ireland, and for years the holy island lay abandoned.

But a few years ago, a band of fearless monks had resettled the island, led by the zealot, Blathmac. He had despised Ragnhild and her shield-maidens.

"You'd think he'd be grateful, after we saved them from the Danes," Ragnhild said bitterly.

"Blathmac hates women and foreigners," said Murchad,

staring at the dwindling island. "But I doubt he'll last long in that defenseless place. The Danes can smell treasure. They'll be back."

The ships veered away from land, crossing open ocean once again, heading for the north coast of Ireland. Ragnhild gave the lands of the Dál Riata a wide berth. There she had been taken captive by the crazed Pictish king, driven by his belief that if he married the woman who possessed the cursed necklace, he would be high king of Ireland. Murchad had rescued her, and they had barely escaped with their lives.

It seemed the entire journey to Ireland was rife with enemies and places where she was unwelcome.

~

Tullynavin

Ragnhild steered *Raider Bride*, straining to peer through the mist. The wind had slackened, and the cries of seabirds told her they were close to land. The question was, at what part of the coast would they make landfall?

Suddenly rugged bluffs materialized through the fog. Ragnhild smiled with pride when she recognized the distinctive form of Inis Eoghain. Murchad clapped her on the shoulder. "That's my expert navigator!"

Ragnhild warmed at his praise, but she couldn't take all the credit. If she had gone astray, Einar would have let her know. Yet she was proud that he had not needed to correct her.

The fog dissipated, and she steered around the rocky headland and through the narrow entrance to the inland sea of Lough Feabhail.

Cian stood at the rail, his eyes scanning the eastern shore hungrily. The peninsula had been part of his father's kingdom, his boyhood home. How must he feel at seeing it now, after all that had happened? Did his heart yearn for all he'd lost?

Murchad followed her gaze. "I think it's best to keep Cian's identity secret until we see which way the wind blows."

She nodded. Murchad was adept at Irish politics, while she was like a goat loose in the hall.

"No one on the western shore is likely to recognize him. The last time he was seen here, he was a boy. I'm sure he's changed a lot since then."

Three years of slavery will change a person, Ragnhild thought. Despite ample food and rest in recent weeks, Cian's face was lean, his cheeks hollow. He had wiry muscles, belying his strength, and there was a wariness in his eyes that made it clear his trust was not easy to gain.

Ursa came to the rail to stand beside Cian, and a smile lit his face. The two outcasts. Ragnhild was glad they had found each other. The girl had made a foolish decision, and now was a critical time for her to recover her self-confidence. The crew still kept their distance from her, but under Ragnhild's watchful eye they had not dared shame her.

The sound of water trickling along the hull told her the tide was with them, pushing the little fleet down the western shore. Soon she recognized the sandbar at the river mouth that led to Tullynavin. Ragnhild called for the crews to drop sail and take to their oars.

After a mad scramble, they got the sail stowed and oars deployed. The ships turned into the river mouth and followed the withy stakes that marked the channel through the shifting sands.

The ship rounded a bend, and the landing hove into view. Shore guards, sighting the ships, sounded the alarm, shouting and brandishing their spears.

Murchad stood in the prow, holding a white shield aloft. "We come in peace," he called as they came into earshot. "I am Lord Murchad mac Maele Duin."

The guards stared for a moment. There were four of them, three young and gangly with barely sprouted beards, barefoot and bare-legged, wearing the knee-length yellow tunics of warriors. The more mature man, obviously their commander, barked an order, and they put their spears aside, standing by to take the mooring lines.

Ragnhild steered *Raider Bride* alongside the rickety dock, constructed of woven withy switches that appeared more complex than sturdy. The shore guard tied them off amid a welter of craft, from tiny hide-covered currachs to seagoing ships fashioned from wood planks.

The rest of the fleet rafted alongside *Raider Bride*. Einar wisely set an anchor to keep the ships steady in the river current. From the looks of the dock, Ragnhild thought it might be needed to keep the whole thing from being blown away by a gust of wind.

The guard commander came forward and bowed. "Greetings, Lord Murchad. It's our honor to have you here. If you will follow me, Lord Aed will be glad to see you."

"Thank you," said Murchad. They scrambled across the rafted vessels and set out after the guards, up the trail to the walled fortress. Ragnhild remembered the battle that had razed this fortress to the ground. She had freed her crew from slavery, and they were fleeing down the river on *Raider Bride* when the stronghold had been attacked in the night. She had turned back to rescue Murchad. That's when she'd truly known her heart was his.

The fortress gate opened, and an honor guard conducted them onward while the dock watch returned to their posts.

Inside, they were met with the redolent scent of the midden, the noise of squawking fowl, barking dogs, and raucous children. Dwellings sprouted like toadstools in the yard, newly thatched roofs still fresh and golden. Folk scurried among them, scattering flocks of chickens and geese. In the center of the chaos rose Aed's rebuilt hall, a roundhouse three times the size of the other dwellings, crowned with its own golden, new-thatched roof.

~

CIAN RECOGNIZED the chieftain who greeted them at the door. He shrank back among the other crew members, hoping he'd changed enough over the years that Aed would not recognize him.

Aed swept a graceful bow. The Irish chieftain was tall and lean, his brown hair and beard streaked with gray. Though he was barefoot like the rest, he wore a fine blue linen robe, embroidered at the cuffs, hem, and neckline with red thread, belted at the waist with a fine leather belt. A silver pin fastened his gray woolen cloak at his shoulder. "Hail, Murchad mac Maele Duin, Lady Ragnhild. Your visit does me honor. You and your followers are welcome." He gestured extravagantly for them to enter.

Cian was swept along with the crew into the roundhouse, keeping to the middle of the pack of Norse, his head bowed so his face fell into the shadow of his hair.

Aed's rebuilt hall, though modest by royal standards, accommodated Ragnhild's four ship's crews along with Aed's forty or fifty retainers. Inside, the structure's newness was apparent. The post-and-wattle walls gleamed with whitewash, the lofty thatch still golden and freshly scented, the gravel floor newly swept. Straw-filled beds lined the walls, and benches surrounded the fire pit. Despite the warmth of the summer's day, an iron cauldron hung on its chain from the roof tree, steaming over the fire.

At the back of the hall stood Aed's high seat, a chair of carved wood with an embroidered pillow for him to sit upon. The steward seated the visitors according to their rank, Ragnhild and Murchad nearest to the high seat.

Cian squeezed in beside Ursa, he hoped hidden among the crew, while close enough to hear Murchad's conversation with Aed.

Through a low door in the back wall, servants entered bearing bowls to wash with and clean linen towels.

Cian was grateful for the traditional Irish hospitality. The servers dipped hot water from the cauldron and mixed it with cold water in the wash bowls. Ragnhild and Murchad washed first, then the bowls were passed along down the ranks. While he waited his turn, Cian's eyes followed Ursa's every move as she dipped a clean linen cloth into the water and washed her face and neck, and pushed up the sleeves of her tunic to wash her arms.

When Cian's turn came, the water had cooled and was no longer very clean, but it still was a luxury to rinse the brine from his skin. Like everyone else, his rough wool tunic and breeks were stiff with salt and grime. Everything could use a good wash, but that would have to wait.

More servants entered, bearing cups and buckets of ale. When the cup came to Cian, the sweet taste of Irish ale, so different from the Norse ale, sent a wave of emotions crashing through him. While the Norse flavored their brews with juniper or yarrow, this ale, paid as tribute to Aed by his tenant farmers, had been brewed to the district's strict legal standards. It was thick and chewy, almost like porridge, sweeter than the Norse drink, but potent. Cian watched Ursa's eyes widen in delight at the strength of the brew.

The scent of food wafted into the room as servants brought in bowls of barley porridge and platters of bread and cheese, along with more ale. Cian's stomach growled in appreciation, and he helped himself, forgetting his worries while he filled his belly.

When the bowls had been licked clean, and the bread and cheese demolished, the harper struck his cláirseach. Cian's soul quivered along with the strings. The room fell silent as the harper strummed a tune and declaimed a tale in a well-schooled, sonorous voice. Most of the Norse crew could not follow the Irish words, but they were captivated by the music and the harper's alluring cadence.

Ursa's hand stole into his. Cian glanced at her, startled, and glimpsed the shimmer of a tear in the corner of her eye. Her touch sent warmth up his arm, straight to his heart. He squeezed Ursa's hand, and their eyes met as the music welled.

Though the performance was not of the highest order, it still had passion. The familiar tune and tale transported Cian to the past, filling him with longing. The music opened his soul as it always did, and he let himself become lost in it.

The harper plucked his last string, waking Cian from his trance. Ursa let go of his hand and moved hers back to her lap. She kept her lashes lowered, and her cheeks were flushed. A faint smile played about her lips.

When the reverberations of the harp faded, Aed turned to Murchad, signaling the floor open to discuss business. "What brings you to Ireland, my lord?" Cian leaned forward to hear the conversation.

Murchad smiled. "I haven't seen my home nor my cousin Niall in a year. How is he?"

"King Niall does very well. We prosper under him." There was an awkward pause. Aed was obviously too wise to say anything that might bring a comparison between Murchad's rule and his cousin's. He hurried on. "The king will be happy to see you. I remember you were as close as brothers."

"That we were, once," said Murchad with a look of regret.

"How long will you grace us with your presence, my lord?" Aed inquired delicately.

"In order to return home before the winter storms set in, we must go to see him as soon as possible. We can stay with you no more than a day. Then we'll sail down to Daire Calgaich and send word to Niall to have men bring mounts to the monastery."

Aed looked relieved at this news. Needless to say, it was a burden to feed and house a royal retinue of one hundred and forty hearty sailors.

Cian fought a feeling of apprehension that nagged him. Surely no one at Aileach would recognize him after all these years. The last time he'd been there, he'd been a boy of eight, before he'd been consigned to the school of harpers. Still the thought of being exposed worried him.

Aed signaled his steward. "You must be tired from your voyage. I will let you retire now. Bless you all and welcome."

The steward conducted Ragnhild and Murchad to a bed alcove on the north side of the roundhouse, a place of honor near the host's bedstead. Cian filed out behind Ursa with the rest of the crew to the guesthouse. He was relieved to lose himself among them, away from anyone who might recognize him.

As they crossed the yard to the guesthouse, Ursa took his hand. After the crew passed through the door, she pulled him aside. In the shadow of the building, her mouth found his.

Though her lips were soft, their touch sent a tingling shock through his body, right down to his feet. A pleasant warmth flooded his belly, leaving him wanting more. He took her face in his hands, pulling her close and returning her kiss.

"Ursa," Tova's voice sounded. "Where are you?"

Ursa pulled away, touching his cheek gently as she slipped inside the guesthouse.

Cian leaned against the building while the strength returned to his knees. He entered the guesthouse and found a pallet among the other men.

All night he lay awake, his whole body alive with the desire Ursa had awakened. This was a new feeling to him. After all his years of captivity, he had no experience with women. He'd been taken by the Danes just as his interest in his female classmates had awakened, before he'd had a chance to explore his desires. As a slave, he'd been starved and beaten and certainly never loved by any woman.

Sleep was elusive as he relived the kisses, the touches, Ursa's scent of herbs. She'd made her desire clear, but he knew better than to rush the shield-maiden. He didn't want his inexperience to scare her away. Somehow he'd find the fortitude to wait.

In the morning they breakfasted on oat porridge and cream,

another taste Cian had missed. Oats did not grow well in Lochlainn, and though their cream was rich, their porridge was always barley.

After breakfast, Cian joined the rest of the crew as they trooped down to the river to bathe. They found a deep pool, dappled with sun and shaded by oaks in turn. They all stripped down, men and women alike, and washed their clothes, hair, and bodies with lye soap.

Cian watched Ursa slide into the water, his desire growing at the sight of her strong, white body, embroidered with battle scars. He dove in and swam to her, and they found each other under water. For the first time Cian's hands were free to explore. She smiled and put her arms around him, drawing him closer. In silent agreement, they made their way to the shore and clambered onto the grassy bank. They found a sunny, secluded spot, where they lay in each other's arms. Glorying in the heady touch of the sun and Ursa's body, Cian brought his lips to hers tentatively. She returned his kisses, stoking his desire. Just when he could stand it no longer, Ursa guided him into her, and Cian made love for the first time.

His years of slavery and loneliness were obliterated by an overwhelming joy such as he'd never felt before, even greater than the joy of playing his harp.

The others had gone by the time their desire was slaked. They lay a bit longer in their sunny spot, then swam lazily back to the other side, where they collected their clothes and dressed.

Tova and Unn grinned at them knowingly when they strolled into the guesthouse. Cian felt himself blush, but Ursa turned a fierce glare on her sisters, and they said nothing.

That evening, Aed entertained them with an even greater feast. Cian sat beside Ursa, so aware of her presence he barely heard the music. All he knew was her scent, her warmth, her breathing. He held her hand, and the heat between them seemed to melt their flesh.

When at last the evening was over and they retired to the guesthouse, Ursa led him to a quiet corner, where they made love through the night. Near dawn they fell into an exhausted sleep, wrapped in each other's arms.

Cian and Ursa were still entwined when they woke. They reluctantly parted, dressing in the cold morning air and eating a hasty breakfast while dodging the grins of their shipmates.

They clambered aboard *Raider Bride* and fitted their oars, following the withy stakes in the river back to the Lough Feabhail. Cian tried to keep his eyes off Ursa, but their gazes met with a jolt like lightning through his body. She broke eye contact abruptly and turned her attention to her oar, but Cian stared at her, mesmerized by a vortex of desires that carried him on a stormy current of emotions beyond his control.

He longed to take out his harp, to express these feelings in the only way he knew how. But that would have to wait.

CHAPTER 8

Skiringssal

Three-year-old Rognvald trotted to catch up with his foster brother, Halfdan, and his blind wolf, Fylgja. Determined as he was, Rognvald's short legs could not catch six-year-old Halfdan, whose limbs had lengthened even more over the summer.

Halfdan slowed, noting the younger boy could not keep up. "Hurry, Ulf is waiting."

They reached the smithy together, where the sound of hammer on metal and the smell of hot iron filled the air.

As the boys burst into the workshop, Ulf glanced up from his anvil. The aging blacksmith watched them take their places, eager for their lessons. Fylgja found a corner near the forge and curled up. The blind wolf was getting old, but he stayed close to his young master.

Today, Ulf took up a hunk of iron bloom with his tongs. He held the iron over the fire until the metal glowed a deep red. "See the color change as the iron gets hotter." The metal transformed from red to orange, lightening to yellow, and finally white.

"Now is the time to forge. If you heat it any longer, the iron will be molten and run all over the place." He pulled the white-hot iron out of the forge with his tongs and laid it on the anvil. "I'm going to beat the slag off of it. Keep your distance!" He hefted his hammer and began to forge the metal. Sparks flew as the impurities fell away from the good iron. "Watch how the color changes as the iron cools." When the iron glowed dull red again, Ulf thrust it back in the forge until it was white once more. Then he withdrew it and forged it again.

"Now you boys practice your forging," he said. Ulf had built the boys miniature anvils on which to practice on scrap wood. It was safe, but satisfied the boys' desire to pound on something. Rognvald bashed his miniature wooden hammer with abandon, while Halfdan, brow furrowed, tried to emulate Ulf's forging technique.

Ulf kept a watchful eye on both of them, especially Rognvald, who showed no fear of the fire even after he'd burned himself trying to pick up hot coals. The smith made sure the toddler could not get near the furnace again.

Once the boys had worn themselves out hammering long enough to sit still, Ulf gave them each a sharpened charred stick and a piece of smooth wood. "Let's see you carve your runes. Do you remember what I taught you yesterday?"

Both boys attacked their wood scraps vigorously, but only Halfdan was able to form the runic letters in a recognizable way. When he'd succeeded in carving the first three runes, Ulf quizzed him. "Can you tell me the names of these runes?"

Halfdan pointed to each letter with his stick. "Fehu, Uruz, Thurz."

"And what do they stand for?"

"Cattle, water, thorn!" Halfdan quoted triumphantly.

"That's right. Keep going," Ulf said. "What comes after Thurz?"

Halfdan pondered for a moment. "Ansuz?"

"That's right! Now, can you cut it?"

Halfdan complied, his face scrunched up in concentration.

Meanwhile, Rognvald was having a grand time, scribing random shapes with his stick and shouting out words that had little to do with runes.

The boys spent nearly an hour carving. Rognvald was just beginning to lose interest when the skáld, Knut, arrived to give the boys their lessons in history and poetry. During his long life, Knut had educated two generations of high-born children in the area, including the boys' parents: Åsa and her brother, Gyrd, as well as Olaf and Sonja. Ulf and the skáld had been friends for many years. Though he was near in age to Ulf, Knut's gray eyes were clear in his tanned face and the old poet still stood straight and moved with lithe grace.

Knut took over, his spellbinding voice enchanting the boys to silence as he regaled them with the exploits of their ancestors: Olaf the Woodcutter, Halfdan Whiteleg, Gudrød the Hunter; Knut described their lineage in terms suited to an adventure saga.

Ulf listened to the skáld while he returned to his work, polishing the blade he'd forged this morning. Skiringssal was a busy trading port this time of year. Word had gotten out that Ulf's blades were superior to others in the trading area, and the demand was high for his swords, though only the most wealthy could afford such a weapon. There were even more orders for the less costly spearheads, axes, and the long fighting knives, seaxes.

Eyvind would be arriving from Tromøy soon to pick up a load of trade goods before he sailed to the eastern ports of Gotland, Birka, and Aldeigja. The trader would return in the fall, his stout knarr laden with goods, and hopefully more ingots of the Wootz steel. Wootz was a superior grade of steel, the secret to Ulf's incomparable weapons. It was manufactured in a hidden location in the East, and could be obtained only in the markets of far-off Serkland. Eyvind had established connections that enabled him to acquire the sought-after metal in Aldeigja and bring it home exclusively for Ulf.

Even on the rare occasions that other Norse smiths got hold of the precious steel, none but Ulf had the skill to forge it. He'd learned the art in his youth, when he'd been captured and enslaved to a master swordmaker in Serkland. The master had crippled his slaves' legs so they could still walk but not run, rendering escape impossible. Of course, he left their upper bodies uninjured so they could wield hammer and tongs.

Åsa's father, Harald, had rescued Ulf and brought him home to Tromøy, where he'd taken up the hammer and served the family ever since.

That had been long ago. Åsa's father was gone, as was the rest of her family. All she had left was her son, Halfdan.

WHEN THE BOYS' lessons were complete, Rognvald's fóstra came and collected the younger boy for his nap, leaving Halfdan free to wander. After his last escapade, he knew his boundaries and had promised not to venture beyond them. He stopped at the kitchen and filched some bread and cheese for his lunch, as well as a leather bottle of small beer.

Trailed by the blind wolf, he entered the forest to visit the landvaettir, who were his friends. They lived behind a waterfall that flowed from a rocky outcropping. In the springtime the water cascaded briskly, but this late in the summer it had dried to a fine curtain of mist. Still, it was cool here and the moss was soft. Fylgja lapped water from a pool, then flopped down in the shade, panting a little.

Behind the waterfall yawned the black mouth of the cave where the spirits dwelled.

Halfdan found the rock with a shallow depression carved in

the surface—an ancient álf-cup. He took the skin of beer from around his neck and poured a little in the declivity.

"Let them come who wish to come, let them go who wish to go, and do no harm to me or mine," he chanted, as Ulf had taught him.

Fylgja whined faintly and the hair on Halfdan's arms prickled. A cool breeze sprang up and caressed his cheek. The vaettir's invitation.

Halfdan took off his boots and walked barefoot beneath the curtain of water that spilled over the rocks. The moss was soft and cold on his bare feet, and the air smelled fresh. Behind the waterfall the shadowy cave beckoned. Halfdan stepped onto the slippery rocks and entered the space behind the flowing water. The air was chilled and thick with moisture.

He called out to his friends, the spirits of the falls. Their silvery voices, so easily mistaken for the sound of water, greeted him and invited him to enter their world. The blind wolf curled up outside and fell into a deep sleep while Halfdan walked into the cave.

The vaettir surrounded Halfdan with delight. They were little creatures, no bigger than Rognvald, though plumper. They wore tunics of cobwebs and red toadstools for hats.

The vaettir brought out their instruments and struck up unearthly music. One strummed a harp with strings of running water, one played drums with the sound of thunder, while another sang with the voice of the wind.

An isolated thunderstorm appeared above the holy hill, for those with eyes to see.

GROA WATCHED CAREFULLY. To any observer, the völva's hugr appeared as a hawk hovering in the sky above the sacred falls. She soared down to the falls and peered inside the cavern, where she watched the vaettir entertain the boy. They were insubstantial creatures, fun-loving and harmless.

This was something she could work with. First she must drive off the vaettir. That was a small matter, for those who lived in rocks and caves were timid folk.

After Halfdan departed, a dark spirit manifested itself in the cave behind the falls. Tall and thin, with sharp-clawed fingers and burning eyes, it trailed malice like a tattered cloak. The vaettir took one look and fled.

Groa settled in to wait.

THE NEXT DAY when the morning lessons were finished and Rognvald's fóstra collected him for his nap, Halfdan prepared to slip away to the falls.

"Wait, lad," said Ulf. Halfdan's shoulders slumped, but he turned back to the smith obediently. "I have something for you." Ulf brought out a small knife, its blade no longer than the blacksmith's finger. Its handle was white and smooth, carved of walrus ivory.

Halfdan's eyes grew wide.

"For you," said Ulf, handing it to him.

Halfdan took the knife reverently. He looked up at the blacksmith, a question in his eyes.

"It's time you started carving the runes with a real knife. But you must keep it here," Ulf cautioned. "It's not a toy, and Rognvald is not to know of it. It will be our secret."

Halfdan nodded solemnly.

"Here, sit," said Ulf. "Let me show you how to cut the runes."

When they finished for the day, it was too late to visit the falls. Halfdan was disappointed, but he could go another time.

As he departed, Ulf said, "We can work on this every afternoon while Rognvald has his nap."

Halfdan's face fell. When would he see the vaettir again? But he could not refuse Ulf's teaching. Mastering the runes was important, more important than playing with his friends. He sighed. He'd have to give them up, for now.

THE DARK SPIRIT lingered all afternoon at the falls and into the night, growing more impatient by the hour. By morning, the spirit was wild with annoyance. She took to the air and circled over the steading to see what was keeping the boy.

She spotted Halfdan crossing the yard, followed by a younger boy. They went into a building, a smithy by the sound of the hammer ringing on iron.

The spirit waited, seething with impatience. After an eternity, a woman arrived at the workshop. She went inside, then came out with the little one in tow.

But Halfdan did not leave the smithy. The dark spirit swooped to the gable end of the workshop and peered in.

There in the glow of the forge, the boy sat beside the old smith. Together, they carved the runes.

That could go on for weeks. It must be stopped.

The spirit hovered over the smithy like a storm cloud, watching until the smith and the boy came out. Together they walked down to the hall, where they had their evening meal.

The spirit waited until the blacksmith trudged back up to the smithy. The spirit scrutinized the old man, seeking weakness.

He had a limp. That was something the spirit could work with. He got to his bed, settling in with a groan.

It took only a small ill-wish, and the aging smith's legs became more inflamed than ever before, so that he could not walk at all. The curse would only last a few days, but that was all that was needed.

The spirit dared not linger, for the vaettir might return and may not be so easily chased away a second time. The dark cloud hurried back to the falls to wait.

THE NEXT DAY when the boys arrived, Ulf could not rise from his bed. While Sonja wrapped the smith's poor legs and fed him tincture of willow bark, Knut gave the boys their morning lessons. When Rognvald's fóstra took him for his nap, Halfdan was free.

He snatched his provisions and hurried down the trail to the waterfall, Fylgja at his side. When he arrived at the site, he performed the ritual at the álf-cups. Then he approached the falls, calling out to his friends.

But today a new spirit met him at the fall's entrance, one he'd never seen before. This vaettr was tall and dark, little more than a shadow. "Hello, young master." The voice was like a gasp.

Fylgja lifted his head and growled. "Don't be rude, Fylgja," Halfdan hushed his wolf, then turned to the spirit. "Who are you? I haven't seen you before."

The shadow spoke in a voice that contained more air than substance. "I am from far away, and I've come to meet you."

Halfdan's neck hairs prickled. "Why would you want to meet me? How would you even know of me?"

"You are famous among my people, young lord. They say you talk to the spirits, and that is rare in one so young."

Halfdan felt a flush of pride rise in his cheeks. He'd learned Ulf's lessons well. But then a worry nipped at him. "Where are my friends, the vaettir who live here?" Halfdan demanded.

"The spirits of the rock and waterfall have gone on a visit to the land of their cousins, the álfar. They send their greetings and invite you to join them. They asked me to wait for you and show you the way." The vaettr's tone had softened to a croon.

Fylgja growled again and snapped at the vaettr. The spirit waved a dark hand, trailing smoke. Halfdan caught a whiff of sulphur. The wolf gave a whine and curled up, burying his nose in his tail.

The vaettr gestured through the falls into the dark cavern. "Come, it's not far. It's just through here."

Halfdan held back, suspicions rising. "What about Fylgja?" He'd promised not to go anywhere without the wolf to protect him.

The strange vaettr paused for a moment before speaking. "Wolves are not allowed in the land of the álfar. But Fylgja will be fine right here. See? He's asleep. He's not worried. He'll be waiting for you when you get back."

Halfdan looked at the slumbering wolf uncertainly. He looked peaceful enough.

"Come, Halfdan, you won't believe the sights in the land of the álfar. Everything is shining and beautiful, and the music is like nothing you've ever heard. Your friends are waiting."

Vivid images of the wonderland of the álfar flickered in Halfdan's mind. Trees in flower, musical waterfalls, dancing creatures such as he'd never seen. Fears forgotten, his eyes sparkled with excitement. "Will I meet the álfar?"

"Yes, they are eager to make your acquaintance. They told me so."

With one final glance at Fylgja, Halfdan followed the vaettr into the dark cave.

WHEN HALFDAN DIDN'T COME HOME for dinner, no one was concerned. The boy often missed meals when he went exploring. Fylgja would see he came to no harm.

But when night fell, worries grew.

"The last time he went missing, he stowed away on my ship to find Åsa," said Eyvind, who had arrived earlier that afternoon. "But Åsa just visited Skiringssal a week ago, and she was safe at home when I left her this morning, so I can't imagine why Halfdan would go looking for her." He put aside the remains of his meal and rose, calling for his crew. "We'll search *Far Traveler*, in case the boy might have stowed away as he did before."

Sonja held up a hand. "Before we scatter, let's ask Rognvald. He knows far more than anyone thinks." She turned to her son and asked gently, "Where is Halfdan?"

Rognvald put a thumb in his mouth uncertainly and shook his head.

"I know you're not supposed to tell, but it's all right. You won't get in any trouble. Halfdan won't be angry. We're afraid he's lost. Please tell us where he went."

"He usually goes to see the vaettir. He won't take me—he says I'm too little."

Sonja hugged her son close. "Good boy. Good boy."

"I'll go," said Ulf. "I know the way."

"But your legs," Sonja objected.

"I'm fine. Your willow bark has worked wonders," he said, stifling a groan as he got to his feet and hurried outside, followed by Eyvind and Olaf. He felt responsible, for it was he who had introduced Halfdan to the spirits in the first place. "You'd best let me go alone," he said. "We don't want to scare the vaettir by tromping into their sacred space. If I don't return soon, you can come looking for me."

Ulf found his way by moonlight to the waterfall where the vaettir lived. At the entrance, he nearly stumbled over Fylgja, asleep by the cavern. When the old wolf did not rouse at the sound of his voice, the hairs on the back of Ulf's neck prickled. Something was wrong.

He closed his eyes and sensed the air. There must be a sleeping spell on the blind wolf. He hoped it was a simple one. He uttered an incantation meant to counter it.

Fylgja jerked awake, howling in distress.

"Where's Halfdan?" said Ulf.

Fylgja loped back and forth at the entrance, whining. A chill passed over Ulf. His last experience here had not been successful. The spirits had put him to sleep rather than deal with him. Fortunately, the vaettir favored Halfdan. They would do the boy no harm, and they might help find him. The spirits had never responded to Ulf in the past, but perhaps this time they would make an exception for the boy's sake.

He picked up the discarded skin of beer. Pouring a sip into the álf-cup, he recited the blessing. Then he squared his shoulders, stepped through the waterfall, and entered the dark cavern beyond.

Ulf called out for Halfdan, but his voice echoed in an empty cave. He lit his torch, and the flame flickered ominously in the uneasy air. He forged ahead as the cavern narrowed to a low tunnel. Ulf got painfully to his knees and held his torch out in front of him, deeper into the cavern. The flame went out instantly. The hairs on the back of Ulf's neck rose as he struck a new light. The torch went out again. With a shudder, Ulf crawled into the dark, fighting down claustrophobia. The sound of the waterfall receded in the distance.

Ulf crawled forward, feeling his way gingerly, until his forehead came up against solid rock. He ran his hands over his surroundings, seeking an opening, but he'd come to a wall.

He called Halfdan's name. His voice echoed through the cavern, and through the echoes he thought he heard a faint reply. He called again, with the same results.

He sensed that Halfdan had come here, that the boy was on the other side of the wall. But Ulf, though he crawled its length, could find no opening, no way in. The spirits, if they were present, ignored him.

The tunnel seemed to close in on him. A chill shivered up his spine. Fighting off panic, Ulf backed out of the passage as quickly as his aching knees would allow.

Once outside, he rested beside Fylgja long enough to calm his breath and slow his pounding heart. Then he relit his torch and began an extensive search of the area, calling Halfdan's name. He got no response, nor did he really expect one. He was certain he'd heard Halfdan in the tunnel, and there the boy remained. It was beyond Ulf's ability to reach him.

CHAPTER 9

Daire Calgaich

The powerful currents of the Lough Feabhail tugged at the steering oar. Ragnhild turned in closer to the western shore, where the back-eddies favored their course. The other three longships followed her like ducklings trailing their mother.

Fishermen's currachs scattered before the longships. Fishing shacks littered the beach, alongside nets spread to dry in the mild Irish sun. At the sight of the Norse ships, the inhabitants dropped their tools and scurried into the hills, where cattle and sheep grazed around raths protected by ditches and palisades. Smoke rose from the conical thatched roofs, scenting the air with the smell of peat.

Ragnhild sighted the sharp bend where the lough narrowed and became a river. The swift current of the flood tide overcame the river's northerly flow and carried them along for an hour, then the waterway broadened once again into a bay. Soon the river narrowed again and swung to the east. At the bend, a massive wooden palisade rose from an earthen embankment.

Daire Calgaich.

The monastery stood on a hill that rose like an island, surrounded by the river on one side and boglands that stretched to the horizon on all other sides. According to Murchad, the island had always been a legendary holy site. Its grove of ancient oaks had been sacred to the druids long before the monastery had been built, but the Christians revered them as well. Saint Colm Cille himself had decreed the trees should never be cut down.

The fortress that stood before them had been rebuilt in recent years by Murchad's clan after his father had destroyed the original settlement in a war with the Connails. This newer monastery was well fortified against any attempts by the clan Connail to take it back, as well as Norse raids.

As the longships approached the shore, monks scurried to close the gates. Ragnhild said, "They'll welcome us as soon as they realize who we are. We've saved them from raids twice in the past."

Murchad turned to Cian. "I trust Father Ennae, but I think it's best we keep your identity secret for now."

"Agreed," said Cian. The Irishman blended in well with the Norse crew. His clothes were the same as theirs, tunic and breeks of wool with soft leather ankle boots. His light brown hair and blue eyes were no different than dozens of Norsemen. Nothing marked him as Irish, as long as he kept his mouth shut.

"Pull hard," Ragnhild ordered. She put the helm hard over to assist the rowers as they rowed against the current.

With one final stroke, the oarsmen drove the longship onto the beach and shipped their oars. Those in the prow jumped over the side to steady the vessel as it swayed in the current, while the other ships beached alongside them. The crews racked their oars and leaped over the side to help drag the ships up the beach out of reach of the tide.

Ragnhild shipped the steering oar and vaulted over the gunnels to join Murchad, who was already striding up the hill. He held his white shield high, announcing himself as he had at Tullynavin.

"I am Murchad mac Maele Duin, here with my wife, the Lady Ragnhild, and her fleet. You know us well. We come in peace!"

Monks peered over the wall at them, tonsured heads glinting in the sun.

"We wish to see Father Ennae," Murchad called.

The gates opened, and a middle-aged monk appeared, a man Ragnhild recognized from their last visit. She reached out to embrace the gatekeeper, who drew back in alarm. "Greetings, Brother Padraig!" she exclaimed, settling for a handshake.

The monk's eyes widened at the crowd of Norse sailors at his gates, but he recovered himself and inclined his head graciously. "You are most welcome, my lord and lady. Please follow me to the guesthouse to refresh yourselves. I will let the father abbot know you are here."

Brother Padraig conducted them through the gates. Within, brown-robed monks hoed garden plots and hauled water from the well, stopping their work to gawk at the Norse party. Daire Calgaich looked much the same as any other Irish settlement. A flock of chickens barely looked up as they pecked and strutted among the round huts of woven withy crowned by conical thatched roofs. Some of the buildings were open workshops, others cells barely large enough for a monk to lie down and sleep. What distinguished the settlement from others was the rectangular church built of stone, guarded by its High Cross.

Brother Padraig led them across the yard to Daire Calgaich's sprawling guesthouse. It was far bigger than Tullynavin's, accommodating Ragnhild's four boat crews with room to spare. Inside the barnlike structure, straw-stuffed sleeping pallets were piled against the whitewashed walls, and the ever-present cauldron of warm water steamed over the central fire.

"Please refresh yourselves," Padraig said with a bow, and backed out of the door. "I will fetch you something to eat."

They took turns washing. Brother Padraig soon returned, followed by several younger monks carrying buckets of ale, wooden cups, and platters of bread and cheese. They set the meal out on the long wooden table by the fire.

"Please eat," said Padraig.

Ragnhild tried not to fall on the food like a ravenous wolf, but her stomach commanded otherwise. Padraig stood by in silence while they ate, his hands folded serenely on his belly. When they'd finished their meal, he said, "Lord Murchad, Lady Ragnhild, I will take you to Father Abbot. He is eager to see you. Your crew can rest while we are gone, and you can join them after you meet with the abbot."

Brother Padraig led them along a flagstone path across the courtyard to the abbot's dwelling, another thatched roundhouse, nearly as large as the guest quarters.

The door stood open to the sunlight. A familiar, gentle voice greeted them from within. "Come in."

Ragnhild followed Murchad inside the low doorway. The dim interior was lit by a single candle on a table. Ragnhild recognized the plump, middle-aged man who sat behind it, a richly-bound book open before him. It was good to see the kind abbot looking so well.

"Greetings, Father Abbot," said Murchad, bowing low. Ragnhild followed suit.

"It is good to see you again, my children," said the abbot. "Please have a seat." He motioned toward two low stools that stood before his desk. "You and your followers are welcome at Daire Calgaich for as long as you wish to stay. Tell me how it is with you."

"Thank you, Father Abbot," said Murchad. "We have a son now, Herulf. He was born in the spring."

"My congratulations," said Father Ennae. "And how do you find motherhood, my lady?" he asked Ragnhild. She cringed inwardly at the hint of doubt in his tone.

Murchad answered for her. "My wife spends her time fighting Danes."

Father Ennae chuckled. "I am not surprised. It's what you were born for, Lady."

Ragnhild brightened to hear approval in the abbot's voice.

"And how is it with you, Father?" asked Murchad.

"We have been blessed. The Danes seem to be preoccupied with plundering farther south. I credit that to Brother Behrt's training. It seems the raiders don't want to deal with monks who can fight. How is Brother Behrt, by the way?"

"He is happily preaching to deaf pagan ears at my brother's court," said Ragnhild. "My sister-in-law is a convert, but my brother and his followers still revere the old gods."

Norse-born but living most of his life in Ireland, Behrt had never seemed to fit in either place. He'd once loved Ragnhild and tried to win her. She'd never returned his love, but held him in the highest esteem as a loyal friend and warrior. After she married Murchad, Behrt joined the monastery here at Daire Calgaich and taught the monks to defend themselves. But Behrt, always a stranger, returned to the land of his birth to become Ragnhild's sister-in-law's spiritual advisor.

The abbot smiled. "Change comes slowly. I am glad Behrt is safe and well and spreading the word of the Lord."

"He has at least found a kindred spirit in my sister-in-law and her followers, and he is respected by all for his fighting prowess."

"I hope that he has found a home at last," said Father Ennae.

"I don't see how he could be happier," Ragnhild said honestly.

Now that they had caught up, the abbot got down to business. "Tell me, what brings you here? The last I heard, you had sailed to Lochlainn."

Murchad replied, "We spent the winter there. Now I have business with my cousin. I would be grateful if you could dispatch someone to Aileach to inform King Niall of our arrival and ask him to send horses for us."

"Say no more; it shall be done," said the abbot.

"Will you make sure to ask Niall to send my pony, Brunaidh, with the horses?" Ragnhild said.

Murchad put his hand on her shoulder. "Of course, *a chroi*. I know how you've missed your pony." He turned back to Father Ennae. "Please ask for my horse, Aenbarr, as well."

"I am happy to be of service." Father Ennae bestowed his blessing on them. Though Ragnhild did not put her faith in gods of any kind, she welcomed blessings from all holy people, just in case.

They took their leave. Once they were outside, Ragnhild turned to Murchad. "What about the ships?" She could not keep the worry from her voice.

"When we ride to Aileach, they will be safe here," said Murchad.

Ragnhild fixed him with a fierce gaze. "Last time, *Raider Bride* nearly burned to the waterline."

"I doubt we need to worry about an attack. Your brother has sworn peace, the Connails are vanquished, and you heard Father Ennae—the Danes are busy in the south. But I agree, we must protect the ships at all costs. What do you wish to do?"

Ragnhild considered. "We should have nothing to fear from your cousin, so we don't need to take all our forces with us to Aileach. We can leave two boat crews behind to guard the ships. Einar and Thorgeir will be in charge. They should be able to fight off anyone."

Murchad smiled. "There's no doubt of that, *a chroi*. A wise plan."

AFTER SO MANY YEARS AWAY, it seemed strange to Cian to be in a monastery. He'd only been to Daire Calgaich a few times as a boy, but he'd spent much time in the monasteries closer to home, seats of learning that carried on many of the traditions of the druid schools of old. The nearly-forgotten sound of the bell calling the faithful to prayer brought the past back to him in a rush.

As heathens, the Norse were not expected to attend. Cian did not want to betray himself, though he longed to join the monks in the church. He contented himself with listening to their voices raised in prayer through the chapel door. Their chants were accompanied by an inspired harper, and soon Cian was lost in the music. Trying to blend with the Norse, he did not bow his head in prayer, but the monks' voices and the harp strings resonated in his heart, stirring a longing he had thought long dead.

When the monks finished, Cian woke as if from a dream to find Ursa beside him, watching him with a gentle smile. His heart swelled near to bursting. He took her hand, and they walked together to join the monks for their evening meal.

After they had eaten, the crew bedded down in the guest-house. Cian said to Ursa, "I don't feel right, lying together in this holy place."

"I understand," she said. They parted and found solitary pallets among the crew.

Though he was exhausted, Cian could not sleep. His mind was enthralled with visions of Ursa.

Once the guesthouse filled with snores, Ursa appeared beside him. She reached out her hand silently and pulled him to his feet. Helpless to resist, he followed her outside into the cool night.

She led him out the gates and down to the shore where the ships lay.

This was all right, a place between the two worlds, neither heathen nor Christian. They spread out their hudfat and spent the night making love beneath the stars.

They fell into a deep sleep in each other's arms. Just before dawn, Ursa woke him and led him back to the gates. Cian stumbled along in a fog of pleasure.

They joined the monks for breakfast, and went out into the yard to await the horses from Aileach. Cian had expected the brethren to set to work in their gardens, but immediately after morning prayers, the monks assembled in the yard. They each took up blunt-tipped poles from a barrel full of them. Their leader, Brother Oengus, approached Ragnhild and Murchad. "I hope your crews will join us. We could use some fresh opponents."

Ragnhild's eyebrows lifted and she grinned at the challenge. "With pleasure! We haven't mown down any Christians since we were last in Ireland."

"I hope she plans to take it easy on them!" muttered Cian. "They're holy men, accustomed to study and contemplation."

Ursa snorted. "Don't underestimate them. They only look defenseless. They've been trained by Brother Behrt, one of the best warriors I've ever known."

Ragnhild cried, "Form up!" She selected a blunt-tipped stave from the barrel. The Norse helped themselves to poles and prepared to meet their foes.

The Norse eagerly spilled into the yard, where they were confronted by a well-organized formation of monks who carried their poles as if they knew what to do with them. Ragnhild took the center position, flanked by Murchad on one side, Einar on the other. Cian lined up with *Raider Bride*'s crew on either side, his heart filled with misgivings. He'd been taught never to strike a holy man. He sneaked a glance at Ursa, who gave him a grin and hefted her pole.

As soon as they were assembled, Oengus cried, "Attack!"

The monks charged, brandishing their staves and screaming battle cries. They maintained their formation with impressive skill.

"Charge!" roared Ragnhild.

The Norse line rushed to meet the opposing formation. Cian let himself be carried along with the rest of his shipmates, though his heart faltered.

Ursa dodged a blow from a monk's pole and whacked him soundly. He swung back and she countered, grinning.

A holy brother jabbed his stick straight at Cian's face. Shocked, Cian barely dodged in time. He stared into the battle-crazed eyes of the monk, who was regrouping for another strike. Cian bashed the monk's stave with his own, sending his aim purposely wide. The brother recovered with surprising speed and came at him again. Cian forgot he was fighting a holy man and threw himself into the battle. Their poles clashed again and again with satisfying thwacks.

The air was filled with shouts and wood bashing wood. Splinters flew from shattered sticks as the monks defended their position with ferocity. The Norse managed to fight their way through the opposing line, but not without sustaining a share of bumps and bruises.

The bells tolled sext, and Brother Oengus called a halt. Ragnhild grinned at him, breathing hard. "I see your monks have lost none of the training Behrt gave them. Woe betide anyone foolish enough to raid Daire Calgaich!"

"The abbot sees the wisdom in being able to defend ourselves," Oengus replied modestly. "Come, let us take some refreshment." He led them to the refectory, where ale and bread were laid out.

Cian's sparring partner fell in beside him. "My name is Eoghain. You fight well!"

"As do you!"

Eoghain stared at him in astonishment. "You're Irish!"

Too late, Cian realized he should not have spoken. He thought frantically for a reply. He decided to stick close to the truth. "Yes, I am Irish by birth, but I have been with the Norse for many years. I was a slave, but won my freedom."

"Well, welcome home," said Eoghain.

To Cian's relief, the young monk did not seem inclined to question him further. He quickly changed the subject. "I had no idea that monks could fight like that."

"It's either fight or die like sheep," said Eoghain. "And why should we? Monasteries don't have to be easy pickings, nor monks helpless victims."

"Agreed!" Cian followed the brother, bemused by this warlike type of monk. Yet it seemed this was just the sort of holy man needed in this age of raiding and pillaging.

As the monks filed into the chapel for prayer, Cian slipped away from Eoghain and lost himself in among the Norse, hoping the young monk would not make too much of his presence. He found Ursa and joined the crew as they prepared to depart.

That night he and Ursa stole away to the ships again. After they made love, she fell asleep in his arms. Cian lay gazing up into the night sky. Everything seemed beyond his comprehension. In the morning he would ride to Aileach, where Murchad would lay his case before King Niall. And then he would march on his uncle, to take his vengeance and claim his birthright, or die trying.

CHAPTER 10

Aileach

The morning dawned fair over the River Feabhail. In the east a great cloud of dust rose. Ragnhild watched in anticipation as a herd of horses emerged from the dust cloud, driven by a dozen mounted men.

As the herd arrived at the monastery's gate, a whinny set Ragnhild's pulse racing. "Brunaidh!" She ran to greet her pony. Brunaidh nuzzled her and breathed softly on her neck as Ragnhild stroked her. Memories flooded back from her first trip to Ireland, when her brother had betrayed her and given her to Murchad as a wife—and hostage. The pony, named for the forest sprites, had been Murchad's gift, her only friend in a strange and hostile land.

She scanned the troops for familiar faces. Like those at Tullynavin, the Irish warriors wore the standard belted linen tunics dyed pale yellow topped with a cloak, and all were bare-legged and barefoot. Ragnhild recognized their leader, Cerball, leading Murchad's horse. He was dressed in the same type of linen tunic, but his status was declared by dark brown breeches, leather shoes, and a green cloak fastened with a silver pin. "Welcome, Lord. I've brought you Aenbarr."

"Thank you, Cerball," Murchad replied, taking the reins and stroking his horse's ears. Aenbarr nuzzled his shoulder and nibbled on his tunic. Murchad's horse was named after the steed of the sea god, Manannán mac Lir, a horse who could run across the sea.

All the horses were tacked in the Irish fashion, without saddle or stirrups. Murchad mounted by leaping onto Aenbarr's back from a dead standstill, legs scissoring, to land lightly on the blanket that padded the horse's back. Cian sprang onto his mount with practiced ease as if he hadn't been away for years.

Ragnhild took a deep breath and flung herself onto Brunaidh's back. She felt a certain amount of pride as she landed squarely on the blanket. She gripped the single rein, attached to the top of the bridle's nose band, leading it straight back over the horse's forehead. From her position astride, Ragnhild watched her Norse crew mount with varying degrees of success. Most of them had attempted this once or twice before, but it was still entertaining to watch. A few of them made it onto their horse's back, but the majority achieved less satisfactory, if more amusing, results. Some slid off the horse's flanks, while others landed on their stomachs and squirmed into a seated position. A few over-shot the mark entirely and tumbled over the other side. The surprised horses sidled away, leaving their prospective riders chasing after them. No one laughed out loud, though there were some suspicious choking sounds.

Svein refused to submit to such indignity. The aging húskarl led his horse to the garden's low wall and used it as a mounting block.

Eventually all seventy Norse were safely mounted. Without stirrups or saddle, their woolen breeches and soft leather shoes struggled for purchase, while the bare-legged Irishmen easily gripped the horses' sides.

Ragnhild had long since mastered the art of riding Irish style. She accepted a long stick from the groom, clucked, and tapped Brunaidh lightly on the flank with the stick. The pony stepped forward obediently. The crew members followed suit, falling in line as the horses moved out. A cart followed, loaded with Murchad's and Ragnhild's sea chests, while the crew's belongings remained on board their ships.

Father Ennae waited at the gate, beside Einar, Thorgeir, and their crews. "Farewell, Lady, Lord. May God bring you back safely to us."

Ragnhild glanced back at her little fleet, hauled up on the beach, covered by their awnings.

Einar followed her gaze. "We will keep the ships safe," he assured her.

"I know you will," she said, squaring her shoulders and turning Brunaidh's head toward the causeway.

Cerball and Murchad led the party out through the gates. With two boat crews plus a dozen grooms, they raised quite a dust cloud on the road. The party skirted the wall to the north, around to the western side, where a wooden-planked causeway at the bottom of the hill served as the only way across the endless marsh.

They descended the hill and stepped onto the wood planks. In the distance, Ragnhild sighted Greenan Mountain, crowned by the Grianan of Aileach, the ancient fort from which she had watched the Midsummer fires with Murchad. The night she had fallen in love with him.

They had ridden a little more than an hour when the planks gave onto higher, firmer ground, and became a well-trodden track through fields of wheat and flax, dotted with circular enclosures. Some protected a collection of roundhouses; others served as pens for the sheep and cattle that grazed the landscape.

The fortress of Aileach stood on a knoll, visible from a great distance across the flat plain. As they came near, Ragnhild could make out its features. The stronghold was defended by a deep ditch, a narrow bridge of land the only way across. Beyond the ditch rose a massive earthen bank faced with stone. The bank was twice the height of a man, surmounted by a wooden palisade. Across the land bridge, a massive oak gate barred the way, crowned with a wooden watchtower.

Cerball halted before the land bridge, and they dismounted, gathering on the bank. He whistled, and the gate opened with an ominous creak. Irish men-at-arms surged across the bridge to surround them. Atop the wall, more warriors aimed spears at the newcomers.

Ragnhild knew she had nothing to fear, but the treatment she'd suffered the last time she was here put her guts in an uproar. She sent a glance to her husband and took comfort in his outer calm. What emotions roiled under his stoic exterior, she could not guess. How must Murchad feel, returning to the fortress where he'd once ruled as king? He'd had ambitions of becoming Ard Ri, the high king of all Ireland.

His marriage to Ragnhild, a pagan and a foreigner, had been his undoing, no matter it was a marriage of alliance to protect Ireland from her brother's raids. When Murchad refused to renounce her, he'd been deposed by his cousin, Niall. Yet he showed no sign of defeat as he dismounted and surveyed the stronghold.

A flock of stable boys appeared to take their mounts. Ragnhild stroked Brunaidh's neck before relinquishing her rein. "I'll see you soon," she murmured into the pony's ear. Brunaidh twitched her ears and lipped Ragnhild's hair before allowing herself to be led to a corral beside the fortress walls. Ragnhild watched her go, feeling abandoned as she was about to enter this place where she'd been accused of thievery and worse.

Murchad strode through the gate with the confidence of one who had been master here. Ragnhild raised her chin and followed him.

Within, another gated wall confronted them. Murchad paused expectantly while two warriors bowed and opened the gate.

A path led forward, lined by a waist-high rock wall that channeled them toward a stout, iron-hinged oak door set in a stone rampart. More spearmen watched them from atop the inner rampart. Cerball opened the door, and Murchad led them into the narrow, stone-lined corridor.

Ragnhild steeled herself and plunged into the dank passage after her husband, focusing on the daylight that glimmered ahead. Suddenly the darkness broke onto a sunlit courtyard teeming with people and thatched round buildings—some living quarters, others animal byres or workshops. Children shrieked and ran through the steading, scattering chickens and geese. A familiar odor revealed the location of the hog pens and the midden.

The royal hall was immense, its whitewashed walls and stout wooden doorframe crowned by an enormous thatched roof. Tullynavin's hall looked like a monk's cell by comparison, though this building showed its age. The thatch had grayed, and the whitewashed walls were dingy, but it took nothing away from its magnificence.

Cerball ushered them along another stone-lined path toward the guesthouse, twice as large as the one at Daire Calgaich. "I'll leave you to refresh yourselves." The man-at-arms bowed and left them. Murchad ducked inside the low door, and Ragnhild followed, the crews filtering in behind. The cavernous guest hall more than accommodated her crew of seventy.

In the center of the room, fires crackled on three stone hearths. Over each one, iron cauldrons simmered on tripods, sending steam fragrant with herbs up into the lofty ceiling. Bed alcoves covered with sheepskins lined the whitewashed walls.

"Lady!" A short Irishwoman rushed to fold Ragnhild in an embrace.

"Fiona!" said Ragnhild, returning the hug. The Irishwoman

had become a dear friend to Ragnhild, despite having once been Murchad's mistress. "How have you been?"

"Very well," said Fiona with a broad grin. "I understand congratulations are in order on the birth of your first child."

A hollow of guilt formed in Ragnhild's chest at the thought of Herulf. She tried to speak but could find no words.

Murchad smiled and ended the awkward pause. "We have been blessed with a son. His name is Herulf."

"I'm sure he's a fine little lord," said Fiona. She seemed to sense Ragnhild's discomfort, for she dropped the subject. "Come this way, Lord, Lady." She ushered them through a low doorway to the private guest chamber, which was a separate, smaller roundhouse butted up against the main building, connected by the inner door.

Within, the obligatory bowl of wash water steamed beside linen towels. Ragnhild and Murchad took turns dissolving the sweat and grime of the road from their face and hands while Fiona chattered.

Guilt pricked at Ragnhild anew. Fiona had once been Murchad's lover, though not of high enough rank to become his primary wife. Still, she could have given him children, and would have proven a far better mother than Ragnhild could ever hope to be.

Her self-reproach was interrupted when the outside door opened. Cerball entered, directing men who lugged in their sea chests.

A manservant appeared and washed Murchad's hair and beard and gave him a trim. From his trunk, Murchad selected his finest tunic and mantle, in blue and purple, the colors only a king was allowed to wear, a reminder that he had once occupied this throne. About his neck he donned a silver torc, not the gold of kingship but rather one of a prince, which had been his since birth.

While the manservant fussed over Murchad, Fiona combed

out Ragnhild's snarled braid and washed her salt-and-dirt-encrusted hair, then opened her sea chest and murmured in approval as she brought out the embroidered linen underdress and fine blue wool gown, carefully stowed by Liv. Fiona helped Ragnhild change into the lovely garments. "You look every inch a queen," she said fondly, pinning the gown's neck closed with Ragnhild's silver brooch. "As queenly as Herself."

"As who?" Ragnhild asked.

"As she who now sits on the throne of Aileach."

"And who is that?"

"Queen Gormlaith, sister of the high king." Shock reverberated through Ragnhild. Niall had married the sister of Murchad's greatest enemy.

Fiona lowered her voice. "They say she is a powerful sorceress."

Fiona would have said more, but Murchad rose. He took Ragnhild's arm and led her to the door.

Cerball conducted them to the door on the western side of the great hall. The guard stood aside to allow them passage into the ambulatory, divided by posts into three aisles. They passed through the central aisle and entered the main room. Though she had been at Aileach before, Ragnhild was awestruck once again by the cavernous hall. The vast room was divided by concentric rings of stout pillars carved from whole tree trunks. White-washed walls glittered with inlaid bronze and gems, and the flagstone floor was strewn with fragrant rushes. The lofty ceiling soared into shadow, its vast height supported by the trunk of an immense oak tree, carved with Ogham symbols. Rich tapestries hung from the crossbeams, glittering with silver and gold and precious stones in the glow of the hearth fire.

The huge room swallowed up Ragnhild's two boat crews, lost among Niall's assemblage on the benches surrounding the hearth. Cerball conducted Murchad and Ragnhild to the raised platform where Niall, king of Aileach, awaited them on the carved oaken throne.

Niall wore robes even more splendid than Murchad's, and around his neck gleamed the massive gold torc of kingship, the torc Murchad had once worn.

The cousins were close in age, but while Murchad was slim and wiry, Niall's build was bull-like. His hair and moustache were the same dark color as Murchad's, but his eyes were so dark a brown as to be nearly black.

Ragnhild wondered if he still blamed her for the theft of the necklace. She could tell nothing from his gaze.

"Greetings, cousin," said Niall. "Please be seated." He gestured to the guest bench beside him. Close by Niall sat a bard dressed in robes nearly as sumptuous as the king's, and next to him the harper, a jewel-encrusted cláirseach resting on his knee. Ragnhild noticed Cian was seated next to Ursa, his eyes fastened on the instrument in awe.

On Niall's other side stood a priest who glared at Ragnhild. Father Ferdia. There was no doubt how he felt about her. She sent him her most ferocious scowl in return.

Enthroned beside Niall was a woman Ragnhild had never seen before, undoubtedly Niall's queen, whom Fiona had spoken of. She was several years older than Ragnhild, fair-haired with piercing gray eyes. Her gown was of the finest woven wool, dyed a deep, costly red.

On her breast gleamed the necklace.

Ragnhild caught her breath, her gaze riveted by the cursed golden treasure she had taken so long ago when she'd fled from Murchad. The necklace that had brought a plague on Tromøy and sent Åsa to Hel to retrieve it. The necklace Ragnhild and her crew had been captured for in the Dál Riata, barely escaping with their lives.

She and Murchad had finally returned the cursed thing to Aileach's treasury, only to be accused by Father Ferdia of trying to steal it. They had only been vindicated when they helped fight off an attack on Daire Calgaich by the Connails.

Ragnhild forced her eyes from the blazing gold up to the woman's face.

Their gazes clashed, sending a shock wave through Ragnhild. She barely heard Niall introduce his wife, Gormlaith, sister of the high king Conchobar, Murchad's mortal enemy. Ragnhild felt Murchad stiffen beside her.

Without breaking eye contact, Gormlaith inclined her head. Ragnhild replied in kind, staring defiantly into those gray eyes. For all her delicate beauty, the Irish queen's gaze was made of steel. Ragnhild's instincts warned her not to turn her back on Gormlaith. She wondered if the Irish queen knew Ragnhild's history with the necklace.

Their staring match was broken when servants brought in mead and served it along with bread and cheese. Good manners required the Irish queen to turn her attention to directing them.

Ragnhild blinked and accepted a cup of ale. Her eyes burned from Gormlaith's searing glare.

"Congratulations to you and your queen, Cousin." Murchad had recovered quickly. His voice betrayed nothing of the shock he must be feeling as he raised his cup to Niall and Gormlaith. "I am so glad you have found happiness."

Ragnhild lifted her own cup, then took a long drink. The liquid trickled down her throat and warmed her belly, easing her nerves. *A powerful sorceress*…Fiona's words echoed in her mind.

Niall raised his cup to them. "And I hear that congratulations are due to you as well, Cousin, on your newborn son."

Murchad's face broke into a broad smile. "Yes, he is a fine lad. We call him Herulf."

At the sound of her son's name, Ragnhild froze. Herulf's mention sent a chill through her. *Silly.* She lifted her cup to her lips and drank hastily, but the Irish queen was staring at her with a strange, intense look. The necklace's three golden disks seemed to glimmer on Gormlaith's breast. A trick of the light.

Or witchcraft. Ragnhild shivered as she recalled Fiona's words.

"To your son," Gormlaith said. "He was born in the spring, was he not? How difficult it must be for you to be parted from him so soon."

Her tone made Ragnhild's hackles rise. It was as if this Irish queen knew what a fraud of a mother Ragnhild truly was.

Her thoughts were interrupted when Niall's master harper plucked the opening strings on his cláirseach. The sound resonated throughout the hall. Under the poet's vigilant eye, the bard gave voice to a mournful ballad of lost love. Ragnhild sought out Cian. He was holding Ursa's hand, his face softened by a blissful smile.

Ragnhild closed her eyes and gave herself over to the music. She let her mind soar into limitless space and time evoked by the master, the story coming to life in her mind's eye as she followed the Irish words.

When the harper's fingers stilled and the bard fell silent, the audience gave an audible sigh. The feast ended, and the diners began to leave the hall, including Ragnhild's crews, who were ushered to the guesthouse. Murchad and Ragnhild waited until only Gormlaith and the priest remained beside Niall.

The king eyed Murchad, his smile gone. "Now, Cousin, I wonder what brings you here to me so late in the season?"

Murchad said, "Cousin, I have pressing business, which I must discuss with you in private. I hope your queen and Father Ferdia will excuse us."

Niall did not look pleased, but he nodded, dismissing his priest, who departed with bad grace, scowling at Ragnhild. She ignored him. He was unimportant.

Gormlaith rose with better poise and bade Ragnhild and Murchad a frosty good-night. Ragnhild could not help sneaking a last peek at the necklace as she departed. Gormlaith intercepted her gaze and raked her with a hostile stare of her gray eyes. Though a chill skittered up Ragnhild's spine, she met the glare with one of her own. The Irish queen averted her head and strode from the room.

Once Gormlaith was gone, a sense of relief came over Ragnhild.

When they were alone with Niall, Murchad spoke. "I have an important reason for my visit, Cousin. I must swear you to the utmost secrecy."

"You have my oath."

Murchad cleared his throat. "What would you say if I told you Cumuscach, chieftain of Ard Ciannachta, was murdered by his brother?"

Niall's eyes widened. "But I thought you…"

Murchad's brow furrowed and his eyes turned stormy. "Despite what has been said, I did not order Cumuscach killed, nor his son and tanist, Cináed."

Niall gaped at Murchad for a moment. Ragnhild watched his face contort as he mastered his emotions—surprise? Dismay? "I cannot believe that Dunchad is responsible. He has long been a loyal ally. Why would I doubt him?"

"Are you doubting me, Cousin?" Murchad's tone contained the hint of a threat.

"No, no, of course not," Niall replied hastily. King or not, Murchad still had power over his cousin.

Mollified, Murchad took a deep breath. "I know Dunchad is a close friend of yours. He may be your ally, but he's no friend of mine. It was he who betrayed me in my war on Conchobar."

Niall stared at him. "Do you have proof of this?"

"I have good reason to believe it." Murchad lowered his voice and leaned his head closer to his cousin. "What I am going to tell you must be kept secret."

"I have given you my oath," Niall reminded him.

Murchad nodded. "I have brought Cian, younger son of

Cumuscach, to avenge his father and brother and take his rightful place as head of the clan."

Niall's expression was even more astonished, and not pleased. "But how did you find him? I understood the youngest son was captured by the Danes three years ago while traveling to his school in Dún Geinhin."

Murchad stared at Niall. "His uncle sold him to the Danes."

"How do you know this? How came he to you?" Something in Niall's tone alerted Ragnhild. An edge of anxiety—fear?

"Åsa, queen of Agder, rescued him from captivity. They escaped together, and she brought him back with her. Queen Åsa has asked my wife to restore him to Ireland." He nodded at Ragnhild.

"I have given my oath to Åsa," said Ragnhild firmly.

Niall stared.

"Cian tried to kill me the moment he saw me," said Murchad with a rueful grin. "But we came to an understanding. He now knows that I am not responsible for his father's death, nor his brother's."

Niall glared at him. "Why should I take the word of someone who claims to be Cumuscach's son, whom no one has laid eyes on for years? How do you know he's not an imposter?"

"I believe the lad," Murchad said simply. "Why else would he risk certain death to kill me and take vengeance?"

"I can't just attack a chieftain who has been loyal to me on the word of some young upstart who cannot prove who he is."

Murchad stared at Niall. "Is that your final word, Cousin?"

"It is."

Murchad's shoulders slumped and his eyes were downcast. "Very well. There is little we can do without your support. We shall return to Lochlainn."

"And take the boy with you. I don't need him spreading lies."

"As you say, Cousin."

Ragnhild could not believe what her husband was saying. He

knew as well as she that Cian was telling the truth. How could he give in without an argument? But a glance at Murchad's face warned her not to say anything.

For once, she decided to obey.

AFTER THEY RETURNED to their chamber and the servants had departed, Ragnhild turned on her husband. "I've never known you to give up so easily. Have you become a mouse?"

Murchad grinned. "Nay, *a mhuirin*. More like a fox." He kept his voice low. "There is no point in arguing with Niall once his mind is made up. I have my suspicions that my cousin knows more about this matter than he is letting on. He did not seem very surprised when I accused Dunchad of betraying me. If Dunchad is an ally of his, then it's best not to stir the hornet's nest." His eyes took on a familiar sparkle. "But we will attack the stronghold anyway. I believe we have enough warriors to do so without his support, as long as we have the element of surprise. Niall does not realize that we have brought only half our forces here today, so he will not expect us to attack Dunchad without his help, nor will he have time to warn him if my cousin decides to break his oath to me. We will depart just the same, but once we enter the Lough Feabhail, we'll take to the eastern shore and head for Dunchad's fortress. But for now, we tell no one."

"Not even Cian?"

"Especially not Cian. Niall doesn't know which of our crew he is, and we don't want anything to make the lad give away his identity. I'll tell him just before we leave Daire Calgaich."

Ragnhild nodded and climbed into the sweet-smelling bed, soft grass and hay covered with a thick woolen pad.

Murchad, snuggling in beside her, said, "Remember the dream I had about the necklace the night before we returned it to the treasury?"

"I remember it well."

In the dream, Queen Medbh of legend had appeared to Murchad and told him how the treasure had been stolen from Connaught by his forefathers. She said that henceforward the sovereignty bestowed by the necklace would belong only to the wife of the high king of Ireland.

But not Conchobar, the current high king.

Ragnhild caught her breath as comprehension shot through her like lightning. "Niall."

"Yes, Niall," said Murchad. "His mother was named Medbh. She was a princess of Connaught, and the rightful heir of the necklace."

Ragnhild sat up. "And Niall has married the sister of the current high king."

Murchad gave a rueful laugh. "Niall has set himself up to be the next high king. My cousin plays a long game, beginning when he had me deposed and himself elected king of Aileach. This has been his plan all along. Let his hotheaded cousin fail, and Niall steps in to save the day. He marries the high king's sister, a woman of unimpeachable lineage. Now he has only to wait for Conchobar to make a mistake, or die, and he'll sweep in and take the high kingship."

A dark mood fell over Ragnhild as she settled back in the bed. "How hard this must be for you, after your own ambitions to become high king were thwarted." She snuggled close to him, pulling the wool coverlet over them. "Do you have regrets now that you are back amid what you have given up, *a mhuirin?*" she asked and held her breath, waiting for his answer.

His arm tightened around her. "No, *a chroi*, not a one," he breathed into her hair. "I am content with our little kingdom in Lochlainn, with our fine son, and the freedom of the seas."

"And a wife who is no kind of mother."

He kissed her hair. "You are the kind of mother I love."

Ragnhild stilled the doubts that niggled in her head and let herself believe his sweet words.

IN THE MORNING as they readied the horses for departure, Gormlaith appeared. She was dressed in lavishly embroidered blue linen and wool, a hooded cloak protecting her hair.

She approached and Ragnhild froze.

"Lady Ragnhild," said the Irish queen, "I wish to send a gift for your son, that he may know he is of royal blood."

She held out a finely carved wooden box, set with brass hinges and a brass hasp. All eyes were on her. Ragnhild took it reluctantly.

"Open it," Gormlaith urged.

Ragnhild lifted the ornate cover. Gold blazed from a bed of fine wool. Ragnhild picked the object up, uneasiness building inside her. Something was not right. She did not trust this woman nor her gifts.

The crowd gasped as she held the item up.

It was a golden rattle, encrusted with precious stones and carved with Ogham symbols. Worth a small fortune.

Feeling Murchad's eyes upon her, Ragnhild managed a gracious bow. She forced words out in a sincere tone. "Thank you, my lady. You do my son great honor."

Gormlaith gave her a satisfied smile, a gleam of triumph in her eyes.

Ragnhild put the rattle back in the wooden box and closed the lid.

Herulf would never touch it.

CHAPTER 11

Skiringssal

Ulf tried to coax Fylgja back to the hall, but though the blind wolf was shivering, he would not leave his post by the cavern entrance. Ulf covered the wolf with his cloak, then trudged back to the hall, where the other searchers had convened after fruitless searching.

They all turned to Ulf, hope in their eyes. "I think I've located the boy. I'm sure I heard his voice, faintly, within the cavern. But I can't find a way to get to him. The way is blocked by solid rock. The wolf will not leave the place. I think he knows Halfdan is there—trapped, somehow."

Sonja said firmly, "We must send for Åsa."

Olaf reluctantly agreed. "I don't know how I'll explain that I've lost her son, again."

"This time it's sorcery," said Ulf. "It's no fault of yours."

"I'll go tonight," said Eyvind.

"But you and your crew have had no rest," Sonja objected.

Eyvind was adamant. "I can't rest while Halfdan is missing.

My ship is ready to sail. I want to be with Åsa. I'll have her here by tomorrow evening."

~

Far Traveler sailed through the night, arriving on Tromøy at midmorning. The lookout had spotted them, and Åsa awaited them on the shore, her face pale with apprehension. She knew Eyvind had stopped in Skiringssal, and with a mother's way, she knew something was wrong with Halfdan.

"What is it?" she demanded. "Is Halfdan sick?"

Eyvind shook his head, taking her in his arms. "He's missing."

"Again?" Anger rumbled in her voice.

"Shhh, love. It's not Olaf's fault, nor Sonja's. We searched everywhere. I tore my ship apart. Ulf thinks it's witchcraft. He found the place where he is sure the child was taken. Fylgja refuses to leave the cavern, so Ulf is certain Halfdan is there, but it's beyond his ability to reach the boy. He sent me to fetch you and Vigdis."

Åsa looked him over. "You're exhausted, and so is your crew. Get some sleep. I'll take my own ship."

"I want to be at your side at a time like this," Eyvind protested.

She gave him a tight smile. "Thank you, love. I appreciate that more than you know. You'll do me no good if you pile your ship on the rocks, and my longship is faster than your knarr. Come to Skiringssal tomorrow, after you and your crew have slept. Depending on what I've found, I may need your comfort more then than I do tonight. At least I am doing something."

Eyvind gave in reluctantly. He and his crew ate a meal and found their beds, while Åsa mustered her boat crew and set them to preparing the ship for the half-day's sail to Skiringssal.

When Åsa arrived at the bower, Vigdis was already packed. "How much do you know?"

"It's Halfdan," the apprentice said simply. "Nothing less would send Eyvind back in the middle of the night."

"He's missing again. But this time there is magic afoot." Åsa filled her in on what she'd learned from Eyvind.

Vigdis gazed at Heid, staring blankly into the fire, wrapped in her shawl despite the warmth of the room. "Now is when we need her most."

"We'll have to make do without her," Åsa said.

"I think we should bring her along just in case."

"But she can do nothing," Åsa objected. "I'm not eager to endanger the völva's health by dragging her onto a ship."

"Even so, I think she must come along."

Åsa was surprised at the vehemence in Vigdis's voice. She decided to trust the apprentice's instincts and comply. She left the bower and found Olvir, who was directing the loading of her ship.

"We must bring the völva with us to Skiringssal."

Olvir knew enough not to ask questions. "I'll send the grooms to hitch up the völva's cart and some men to assist in bringing her out. Let me know if there's anything else I can do."

"Thank you, Olvir."

Åsa hurried back to the bower. Catching her breath, she sat down beside her mentor and took the gnarled hands in her own. "Heid, Halfdan is in trouble. We need your help to save him. You must come along with me to Skiringssal."

Heid gazed at her with vacant eyes. Åsa despaired of the völva's ability to help, but she coaxed the aging sorceress to her feet and wrapped her in her warmest cloak. She took Heid's arm and guided her as she shuffled to the yard, where the stable hands had her cart ready. The apprentices bundled their mistress into her seat and tucked a blanket around her. Åsa drove the cart down to the shore, Vigdis and the ship's crew following on foot.

A burly oarsman picked Heid up as if she were a wisp of straw and set her gently on *Ran's Lover*. Heid had no reaction to the handling. Normally she would be cursing the man and threatening to make his penis shrivel up and fall off. Her silence sent a chill of dread through Åsa.

Vigdis climbed aboard and settled the völva in the shelter of the stern. Åsa took the helm, listening to Vigdis explain Halfdan's plight to her mistress once again. Heid made no sign that she heard or understood what her apprentice was telling her, but Vigdis persisted.

They had to try.

THERE WAS no wind when they set out, and the crew had to row half of the way to Skiringssal while Åsa stalked the decks anxiously. Finally a breeze filled in for the end of the journey, giving the tired sailors some relief. They pulled into Skiringssal's harbor just before sunset. Ulf was waiting on the pier. It was obvious the aging blacksmith had not slept.

He told them about hearing Halfdan's voice in the cave behind the waterfall and finding Fylgja in a trance-like sleep beside the cave. Åsa's alarm increased, and Vigdis turned pale, but Heid seemed not to hear.

Olaf had driven down in a wagon to meet them. He and Ulf lifted the völva into it as if she were made of eggshells. All the while, Heid uttered not a word, when she would normally be protesting vigorously. As Olaf drove them up the trail to the hall, Åsa and Vigdis cradled the frail sorceress between them, trying to shield her from the worst of the jolts.

When they reached the yard, Ulf got off the wagon and received the völva as Åsa and Vigdis handed her down. Heid was unresisting as a rag doll. As Ulf carried her to the bower, Åsa noticed that the smith's limp seemed more pronounced. Apprehension clutched at her heart. Was it just old age catching up with him?

Sonja awaited them outside the bower, pacing and worrying the edges of her shawl. When she saw them, she threw her arms around Åsa. "I'm so sorry!"

"It's not your fault," said Åsa. "I know you've done everything you could to keep him safe. There are powers at work beyond ours."

Sonja eyed the sorceress, slack in Ulf's arms.

"I don't know what Heid can do," said Åsa, "but Vigdis had a feeling we might need her, and I trust her intuition."

"We'll make her comfortable in the bower."

Ulf carried the völva inside, where he set the sorceress on a bench by the fire. Sonja tucked a thick down comforter around her.

As soon as Heid was settled, Åsa turned to Ulf. "Take me to my son."

The blacksmith's eyes were bleary, but he led Åsa to the yard, where horses were waiting. With effort, Ulf hoisted himself into the saddle and took the torch Olaf offered him. Åsa and Vigdis got on the other two horses and followed him out past the steading.

The full moon cast an eerie light onto the trail, making Åsa stifle a shudder of foreboding. It seemed they followed the rocky way forever. At last they reached the falls, where Fylgja waited at the waterfall entrance. When they approached, the blind wolf got to his feet, barking anxiously.

Åsa dismounted and turned to Ulf. He looked exhausted, and she feared for him. "You stay here with Fylgja," she ordered in a tone that brooked no argument.

The blacksmith dismounted and sat down gratefully, slumping against the rock. He coaxed Fylgja to him. "We can do no more, old friend. Rest with me." The wolf settled down with a reluctant whine and laid his head in Ulf's lap.

"The air reeks of sorcery," said Vigdis.

Åsa nodded. "Wait here while I try to get through." Drawing

her belt knife, she scratched protective runes on the wood handle of an unlit torch.

Sheltering her torch with her shawl, Åsa plunged through the waterfall. She gasped as the cold water shocked her. Emerging from the frigid spray, she wiped the water from her eyes and peered into the darkness. The passage yawned before her, shadowy and foreboding.

She rummaged in her leather belt pouch and drew out flint and steel as well as a stick of heartwood shaved into thin curls. She knelt on the floor and carefully struck the flint, scattering sparks on the dry curls of wood. After a half-dozen frustrating strikes and showers of sparks, she was rewarded by a wisp of smoke that quickly faded. She cupped her hand around the stick and blew on the curls gently until the sparks caught. Åsa nursed the tiny flame until it steadied, then touched her glowing stick to the torch's char cloth. The cloth flared and she breathed an audible sigh of relief.

She stepped into the cave's maw. The ceiling was too low for her to stand upright. Stooping, Åsa crab-walked into the darkness, holding the flame before her.

As the tunnel constricted, she had to lower herself to elbows and knees to keep going. The dank rock walls were too close to allow her to turn around or even look back. She tried to steady her nerves by chanting a vardlokkur as she crept deep into the cavern.

The torch guttered, then went out. Her breath caught in her throat and she stopped short, afraid to go on. In utter darkness, she called Halfdan's name, then held her breath, listening.

"Mama?" Halfdan's voice, barely audible, but it was her son.

Her heart began to pound and she forged ahead as fast as she could. "Halfdan! I'm coming!"

The deeper she went, the darker and narrower the tunnel became. The dank walls closed in on her so she could barely squeeze through. She fought down the feeling of suffocation and forced her way forward, the rock scraping her skin. She told herself it was no worse than the passage to Hel.

"Mama?" His voice sounded close. He must be right beside her.

"Halfdan! I'm here, son!"

She groped in the darkness and her hand found him in the small space. For a moment, she went limp with relief. Then she took him in her arms and held him close. His face was wet with tears.

"How did you come here?" she said.

Between sobs, Halfdan said, "A spirit led me here. The vaettr promised to take me to my friends in Álfheim, but it was a lie. The spirit left me here all alone, and I can't find a way out."

Åsa hugged him even closer. "Now that I've found you, I'll take you back."

She squirmed around in the tight space, keeping a grip on her son, and began to crawl back the way she'd come. A rock wall blocked her way. She turned in another direction, seeking the opening, but there was nothing but rock everywhere.

The tunnel had vanished.

Vɪɢᴅɪs ᴡᴀɪᴛᴇᴅ outside the cave beside Ulf and Fylgja. The moon set, and a breeze ruffled the ferns.

"Åsa should have returned by now," said Vigdis, her apprehension growing. "I'm going after her." She took their other torch and crawled into the tunnel, leaving Ulf and Fylgja in the dark.

She backed out again quickly, her torch gone out. "I can hear her in there, chanting. But I can't see her and I can't get to her. There are no openings in the wall—it's solid rock. It's like she's on the other side. There's some kind of enchantment here. Ulf, come with me, there are incantations we can try."

The apprentice and the blacksmith crawled back into the

cavern and halted near the rock wall. They could hear Åsa's voice, a faint murmur through the rock.

"Let's try a galdr chant to help the lost find their way," said Vigdis. After she'd repeated it a few times, Ulf added his voice to hers. Even Fylgja joined in with a mournful howl.

Nothing happened.

Vigdis tried another chant, this one to open doorways, to no avail.

They fell silent. Vigdis and Ulf stared at each other in dismay.

"We need the völva," said Ulf.

"I know we do. Whether she'll be in any condition to help, I don't know, but we'll fetch her."

VIGDIS AND ULF rode back to the hall, leaving Åsa's horse tethered to a tree branch outside the cave. The blind wolf refused to leave, so they left him guarding the cavern's entrance.

Once back at the hall, Ulf waited by the fire while Vigdis explained the situation to Olaf. "We have to bring Heid. I don't know what she can do, but we have to try."

"Agreed," said Olaf. "Tell me what you need."

"A cart could never navigate the trail to the falls," said Ulf. "I'll go on horseback and take the völva up in front of me."

"You're exhausted," Vigdis objected.

"I cannot rest until I've set this right," said Ulf.

Vigdis realized by his tone that he would not give in. "Very well," she said.

She hurried to the bower, where she found Heid huddled by the fire as usual, shawl clutched around her frail form. Vigdis laid a hand on the völva's shoulder and said gently, "Lady, Halfdan and Åsa have vanished. It appears that they are trapped by an enchantment in a cave. I have tried everything I know without success. You must come with me and release them. Please, Lady, you're the only one who can save them."

Heid stared at her blankly. Vigdis could not tell if her mentor understood what she said or not. She gently pulled the völva to her feet and guided her out to the yard. Heid went willingly enough. Ulf dragged himself into the saddle, and Olaf carefully lifted the sorceress up to him.

Ulf pulled the völva up gently and situated her astride the horse's withers before him, tucking her shawl snugly around her. He held her tight with one burly arm and took the reins with the other, guiding the horse with the pressure of his knees.

Sonja had packed saddlebags with food and ale for them to take along. Vigdis drank a cup of ale in the saddle before they set out, realizing she had not stopped to eat in hours. She chewed on some dried meat as she rode.

They rode on, the horses' hooves falling softly on the dirt trail. Vigdis eyed Heid's form, slumped against Ulf in the saddle. As they neared the cavern, her apprehension grew. How could the völva help when she was barely conscious? It was foolish to risk bringing her here. But what choice was there? She'd exhausted her abilities, and Ulf's. There was no one else.

ÅSA HELD HER SON CLOSE. The space they were confined in allowed only a few inches of movement in any direction. The air already seemed stagnant. She reminded herself that she had been lost in a cavern in Svartálfheim, but then she'd been utterly alone. "Halfdan, do you know where the bad spirit came from?"

Halfdan's sobs had dwindled, and now his breath came in gulps. "I didn't know before, but now I think it's Horik's völva," he said between hiccups.

Groa had tried to lure Halfdan in Erritsø, but the boy had resisted the völva. Åsa shuddered, thinking of the living corpse of

Groa she'd glimpsed in Erritsø. What kind of power kept a woman alive in so much agony?

Power like Heid's.

Åsa doubted she herself had that kind of stamina, not yet. A chill crept up her spine as she imagined what she would have to suffer to gain it. *Oh, Heid, where are you when I need you?*

She resumed her chanting.

ULF AND VIGDIS helped the völva through the curtain of the waterfall, trying to shield her from most of the water. They entered the tunnel, and the old sorceress moaned as they maneuvered her onto her knees. Together, they crawled into the constricted passage, coaxing Heid along between them. In spite of her obvious pain, the völva moved forward as best she could.

When they came to the end of the tunnel, the völva's breath hissed in her throat. Her gaze riveted on the rock wall. She reached out trembling hands to touch the rock.

"Åsa," she whispered, feeling the rough surface.

"Yes," said Vigdis. "Åsa and Halfdan are trapped behind this rock. We must release them. I've tried everything I know."

The völva turned toward her apprentice, her eyes wide. For the first time there was comprehension in them. Heid faced the wall and closed her eyes. Her fingers searched the rock as she mumbled under her breath. Suddenly she gasped, and her hands moved frantically, seeking. Her muttering became faster, more insistent.

Heid began to wail.

The eerie sound echoed through the cavern, loud and urgent. The völva rocked back and forth, gripping the rock as she keened. Vigdis's skin crawled and her ears rang.

Heid collapsed onto the cavern floor.

CHAPTER 12

Dún Ciannachta

After Murchad gave him the news that Niall had refused to support him and that he was to return to Lochlainn, Cian was in a turmoil. He was released from the onerous burden of ruling his clan, but he was even further from the dream of resuming his studies.

As he readied his horse, Ursa found him pondering these issues. "You're awfully quiet."

"The king will not support my cause," he confessed. "I am to return to Lochlainn with you."

Ursa laid a hand on his shoulder. "I'm glad not to lose you."

Cian took her hand in his. "I would hate to part from you. But I wish I could remain in Ireland and resume my harper's training."

Ursa nodded. "I understand your longing. But even if you never study again, you will always be a great harper."

A calm came over Cian. Ursa was at his side. Ragnhild and Murchad had forgiven him for his attempt on Murchad's life. Perhaps others would come to as well, given time.

Ursa leaned forward and kissed his lips.

He put his arms around her and drew her in, savoring her scent of leather and soap. Then he released her and turned to his work.

Cerball and Niall's grooms accompanied them on the ride across the marshland to Daire Calgaich, to take the horses back, and perhaps to ensure they departed as promised. Cian rode among them morosely. He'd barely found his homeland, only to leave it again and live in exile.

Ursa rode beside him, keeping a companionable silence. He appreciated the way the shield-maiden did not chatter incessantly, as if she sensed his mood. At least there would be one person in Lochlainn who understood him—but he would always be a foreigner. Even her companionship could not diminish his longing to remain here, where he belonged.

Father Ennae greeted them enthusiastically at the gates. "Welcome, welcome back, my friends! Come, make yourselves comfortable. Are you hungry? Come and wash while we cook some porridge." The abbot seemed barely able to contain his excitement at their arrival.

Murchad dismounted and gave Aenbarr's reins over to one of the grooms. "Thank you, Father. I'm afraid we can't stay long. We must sail for Lochlainn in the morning. We need to get home before the autumn storms rise."

The abbot's smile collapsed, but he covered his disappointment with a one-shouldered shrug. "I'll be sorry to see you go. How was your visit with the king?"

"Not as successful as I would have hoped," said Murchad. "But it was good to see my cousin again, and to meet his new queen."

The grooms watered and fed the horses but made no effort to return to Aileach. They obviously had orders to ensure that the Norse ships departed as promised.

Father Ennae directed the monks to supply the Norse fleet for their return trip. They laid in a generous store of the monastery's good ale, plenty of flatbread, dried meat and fish, oats and barley, apples and cabbages. Cian skulked in the background, scheming of ways to remain in Ireland. Perhaps he could persuade Murchad to leave him behind at the monastery. A two-day walk would bring him to the school.

But Murchad was busy with preparations for departure, and no opportunity arose to speak to him.

Cian sat numbly as they paid their respects to the abbot and shared a meal with the brethren. Even Father Ennae's harp music failed to stir him. That night he slept alone in the guesthouse. He and Ursa had not found an opportunity to slip off together. A hollow feeling of homesickness lay on him like a heavy weight. After all he'd been through, to come so close to home and then leave again without even seeing it. He imagined hiding, staying behind after the ships sailed and joining the monastery under an assumed name, then finding his way back to Dún Geimhin to study the harp. Perhaps he would persuade Ursa to come with him.

He finally fell into an uneasy sleep, but no sooner had he dozed off than something woke him. He turned, thinking it was Ursa slipping into bed beside him, but his hand connected with something hard.

And sharp. His eyes flew open to see a dark shape, a blade glinting. He gripped the wrist and shouted.

The assailant wrenched free from Cian's grasp and fled.

The others came running. "Stop him!" cried Cian.

"Stop who?" Thorgeir was beside him, gripping his seax.

"Someone was here, with a knife," Cian stuttered.

"There's no one here but us," said Svein.

"I think you had a nightmare, lad," said Thorgeir kindly.

Shame rose in Cian's chest. Had he dreamed it? "Sorry," he said. Now everyone in the crew would dislike him even more for disturbing their sleep.

"Everybody back to bed," said Einar.

Cian could not go back to sleep. What if it wasn't a dream? What if Niall had sent an assassin after him to make sure he couldn't claim his birthright? But how would Niall's assassin recognize him? He'd done nothing to give himself away at Aileach.

Then he remembered the monk, Eoghain, who recognized him as an Irishman. A cold hand clutched his heart. He slumped against the wall, hand on his seax, eyeing the shadows.

Something moved in the dark, and he steeled himself, clutching his knife as a figure approached.

"Are you all right?" Ursa whispered.

He caught his breath. "Yes. I-I had a bad dream. I'm an idiot."

"No, you're not," she said, making herself comfortable beside him. "I'll stay here with you." She took his hand, and in her reassuring presence, Cian's heart slowed. His eyes fluttered.

He fell asleep holding her hand.

In the morning when he woke, Ursa was already gone. Shame overcame him as he remembered making a fool of himself over a bad dream. Hoping no one would mention it to Murchad or Ragnhild, he rose and skulked out to the yard, where the crews were finishing breakfast. Ursa was seated with the others. She spotted him and sent him a reassuring smile.

After breakfast, they waited while Ragnhild bid a reluctant good-bye to Brunaidh. "I wish I could take you back to Lochlainn with me," she told the pony. "Our longships could not accommodate you on such an arduous voyage. The sea would make you very unhappy. I will miss you, old friend. But I will return." Brushing away tears, she hurried to the beach, followed by a crowd of sailors and monks.

Father Ennae blessed their ships and sprinkled the prows with holy water. The sailors climbed aboard and took up their oars, while the monks launched them into the river.

Cian was assigned to the off-duty crew. While his shipmates

rowed north, Cian stood by the rail, gazing despondently at the shore passing by. Would he ever see his home again?

Murchad called him over. "I have something to discuss with you in private." Ragnhild joined them, an expectant look on her face.

Cian's hopes rose. This might be the opportunity he'd hoped for. It wasn't too late to ask to be put ashore. He could make his way back to Dún Geimhin on foot.

His shoulders sagged as he realized that would mean parting from Ursa. Ragnhild could afford to lose one crew member, but not two, especially someone as skilled as the shield-maiden.

Murchad placed his hand on Cian's shoulder and squeezed. "I understand you had a scare last night."

Cian hung his head. "A bad dream. I'm sorry I disturbed everyone."

"Perhaps." Murchad studied him, then shrugged. "But never mind. I have good news for you. I've found a way to fulfill your mission after all."

Cian stared at Murchad, openmouthed. "But King Niall has refused to support us."

Murchad gave him a crafty grin. "We have enough warriors to succeed without Niall's forces. We'll stage a surprise attack from an unexpected direction. Once Dunchad is defeated and you are in control, with our support, Niall will have no choice but to accept you as the only living clan member eligible to be chieftain. My cousin won't go to war against us, especially when we can prove him in the wrong. But we do need the element of surprise."

A knot formed in Cian's gut. Murchad's plans were going in the wrong direction.

Murchad pressed on. "We need to be able to land the ships and ready an attack without your uncle being forewarned. Do you know of a place where we can hide the fleet while we launch an attack? Somewhere four ships and their crews would not be noticed and reported to your uncle."

Despair sickened Cian as he began to grasp the plan. He could not bring himself to lie, much as he'd like to. After attempting to kill Murchad, Cian was honor-bound by his obligation. There was no way out of this trap.

"There's a river mouth a safe distance north of the fortress," he said reluctantly. "At night, even fisher folk do not go there—they believe it's haunted by the Fae Folk. If we arrive after dark, we can go upriver and find a place to hide the ships."

"You will lead us there," Murchad commanded, leaving no room for objection.

Hope and dismay warred in Cian's chest. He owed Murchad, and he wanted to do his duty to his father's and brother's memories and take vengeance. He desperately wanted to stay in Ireland and pursue his music. But he did not want to become a chieftain, nor to lose Ursa. If he became the head of his clan, he would be forced to marry for alliance. Ursa would never agree to be a second wife, nor would he ever ask her to.

His situation was hopeless. He could see no way to achieve his dreams. In a few days' time, he'd either be ruling his father's stronghold, or lying dead.

THE SHIPS LEFT the river and entered the Lough Feabhail, out of sight of the monastery and Niall's lookouts. Ragnhild steered them toward the eastern shore, seeking the haunted river's mouth.

When they reached the deepest waters in the middle of the Lough Feabhail, Ragnhild called a crew member to take the helm. She glanced forward, locating Murchad on the bow, speaking to Cian. Good, he was preoccupied. She did not think he'd understand what she was about to do. She could not explain it to herself, but she knew she must take action.

The helmsman minded his course and took little notice of her as she made her way past him to the stern. With her back to him, Ragnhild reached into her belt pouch and brought out the rattle Gormlaith had given her for Herulf. Her pirate's heart viewed the jewel-encrusted thing with regret, but she leaned over the stern and dropped it overboard. The gold and jewels sparked and glimmered as it sank into the depths of the Lough Feabhail.

She'd had enough of Ireland's cursed jewels. None would reach her son.

THE LATE SUMMER sun was setting when Cian spotted the familiar entrance, low and flat and fraught with sandbars. The years had changed their shapes, but he still recognized the place. It was the only large estuary on this stretch of shore.

He guided them to the broad, shallow entrance. As they wended their way silently between the sandy shoals, Cian's boyhood memories flooded in. He and Cináed had explored the river in their hide-covered coracle, shivering at the thrill of encountering the Fae lurking among the trees.

The ships grounded several times in the dimming twilight, but the crew shoved off the soft sandbars easily enough on the flood tide.

They rowed upstream until they found enough foliage to provide cover. When Ragnhild approved the location, they pulled the ships onto the sandy bank, camouflaging them among the scrub brush.

Einar set guards while they made a cold camp. They had no fire, no music, no stories tonight. Just a supper of dried meat and flatbread washed down with the monastery's good ale.

After the scant meal, Murchad looked at him. "Are you ready to guide us to scout the fortress?"

Cian nodded and rose. He led Ragnhild, Murchad, and Einar into the forest. They went silently on foot, following Cian along deer paths that wove through the undergrowth. Even after all these years, he still remembered how to stalk game without making a sound.

As they forged through the darkening forest, his brother's laughter seemed to echo in the trees. An uneasy feeling stole up Cian's spine, raising the hairs on the back of his neck. Thinking he caught a flash of movement, he scanned the shadows with a shiver.

Murchad leaned over to Ragnhild and whispered.

"What is it?" asked Cian.

Ragnhild murmured, "We're being watched. Act as if you don't notice."

"Do you think they're Dunchad's men?"

"We have to assume he knows we're here."

Dread congealed in the pit of Cian's stomach, churning up his last meal. He swallowed hard and moved on.

The forest had grown and changed since he was last here, but still Cian knew the way home. The smell of woodsmoke curled into his nostrils, thickening his throat and stirring up memories.

The others sniffed the air, catching the scent.

They halted on the verge of the forest. In the clearing beyond, the enormous thatched roof seemed to rise out of the ground like a gigantic mushroom, overlapping the outer palisade of the fortress. A ditch encircled the wall, deeper than the height of two men. The only way across was a narrow land bridge, leading to a stout oak door set in the timber wall. Two spearmen guarded the door, but they leaned on their spears casually, chatting with each other. Within such a fortress, Cian's home had always been secure.

The land surrounding the fortress had been cleared of trees, so it could not be approached by stealth. Fields patterned the landscape, and folk herded cattle and sheep into circular enclosures. Cian peered out from among the trees, watching the livestock enter their pens and the herders retire to the hall for the night.

The fortress door stood open, just as it had in his father's day. He could not remember ever seeing it closed. The two spearmen who guarded it peered into the hall, seeming more interested in the goings-on inside than keeping watch.

"These people don't fear attack. I don't think they know we're here," said Murchad.

"Then who are the watchers in the wood?" Ragnhild asked.

Murchad frowned. "That we must discover."

A shiver ran through Cian as he thought of the Fae, lurking in wait for them.

They observed the fortress awhile longer. Firelight flickered in the doorway, and the faint tinkle of music and laughter echoed from within. Cian remembered this time of night, the day's work done, the promise of food, good company around the fire, a snug bed. A longing rose in his chest. His throat constricted and he swallowed hard.

"Even if we take out those two worthless guards, we'll never get past that land bridge," Murchad growled. "The warriors inside would pick us off from the doorway as we crossed. Let's go back to camp. We'll have to think of another way."

"What about the souterrain?" Cian asked.

Murchad studied him and nodded. "Do you think you can find it?"

"Not in the dark. I can try in the morning." Cian's heart was full of doubt. He had been so young the last time he'd been at the hidden entrance to the souterrain, years ago with Cináed.

"Good. At first light we'll try to locate it."

Cian's mind worked furiously. Here, he was only a half-day's walk to the harper school at Dún Geinhin. If he left tonight after everyone was asleep, he could be there by midmorning. None of the Norse knew where the school was.

But Murchad did. Even if he got away, Murchad would track

him down and drag him back in shame. Ursa would never speak to him again. He'd lose her too.

It was hopeless.

He led them back through the woods to their camp. The sensation of being watched crept up Cian's spine once more. His neck hairs bristled.

The tree above him rustled, and he glimpsed a dark figure just before it landed on his back. He struggled and drew breath to scream, but a rough hand clamped over his mouth. His arms were held in an iron grip as he glimpsed other dark shapes attacking Einar, Ragnhild, and Murchad. The assailants were all but invisible—the gleam of an eye in the moonlight, the flash of a dagger's blade. Cian's heart pounded in his chest. The Fae!

Ragnhild managed to twist out of her attacker's grip and drew her seax. She whirled and thrust her blade at him, but he dodged away from her. Ragnhild recovered instantly and went after him. Murchad and Einar shook off their own assailants and fought side by side, seaxes in hand, barging their way toward Ragnhild. Cian succeeded in wrenching himself from his captor's grip. He drew his own blade and joined Murchad and Einar.

Ragnhild was still fending off her foe, and Murchad had nearly reached her when her attacker gave a shrill whistle. All the assailants converged on Ragnhild. She fought like a cornered wolf, slashing and stabbing with blows that had to draw blood, but her attackers made no sound, nor did their attack relent. They went after her in a systematic method. Two grappled each arm, tangling her legs between theirs. One gripped her hand and peeled her fingers from the seax hilt. The one behind her grasped her braid and yanked her head back, pressing his knife against her throat. "Stop or she's dead," he growled.

Cian froze beside Murchad and Einar. More dark-robed assailants swarmed out of the shadows and took their knives. Eyes fixed on the blade at Ragnhild's throat, the three allowed themselves to be bound and gagged.

Despite her kicks and elbows, Ragnhild's attackers succeeded in tying her hands and stuffing a rag in her mouth. With everyone subdued, her captor released her braid and removed the knife from her throat. She immediately twisted around and head-butted him, but he was ready for her and dodged the full force of the blow.

The captors crowded in, blocking any escape, and marched the four of them through the forest without a word, moving as silent as wraiths.

Despair sapped Cian's strength. These were no Fae, but flesh-and-blood warriors. His uncle had been watching them all along. Of course. Niall had suspected their plan and had warned Dunchad. By morning Cian would be dead, and Ragnhild, Murchad, and Einar with him. When they'd set off from home, he'd known the risks, but they hadn't seemed real. He'd never imagined that his companions might die because of him.

He racked his brains to find a way to get them out of this. How could he convince his uncle to let them go? He'd gladly offer his own life for theirs. But would Dunchad agree when he had the advantage?

Their captors led them on a circuitous route, sometimes backtracking then forging ahead, until Cian had no idea where they were. They had traveled some distance when he caught the scent of woodsmoke.

They broke into a clearing hidden by trees and thick under-growth. A crowd of dark-clad people were silhouetted by a cooking fire. They turned their pale faces toward him, other-worldly in the firelight. Icy fingers walked up Cian's spine. Perhaps they were the Fae Folk after all.

A figure rose from the fire and approached them. Though garbed in tattered robes like the others, this one bore himself with an air of command.

He walked up to Cian and jerked the rag from his mouth. Apprehension boiled up in Cian's chest.

The figure gripped Cian's chin, forcing him to turn his face into the firelight.

Though the man's face was obscured by shadow, there was no mistaking his voice.

"Hello, brother."

CHAPTER 13

C ian gaped up into Cináed's face. "You're alive!" he cried.
"I could say the same for you." Cináed's familiar voice with its wry humor squeezed Cian's heart.

"Dunchad told me you were dead."

Cináed untied his hands and hugged him hard. "He did his best to make it true, but he failed. He believes I'm dead, but I managed to escape his murder attempt. I've been hiding out in the forest for the past three years with a few of my trusted followers who survived."

"How have you managed to stay hidden so long?"

Cináed shrugged. "When his scouts venture too close to our lair, they disappear, never to be heard from again. Most of them join with us. The few who don't..." He trailed off with a wolfish grin. "The legend has always been that these woods are haunted, and we have become the Fae."

"That is a miraculous tale, brother. I am so happy to see you!" Cian nodded toward Murchad and Ragnhild, who were still being restrained by Cináed's men. "Brother, may I present Lord Murchad mac Maele Duin and his wife, Lady Ragnhild of Lochlainn. They have brought me here to take vengeance."

Cináed drew a sharp breath and stared at Murchad. "Lord Murchad! It is an honor to have you among us." He bowed, then turned to the men who held him. "Remove their gags and untie them. Please, come and make yourselves comfortable. I apologize about having to gag you—we had to take precautions lest my uncle's spies were near. Here it is safe, for we are deep in the forest. We keep a cold camp by day lest our smoke rise above the trees and reveal our location. At night we are hidden well enough by the trees that our firelight cannot be seen."

Cináed led them to a downed tree on which several other dark-garbed folk sat, cooking over the fire. Their teeth and eyes gleamed in the firelight as they smiled and bowed to Murchad. It was hard to read Murchad's expression in the dark, but it seemed as if he stood taller.

Cináed called for ale and food. "Lord Murchad, I understand that my uncle blamed Father's murder on you. I see that my brother does not believe his lies."

"He did at first," said Murchad, a bit of humor in his tone.

Cian flushed in shame. "I confess, I tried to kill Lord Murchad to avenge your death and Father's, but then I discovered our uncle was the one responsible."

"I'm glad to hear that," said Cináed. "Truth will out. Now what of you, brother? I heard that you were taken by the *dubh gaill*. How did you come to be here in my forest with Irish royalty and a crew of foreigners?"

"What you heard was true. I was sold to Horik, a *dubh gaill* king, but I escaped a few weeks ago with the help of Åsa, a queen of the *finn gaill*. She is the sworn enemy of Horik, and she asked Lady Ragnhild and Lord Murchad to restore me to Ireland."

Cináed turned to face Ragnhild and Murchad. "I thank you, Lady, Lord, for bringing my brother to me."

"You're welcome," Murchad replied. "We've also come with four fully-crewed ships to overthrow Dunchad."

Cináed smiled. "Yes, my scouts have seen your ships and counted your crew."

Murchad said, "I brought Cian's case to Niall mac Aida, but he would not support us against Dunchad."

"No, Niall favors Dunchad and would never support anyone against him," Cináed scoffed. "I did not even try to let Niall know I was alive. I knew he would not help me, and I feared he would betray me to our uncle."

"He accused me of being an imposter." Cian paused uncertainly. "After we succeeded in overthrowing Dunchad, our plan was that I would take the place as chieftain, but now that you're alive…" Cináed gave him a look, but in the dark Cian could not read his brother's face. "I don't want to be lord," Cian said quickly. "You're the tanist. You were raised for it, and I support your claim. I only want to return to my studies and become a master harper."

Cináed's shoulders visibly relaxed. "And so you shall, little brother."

Several men and women emerged from the shadows, bearing wooden boards loaded with meat, while another man rolled out a keg. The impromptu meal was served on rude wooden trenchers and cups carved from wood, but the food was excellent—cold smoked venison and surprisingly good ale. "Courtesy of our dear uncle," Cináed quipped, raising his cup.

Murchad, Ragnhild, and Einar had rubbed the circulation back into their arms, and now they accepted the ale offered with grace. "Lord Cináed," said Murchad. "I assume you've given some thought as to how to take the fortress."

"That I have," said Cináed. "There are not many ways to succeed. I've never been able to raise enough fighters for a full-scale attack on our uncle."

Murchad nodded. "How many do you have?"

"Twenty able-bodied warriors, and their families. Some of the others can be relied upon in a fight."

"That gives us one hundred sixty fighters." Murchad glanced at Ragnhild. "Though twenty will be left to guard the ships. How many warriors does your uncle have?"

"I've counted a little over one hundred, though some barely deserve to be called warriors. I have no doubt that your party could overcome them in an open battle."

Ragnhild frowned. "How will we attack the fortress? Even with superior numbers, the land bridge is the only way in. Even if we were able to dispatch the guards without raising the alarm, at best, we could cross it three abreast. Your uncle's bowmen would pick us off from the doorway."

Cináed said, "We've gotten quite close without being detected. Dunchad no longer posts lookouts in the forest, after a number of them mysteriously disappeared. Their bodies were never found, because they've joined me." Cináed smirked. "He probably has trouble finding volunteers."

Murchad said, "How long could your uncle hold out during a siege? From what Cian tells me, the fortress has a good well."

"Yes, and Dunchad keeps plenty of stores inside his walls. He could hold out for weeks during a siege."

"We don't have weeks," said Ragnhild. "We need to draw his forces out into the open, but what could bring them out of the safety of the fortress?"

"My uncle is a coward," Cináed scoffed. "He would never come out and fight. He'll sit tight inside his walls and wait us out."

"Fire," said Einar. "An old-fashioned Norse hall burning. That would bring him out."

Cináed bristled. "Then I would be chieftain of nothing. Those within are my people, and I will not have them killed."

"I don't see them flocking to you," said Einar.

Cináed glowered at him. "They don't even know I'm alive. I've had to keep that a secret. If he knew I had survived, even a coward like my uncle would scour the forest and never rest until he had my head hanging from his gate. I've survived this long because I'm nothing more than a faerie story."

Murchad stepped in before this became a brawl. "If you can offer us an alternative way of attack, we will not burn the hall."

"The souterrain," said Cináed. "My people can sneak in that way and draw their attention away from the entrance, while the rest of you storm the hall."

"It's a risky plan," observed Murchad.

"A risk I'm willing to take. I've given this a lot of thought. I can't spend the rest of my life as a ghost in the forest. This is my only chance to take what's mine."

"Let's see this souterrain," said Murchad.

"Follow me. We'll take a look."

Murchad, Ragnhild, and Cian followed Cináed back through the dark wood toward the fortress. Cináed moved with the sureness of a man accustomed to the shadows.

They came to the verge of the forest and circled the fort, keeping to the cover of the trees. The trees and shrubs hid them well, but by the light of the crescent moon, Cian spotted the weathered Ogham sign carved on the fortress wall.

Cináed took a bearing on the Ogham symbol and led them back into the forest. Nothing looked familiar in the dark, and for a bad moment Cian feared the entrance was no longer there.

But then he recognized the stump, now overgrown and almost completely rotted. It was obvious that no one had used it in years, but Cináed led them right to it.

"I've kept it hidden, but I've never had enough warriors to attack successfully. Of course my uncle knows the tunnel is here, but the passage hasn't been used in years. He doesn't fear attack. Help me." Murchad and Cian lent their strength to him and they heaved the stump aside. Ivy and shrubs camouflaged the hole.

When they had pulled the foliage aside, a yawning, black hole was revealed.

"Where does it come out?" asked Murchad.

"The cold stores," said Cináed. "I've crawled through it a few times, spying on Dunchad and pilfering the odd barrel of ale or round of cheese. Never enough to be missed."

Murchad nodded.

"We'll come back later tonight," said Murchad. "When everyone in the fortress will have drunk their ale and hopefully be sound asleep."

"You can count on it. They fear no enemy, as long as they stay out of the forest." Cináed led them back through the forest to the Norse camp. "Get some rest, and ready your warriors. We'll come for you tonight." He put his hand on Cian's shoulder. "Brother, stay with me. This may be our last chance to talk, and we have much to say to each other."

Cian followed his brother on a meandering route through the trees. He was surprised when they broke through into the clearing, having no idea they were even close. Cian was certain he would never find the camp again on his own.

Now that he knew to look, Cian picked out shelters scattered among the trees, constructed of branches and thatched with bracken. If he hadn't known folk lived here, he'd have mistaken the huts for thickets.

Women and children peeped out from among the foliage. When they saw who had come, they began to emerge and take their places by the fire.

Cináed spoke in a determined voice. "Our opportunity has come. My brother brings us enough warriors to overcome Dunchad and take back what is rightfully ours." No one cheered, but a positive murmur rose among the people. "We will depart in a few hours and enter the fortress through the souterrain. Our party of twenty should be enough to cause a diversion within the fort, while Lady Ragnhild leads her crew to fight their way across the land bridge. Everyone, make ready. Get some rest."

Babbling in excitement, the warriors retired to their huts with their families to prepare. Cináed took a seat on a fallen log and patted the space next to him. "Brother, tell me of your years of captivity and your escape. How did you survive the Danes? They are cruel brutes."

Cian closed his eyes and began. "When the Danes took me, I managed to keep my harp. When they tried to take it from me, I played for them. That is how I came to the Danish king. Even the *dubh gaill* love music, and the raiders knew their king would appreciate my ability on the harp. My playing kept me alive all those years with the brutal Danish king. When they captured the *finn gaill* queen, Åsa, I befriended her. Her allies came to rescue her, and we escaped together. Though they were sorely outnumbered by Horik's forces and defeat was almost certain, her allies' diversion gave us an opportunity to get away. The hall caught fire, and that enabled Åsa's allies to escape the Danish forces. She brought me back across the sea to her home. The Danes pursued us, and we met them in a sea battle. I fought by Åsa's side. Lady Ragnhild came with her fleet to support Åsa. After we defeated the Danes, Queen Åsa offered me anything I desired in thanks. I chose to come home to Ireland to resume my studies." He closed his eyes. "When I found out that Lady Ragnhild was bringing me to Lord Murchad, I believed my opportunity for vengeance was God-given. I am so glad I failed."

"What a tale you have, brother. The bards will sing of us both through the ages."

By the dim firelight, Cian noted that his brother had changed. His face had taken on a leanness, and his eyes betrayed a hardness Cian had never seen before. "Now please, tell me of your life the past years. Everyone believes you were dead. How did you escape Dunchad?"

Cináed bowed his head so his face fell into shadow. "After our uncle's men murdered Father, I fled into the forest, but Dunchad's men caught up with me and cast their spears at me. They found their mark, and I fell into the river, mortally wounded. My body was carried downstream by the swift current, out of my enemy's reach. I finally washed up on a bank, where I would have died, but a hermit found me and nursed me back to health in secret, here in the forest. Once I was healed, those loyal to me, who'd been in hiding, found me. They remain with me to this day." Cináed paused. When he resumed speaking, his voice vibrated with emotion. "I will have back what is mine. I have bided three long years here, living like a wild animal, waiting for a chance to avenge Father's murder. My people here have escaped Dunchad's brutality to live free." He broke off abruptly. "But now our tales are told, brother. We should both get some rest."

Cináed brought him to his own hut, and they burrowed into the leaves and fronds that made up their bed. Cian tried to sleep, but excitement and fear kept him awake. Cináed was alive! He'd mourned his brother for three years. And soon he'd see the inside of his home again for the first time in years. He would fight Dunchad and avenge his father, but he would not have to be the lord of the Ciannachta.

By this time tomorrow he would be a free man, or a dead one.

He must have dozed after that, for Cináed woke him and he rose with the others. They armed themselves with long knives and the small round buckler shields the Irish used. They were not much bigger than the boss of a Norse shield, but they would be less cumbersome to carry through the underground passage. Cian had trained with bucklers in his youth, and was confident in his ability to defend himself with one.

He set off with Cináed and his twenty fighters through the forest. They found Ragnhild and her warriors gathered in a cold camp hidden in the forest, close to the riverbank, where they could watch the ships.

When Murchad explained the plan of attack, Svein groaned. "My poor back has barely recovered from the last underground tunnel. I'm getting too old for this creeping around."

Ragnhild grinned and patted him on the shoulder. "You won't

have to, old man. You will stay here and guard the ships." She counted off nineteen to remain with him, including Tova and Ylva, the youngest of Ursa's sisters.

"When you make it into the fortress, we'll need a signal," said Ragnhild.

"We will send one man back through the tunnel to alert you that we're inside. If possible, another of us will come to the doorway and make the sign of the cross with the torch." Cináed demonstrated.

"You mean the sign of Thor's hammer," said Thorgeir with a grin.

Cináed shrugged. "Whatever gets your attention, heathen!"

"I will go with you into the souterrain," Murchad said. "You need someone with experience in strategy. I'm accustomed to tunnels, and I'm slim enough to fit. But Lady Ragnhild will need an Irishman to advise her. Lord Cináed, please choose one man from your people to send with the main force."

"Dermot, you speak a little of their *finn gaill* language." Cináed singled out a man to go with Ragnhild.

The party of one hundred forty warriors set off through the dark forest toward the fortress, walking single file, stepping carefully to make as little noise as possible. When they came to the fork in the path, Cináed and his men split off from the Norse, taking Cian and Murchad with them.

CHAPTER 14

Skiringssal

Åsa ceased her chanting. She strained her hearing—a faint voice, scrabbling on the rock—

An eerie keening rose. Her hands flew to cover her ears, and Halfdan began to cry.

"Hush, hush, dear," she said. The horrid noise ceased abruptly, and Halfdan's crying subsided to muffled sobs. The silence brought relief, but also desolation. Despair fell on her like a shadow. She sat back, cradling her sobbing boy. "Shhh—shh." Åsa tried to soothe herself as much as Halfdan. She barely had the strength to hold him. He rested his head on her chest, breath rasping. Åsa rubbed her son's back.

She did not know the cause of the terrible feeling, but it overwhelmed her. What could it mean? Åsa reached out with her senses, trying to penetrate the rock. She felt a glimmer of spirit beyond.

Heid. Not the vague Heid-gone-missing of recent times, but the woman's keen intelligence, trying to connect with her. And the grief of failure, alive and palpable.

A failure that meant all was lost. Not even Heid could help her. Groa had won. Åsa slumped against the cavern wall, stroking Halfdan's hair.

She had to save her son. There had to be a way, no matter what the odds. She'd come so far with him, survived so many perils together; she couldn't give up. She wouldn't.

A new determination welled up inside of her. She felt Halfdan stiffen in her arms, as if he sensed her resolve. She gently set him on the ground beside her and moved to the spot from which the noise had emanated.

"Heid," she called. "Lady, are you there?"

She pressed her ear to the rock, straining to hear.

No answer.

"Heid, I'm here with Halfdan! You must help us get out."

It was useless. She could not hear well enough through the rock to make out the völva's words, even if Heid was coherent enough to give instructions.

Åsa racked her brains, trying to think of a chant to release herself. A galdr to penetrate a rock wall. She thought back to when Halfdan had helped her find the way out of Svartálfheim. That had been different. She hadn't been trapped inside a rock, but lost in the dark. Halfdan had reached out to her between worlds. Could she do that with Heid?

Åsa sent out her mind, directing it into the rock the same way she entered Stormrider. She strove to pass through the barrier, seeking Heid.

In a surge of revelation, she sensed the völva's hugr. It was strong, but utterly uncontrolled. If only she could tap that power, use it to break through the rock.

A wave of darkness and despair crowded in, casting a shadow on her mind. Another hugr loomed over them, grim and full of hate.

Groa.

The hair rose on the back of Åsa's neck. She'd played mind

games with Horik's sorceress before, but this was a different Groa. More potent, filled with hostility and rage.

Åsa quailed inwardly. How could she prevail against this force of nature? It was like forging into a storm.

What did she have to work with? She had time, at least until they both died of thirst and hunger. That was beginning to feel like a real possibility. Halfdan had been in here for more than a day without food or water, and he was becoming listless. The cavern was cold and damp, further sapping their strength.

Åsa turned her focus on Heid, sending out thoughts to the völva. *Heid, you must help me. Instruct me. How do I open the rock?*

The air seemed to be getting thinner. Her head started to ache and she struggled to breathe.

Heid, hear me. I need your help. Lend me your strength. Send me your hamingja.

She felt a glimmer of response, but with it a tide of confusion flooded in. She shook her head, trying to disperse the chaotic wave of images and feelings.

Heid, Lady, you must gather your wits and send aid to me and to Halfdan. We need you.

Halfdan began to cough. She could hear him wheeze.

Heid! Wake up! We are dying in here!

Åsa fought the despair that gripped her mind.

I will not fail. I cannot fail.

Darkness took her.

Wake, Queen. Rouse yourself.

Åsa roused from her stupor, a flicker of hope in her chest.

I've been waiting for you.

Terror crashed down on Åsa. Not Heid. Not Vigdis.

Groa.

Åsa forced herself to breathe deeply and calmly. She

summoned her power and blasted an answer. *What do you want, witch?*

A chuckle reverberated through the small cavern. *I've got what I want. You and the one you hold most dear, in my power. My revenge.*

You only got what you deserved. You are due no vengeance.

Another chuckle, even more malevolent. *Nevertheless, I suffered greatly because of you. I will have vengeance for that.*

It was obvious Åsa could not reason her way out of this situation. She would have to outwit her enemy. She probed again. *What will you do with us?*

I need do nothing at all, just watch you suffer and die all on your own.

But Halfdan is a little boy. He's done nothing wrong.

Little boys grow up to become warriors who take revenge. Watching him suffer will make it all the worse for you.

My völva will save us.

Ha! Your völva is a helpless old wreck and her apprentice too green. When I overcame death, I gained more power than any mortal. There is no one on this earth who can touch me.

No one on this earth. The words echoed in Åsa's mind. She gathered her thoughts and sent a plea to the dísir. Her mother, and her ancestress Estrid, living in the other world, watching over those who still were on Midgaard. Åsa used no words, for fear that Groa would intercept her prayer. Just a feeling of need, as strong as she could make it.

Åsa could sense no answer. She tried again, but she was too weak to muster another call of that potency. She pulled Halfdan close, burying her nose in his soft hair, inhaling the sweet smell of him, feeling the warmth of his small body. He was quiet now, though his breathing was labored. She stroked his hair and kissed his head, murmuring soothing words. Her brave child who had saved her more than once. She must save him.

She mustered all her strength and sent her thoughts through the rock again, to the dísir, to Vigdis, and to Heid. She called them all to help her take control of the völva's power and bend it to her will.

GROA WATCHED her victims with triumph. She could see them in the darkness, though they could not see her, only feel her malevolent presence. They were weakening. The queen had all but given up. Groa's spirit gorged on the woman's despair, the little boy's fear. There was no escape for them. The Danish völva relished their final moments. Her hugr bloated with gratification.

A blast of power shot into her, discharging all the satisfaction and triumph.

Clouds gathered and swirled around her. They coalesced into shapes of women, wearing cloaks of the night sky.

"You!" Groa cried. "You're dead!"

"No more than you," came the reply as another gust of power shot through her.

Groa desperately rallied her strength and consolidated it, then sent out a blast of her own. Darkness flowed into the vision like blood in water. The specters quivered and dissolved, then shrugged off the dark stain and regained their forms.

Groa gathered her power and sent it forth again. As darkness enveloped the phantom women, their light deflected it, and the blast rebounded onto Groa. The force of it sent her reeling.

A sliver of real fear pierced her hugr.

She mustered every bit of strength and hate within her. It coalesced into a ball of darkness so dense no light could escape. Instead of hurling her power at the vision, she drew everything toward her. She could feel the insubstantial light drawn inexorably into her dark center. She would consume her enemy and grow larger, more powerful.

She would become a god.

Closer and closer the light mass drew. Groa could taste the

power, feel it swell her already enormous mass.

Just a little closer now…

As the opposing force was sucked toward her maw, Groa realized it was not being dragged to her. It was hurtling at her with immense power, rolling Groa's own force up into it.

A collision was imminent.

Her enemy was far bigger, more massive. Groa would be obliterated.

She stopped drawing in and tried desperately to back away, but the vision was locked onto her and coming faster and faster…

The world exploded in a blast of light.

THE EXPLOSION THUNDERED through the rock wall. Bits of rock crumbled and slid. Åsa jolted out of her trance with a sense of urgency. She grabbed Halfdan and fled through the now opened tunnel. Outside she found Ulf and Vigdis, the blind wolf…and Heid. The sorceress lay motionless on the ground, eyes closed. Vigdis was leaning over the völva.

"Is she alive?"

Vigdis shook her head. "I can't detect her breath."

The ground rumbled ominously.

"Hurry!" Åsa said. "We have to get out of here before the hillside comes down on us."

Ulf picked up Heid's head and Vigdis her feet, and they carried her to the horses. Holding Halfdan close, Åsa dashed ahead.

The horses whinnied in distress and milled restlessly. One jerked its reins free of the tree branch and bolted into the night. Åsa set Halfdan down and grabbed the reins of the other two, speaking soothingly to them. Ulf and Vigdis arrived, lugging the sorceress's inert body between them. Ulf mounted and took the reins, reaching down to pull Heid up onto the withers of his horse while Vigdis pushed.

Åsa mounted the remaining horse, setting Halfdan up before her. She felt him shiver with the cold. She reached down to help Vigdis up. "We'll ride together."

But when the apprentice swung onto his back, the horse lowered his head and started to buck. Åsa quickly reined him in and regained control, but Vigdis slid off.

"That horse won't take all three of us," said Vigdis. "You ride with Halfdan. I can walk. It's not far—I'll be all right."

There was no time to argue. "I'll send someone back for you," Åsa promised.

She urged her horse after Ulf. Much as she hated to leave the apprentice on foot, there was no other way to save Halfdan and Heid. She kept glancing behind. Vigdis was maintaining a good pace, though falling behind the horses. To Åsa's relief, the blind wolf shambled along beside the apprentice.

Åsa lost sight of them in the darkness, and a foreboding grew within her, but Halfdan was shivering harder now. She kept going.

When they arrived at the hall, Olaf and Sonja met them at the door.

"You must send a horse back for Vigdis," Åsa said urgently. "One of our horses bolted. The hillside is collapsing, and she's on foot."

Olaf called for a groom to ride out, leading another horse for the apprentice.

Sonja supervised her women as they took Heid's limp form from Ulf and carried her off to the bower. The blacksmith slid off his horse and hobbled stiffly into the hall.

Eyvind swept Åsa and Halfdan into his arms. "Thank the gods you're all right. I arrived a short while ago. I was just getting ready to come after you." He gestured toward the groom's horse. "That horse was saddled for me."

Åsa returned his embrace. "Halfdan needs to be warmed. I must go back for Vigdis."

"You're exhausted. The groom will find her."

Åsa knew she would not be able to rest until Vigdis was safe.

"Why are you so worried?"

"I just have a bad feeling." It was more than just guilt for leaving Vigdis on foot.

She took Halfdan from Eyvind and carried him to the bower. She wrapped the boy in furs and sat by the fire, holding him close. Sonja brought some warm broth, and Åsa coaxed her son to sip a little. After a while, his trembling subsided. "Let's get you into bed," she murmured. Sonja and Rognvald's fóstra helped her put the exhausted boy to bed beside his foster brother. He fell asleep immediately.

She stopped to check on Heid. The sorceress lay on the bed, still as ice. Åsa knelt beside the völva, her ear to Heid's mouth. Was there breath? She couldn't tell. She stared at the völva's inert form in despair.

"You're dead on your feet," said Sonja. "There's nothing more you can do here for now. Come to the hall for a cup of ale." Sonja took a firm grip on her arm and led her across the yard to the hall. Åsa was glad to see Ulf snoring on his bench near the fire, an empty ale cup in his hand. Eyvind, Sonja, and Olaf kept her company while they waited for the groom to return with Vigdis.

Åsa had finished her ale and nearly fallen asleep herself when the clop of hooves roused her. She hurried out to the yard. Her heart missed a beat when she saw the groom led a riderless horse.

"Where is she?" Åsa demanded.

"Lady, I rode the trail to the rockfall, but I met no one. I called her name but got no answer. The trail is completely blocked by the slide."

"Get down from the horse," Åsa ordered.

"Lady, I'm sorry."

"I don't blame you. Now get down."

The groom dismounted, and Åsa hoisted herself into the saddle. She took hold of the spare horse's reins and set off toward the rockfall, cursing herself for not going after Vigdis in the first place.

She heard hooves behind her and looked back to see Eyvind, mounted and following her. He caught up. "I can't let you go alone," he said.

Before long, several more riders had joined them, including the groom and Olaf. They rode down the trail, calling Vigdis's name.

Their voices echoed in the silent night.

Åsa reached the rockslide first. It was far more extensive than she had imagined. The groom had spoken truth when he said no one could ride past it. The footing was too uneven for a horse. She dismounted and scrambled over the slide area, calling Vigdis's name.

Fylgja materialized out of the darkness. He ran to Åsa and barked, then back to the slide. There he stayed, whining and scrabbling at the rock. He snuffled the earth, seeking Vigdis's scent.

The others arrived and dismounted. "Vigdis must be between here and the end of the slide," Åsa said.

Fylgja began to bark and dig with his paws. Åsa hurried over to him. She fell to her knees and scrabbled in the gravel and rock. "Here!" Åsa cried. "Start digging."

It was slow going. They had to be very careful not to accidentally injure the apprentice in their digging. They dared not use shovels or picks, but only their hands. They dug as fast as they could, ignoring broken nails and bloody fingers.

Fylgja stopped digging and barked. Åsa scrabbled at the ground with as much haste and care as possible. Vigdis's face surfaced. "I've got her!" The apprentice was semi-conscious and moaning.

The others joined Åsa, carefully scraping away the dirt and

gravel with their hands. They unearthed Vigdis's body and tried to gently lift her. The apprentice gave a short cry of pain and fainted.

"We need a stretcher," said Eyvind. "Get some saplings and green branches."

In a short time the men had cut the required wood and assembled a stretcher, tying the branches between the two saplings. Olaf flung his cloak over it, and they carefully eased Vigdis onto it. Thankfully, she did not regain consciousness while they moved her. Eyvind strapped her in place with ropes and covered her with his own cloak.

"Easy, now," Åsa cautioned as Ulf and Eyvind picked up the makeshift stretcher. Though the apprentice had gone hours without food or drink, Åsa didn't dare try to give her anything to drink in her unconscious state. The best she could do was keep her warm.

Olaf sent two riders ahead to alert Sonja of their return. Ulf and Eyvind carried the stretcher while Åsa led the horses, Fylgja at their side.

The trek back was long and arduous, as the bearers tried not to cause Vigdis too much pain. She moaned without regaining consciousness. By the time they reached the steading, Sonja had a fire roaring in the bower and a bed prepared nearby. Broth and potions steamed over the fire, scenting the air with herbs and the strong odor of leeks. Sonja and her women received Vigdis as the men lowered her onto the bed, and the women tucked her in with care. Fylgja left her side for the first time and went to lie at the foot of Halfdan's bed.

Vigdis roused into a semi-conscious state. She was able to sip at the cup of broth Åsa held to her lips, while Sonja went over the apprentice's body carefully, testing for broken bones or internal injuries. Though Sonja was gentle, Vigdis moaned and lapsed back into unconsciousness.

Sonja turned to Åsa and reported, "She's bruised and beaten, at least one rib broken, and between the cold and shock it's a wonder she's alive, but she is. I think she'll mend, but it will take some time."

Åsa did not know the results of what had happened back at the cave, or whether Groa was still a threat. Whatever danger was still out there, she must face it alone without Vigdis or Heid.

With Vigdis as well taken care of as possible, Åsa turned her attention to Heid. The sorceress lay on a bench against the wall, pale and still. Åsa sat beside her, smoothing the frizzy white hair back from the völva's face. Once again she bent her head to Heid's to try and feel any sign of breath. She was met with stillness.

But the sorceress's body was still warm to touch. If she were dead, she'd be stone cold and starting to stiffen by now. This gave Åsa hope. It was possible that the völva's breath was too faint to detect. She took Heid's hand in hers and rubbed it, working her way up the sorceress's arm. All the while she murmured to her mentor. "Do you remember when first we met? You stopped Gudrød from raping me, though you were my enemy. Remember when I thought I tricked you and escaped in the boat, yet you knew all along. You arranged for that boat to be there, and for Olaf to come after me. I could never fool you. You've always been two steps ahead of me. You've always been there to protect me, to guide me. I'm not ready to do this alone, not yet. Neither is Vigdis, nor Halfdan. We still need you. I know you're tired. I know you want this to be done. But please, just a little longer. Just a few more years." A teardrop traveled down Åsa's cheek and dripped off the end of her nose to land on Heid's eyelid with a plop.

The völva winced and blinked, sucking in a huge breath. Her eyes flew open.

"What do you want?" she grumbled.

CHAPTER 15

Dún Ciannachta

Ragnhild choked back the dread that roiled up from the pit of her stomach. She didn't like being separated from Murchad, but she understood the wisdom of his plan. Cináed and his outlaws were effective at ambush tactics, but they were young and inexperienced in the ways of war. They would need Murchad's guidance. *He'll be fine*, she told herself.

Ragnhild studied Dermot, the man Cináed had assigned to her. He was in his mid-twenties, ragged and lean from years living off the land, but strong enough. She doubted he was as experienced in battle as Murchad, but he'd been with Cináed in hiding all these years, so he knew the lay of the land. His knowledge of the Norse language enabled her to communicate with him, and he would have a good understanding of the nuances of Irish tactics and warfare.

Einar and Thorgeir were at her side as Dermot guided the main force of warriors toward the fortress. Ragnhild was glad she had the two húskarlar, experienced in the ways of war, to advise her in the coming siege. She had fought plenty of battles, but she knew herself to be rash. She needed older, cooler heads to guide her. If she couldn't have Murchad with her, Einar and Thorgeir were the next best thing.

Stalking through the dark forest with her warriors, Ragnhild was in her element. Despite the size of their army, the Norse were experienced hunters and followed deer trails with little disturbance. Birds fell silent as they passed, but Dermot assured her Dunchad had no lookouts in the forest canny enough to take notice.

They reached the verge of the wood, where they studied the fortress from the cover of the trees. All was silent and dark. The door stood open, the guards leaning on their spears, half asleep. The livestock were quiet in their pens.

Dermot observed, "The door is open now, but if they see us coming in time to bar it, we'll have to break it down. It's a stout oaken door."

"Thorgeir and I will take a party to find a heavy log suitable for ramming." Einar tapped four burly men to accompany them in their search.

While they waited for Einar and his party to return, Ragnhild and Dermot studied the fortress. Now all they could do was wait for Cináed and Murchad's messenger, or their signal.

CIAN FOLLOWED his brother and his fighters through the forest. Cináed found his way unerringly in the dark to the rotted stump. They heaved it aside to reveal a hole darker than the night—the entrance to the tunnel.

"I'll go first," Cian volunteered. "I'm younger, and I know the passage." He got to his knees and gazed down into the dark opening, instantly regretting his rash offer. He swallowed hard and dove in head first, slithering down the dirt hole on his belly. The opening was tighter than he remembered. He'd grown since he'd been down here last, more than five years ago.

He ignored his terror of getting stuck and squirmed into the darkness. The gravel floor beneath him tore at his hands; his back scraped the walls and ceiling of dry-fitted stone. There was barely room for a grown man, and a flexible one at that.

Murchad grunted as he climbed down behind Cian, letting out a faint groan as he slithered in. Cian heard the scraping and curses of other men fitting themselves into the narrow tunnel.

Soon the passage widened, and Cian was able to get off his belly onto his hands and knees. "It gets bigger," he called back softly. A rat skittered over his hands and he bit back a yelp. He crawled on a little further and sensed air above him. Carefully lifting his head, he rose to a kneeling position, expecting to collide with the ceiling. When he didn't, he carefully straightened to his full height. His hair brushed stone, warning him of the roof's proximity. It was a relief to straighten up, although he had to keep his head hunched between his shoulders. When he was a child he could stand up here, but the ceiling was not high enough for a grown man. "Careful," he said over his shoulder. "You can stand here, but watch your head."

Behind him Murchad scrambled to his feet and cursed softly as his head bumped the ceiling. He passed Cian's warning back along the ranks as the warriors straightened up with grunts and groans.

Cian felt his way along the cool, dank passage. Their shuffling feet resounded on the gravel floor. He hoped the noise didn't carry. The dim light from the opening faded completely, and he felt his way along in utter darkness.

The tunnel went straight for a way, splitting off twice into dead-end rooms, but Cian remembered the passage from his childhood explorations. He proceeded cautiously, feeling his way ahead of him, for there were places where the tunnel narrowed and the ceiling dropped abruptly. Each time he came to an obstacle, he murmured a warning to those behind him.

Then he ran face-first into a wall. Fortunately, he'd been moving slowly, and the surface was wood, not stone. The bump stung his nose, but he thought there was no serious damage. Murchad ran into him before he could warn him, pressing Cian into the wall again. "Stop!" he whispered. Murchad echoed his warning as the men bunched up behind him.

Cináed said, "It's just a door to keep out animals."

Cian ran his hands over the wooden surface, contacting hinges. He felt his way to the other side, found the handle, and pulled. To his relief the door creaked open. Everyone pressed up against the passage wall as the door opened into the tunnel, hinges protesting after years of neglect.

Cian slipped around the door. The space broadened and the air smelled of cheese and sour milk. He felt Cináed beside him, heard the shuffle as the group crowded into the space. "We're in the cold stores," said Cináed. "There's another door up a few steps at the far end."

"Wait until everyone is here," Murchad whispered.

Eventually the shuffling stopped. The only sound was the breathing of twenty warriors.

"We're going to go through the door," Murchad said in a loud whisper. "Ready?"

Weapons rasped as they were drawn, and the men murmured, "Ready!"

Murchad hissed, "Cian, open the door!"

Cian climbed the three steps to the door, where a faint light glinted through a keyhole. He put his eye to it. His view was limited, but he could glimpse the dim glow of dying embers and the dark shapes of sleepers. All was silent but for a few snores.

Drawing a deep breath, he grasped the handle and pulled, but the door wouldn't budge. He was sure it opened into the store room, but just in case he tried pushing. The door didn't move. "It's locked," he whispered. His father had never locked the store room, but it seemed Dunchad kept it locked against thievery. Perhaps he had noticed Cináed's pilfering and blamed his own people.

Murchad sucked in his breath. "I don't want to send the messenger to Ragnhild before we get in, but if I don't, she might attack anyway, thinking that we're in danger."

Cináed said, "Dunchad's archers would pick her fighters off the bridge before they crossed. That has to be prevented at all costs."

"Einar and Thorgeir won't let her go in without the signal," said Cian.

"I'm not sure they would be able to stop her if she thought we were in danger," said Murchad. To Cináed, he said, "Have your messenger get ready. We need some light. Give me the torch." Cian brought out the torch he'd carried in his belt, while Murchad rummaged in his belt pouch. He drew out his flint and steel and some dry tinder, and struck a light.

Murchad took the torch and shone it on the door. It was stout, made of oak with an iron lock-plate housing the keyhole. The hinges were also iron, the pins peened firmly into place.

"Perhaps there is a key here somewhere." Murchad cast the light around the walls again, but no key was evident. He shrugged. "I'll force the lock."

He handed Cian the torch and brought out a thin-bladed knife. Cian kept the torch shining on the lock while Murchad inserted the tip of the knife into the keyhole. Metal scratched on metal as he fished around, trying to trip the lock.

The door flew open, flinging Murchad off the steps. Armed men crowded the doorway, pointing spears.

Cináed knocked the torch from Cian's hand. It fell to the floor, and Cináed stomped the light out while his warriors withdrew into the shadows. Cináed dragged Cian into the dark with him. Cian drew his seax, though he knew their long knives were no match for spears.

His brother's warriors crowded the store room, packed close together, their long fighting knives and bucklers ready. Dunchad's men were jammed three abreast in the doorway, peering into the darkness. Though they could not see their foes clearly, the steps up from the store room and the length of their spears gave them the advantage.

"Cináed, send your man back through the tunnel to warn Ragnhild," Murchad whispered. Cináed's man did not hesitate but scurried back into the tunnel. "We have to fight our way through."

"We're ready," murmured Cináed, quietly echoed by the warriors in the store room.

"Charge," said Murchad.

Murchad, Cian, and Cináed were the first to assault the stairs. Dunchad's warriors jammed the stairway, silhouetted against the light, stabbing spears blindly into the dim recess. A spear flashed toward Cian's face. He flung up his buckler and knocked the spear out of the assailant's hands, and it clattered to the store room floor. Cian ducked and swept the spear up, thrusting it into the crowd on the stairs. It found its mark in an enemy's throat. The man fell, clutching the shaft. Cian yanked the spear out of the fallen man's grasp.

Another warrior blocked the light, kicking the corpse of his comrade down the stairs. Cian lunged at the man, thrusting the spear into his belly. The man screamed and doubled over, pulling at the shank. He collapsed onto the stairs, momentarily blocking the warriors behind him. Then he too was kicked aside, and Dunchad's warriors surged into the store room.

Despite the poor visibility, they could hardly miss hitting someone among the tightly packed men who thronged the store room. In the darkness, Cináed's fighters screamed and fell, but others yanked spears from their enemies' hands and thrust them back at the guards. Cináed's fighters were bringing the enemy down, but as soon as one fell another took his place. Dunchad could well have more than one hundred warriors within the huge fortress. It was only a matter of time before they decimated Cináed's force.

By now the floor was clogged with downed fighters from both sides. Their groans filled the air and the room stank of blood. Barely a dozen of Cináed's men still stood. Murchad and Cináed had survived the onslaught, and now they rallied the survivors together, forming a shield wall of sorts with their bucklers edge to edge.

"Charge, you cowards!" a voice screamed from the doorway. Cian's heart raced as he recognized his uncle's voice.

Dunchad's warriors plunged deeper into the room, spears jabbing into the dark, seeking flesh.

"Stay together," Murchad said. He guided his shield wall, dodging right and left, thrusting captured spears into the throng of attackers. Cian knew it was a lost cause, outnumbered as they were, yet the fate that awaited them at his uncle's hands was far worse. Better to die fighting.

Cian rammed his spear into the belly of the enemy in front of him, and in the dim light watched the man's eyes widen, his face contorted in agony as he slid off the spear.

The floor was slick with gore, and Cian struggled to keep his feet under him. Dunchad's warriors slipped on the blood and tripped over bodies in the gloom.

Cian cocked his arm back to hurl a spear into the advancing enemy. Something heavy hit his head.

His fingers lost their grip on the spear and he fell.

Crouched in the foliage, Ragnhild scrutinized the fortress in the pre-dawn gloom. The two guards on the land bridge peered into the hall, distracted by something. Was it Murchad's attack?

Ragnhild grasped her braid and twisted it around her wrist. "Shouldn't they have made it inside by now?" she whispered to Einar. He grunted in agreement.

A runner barged his way through the foliage. "Lady!" he gasped, doubled over, struggling to catch his breath. "I have news from the tunnel."

"Report!" Ragnhild ordered.

"The enemy surprised us in the store room. I fear by now everyone is down or captured. I am the only one who got away."

Ragnhild hid her terror with a scowl, gripping her braid and twisting it in her fist. As they watched, the two door guards hefted their spears and dashed into the fortress. Faint sounds of shouting emanated from the doorway.

"Now!" she hissed. "We must attack now." She charged out of the forest and dashed across the clearing to the land bridge, followed by Thorgeir and Einar. One hundred twenty warriors materialized from the forest edge, their footfalls pounding as they converged on the fortress.

The sound of fighting resounded from within. As Ragnhild's forces bore down on the land bridge, a warrior appeared in the doorway, armed with spear and buckler. Ragnhild launched her javelin and took him in the chest. She rushed across the land bridge as he thudded to the ground. Another warrior grabbed the downed man by his legs and dragged him inside, slamming the door just as Ragnhild reached it. Her shoulder hit the solid oak hard, sending her rebounding with a curse of pain. A thunk sounded inside as the wood bar dropped into place.

"We'll have to ram it," she ordered. A dozen warriors had crowded the bridge behind her. She herded them off the bridge to clear the way as the battering ram was passed up through the ranks. Thorgeir, Einar, and four other stout men took hold of it.

With a roar they stormed the fortress, footsteps resounding as the six big men thundered across the land bridge.

They rammed the tree trunk into the door with a deafening crack, but the stout planks rebuffed them. Cursing, they backed down the ramp and charged the door again without any visible weakening of the oak.

CHAPTER 16

C ian woke in the dark to the sound of groaning. He realized the noise came from his own throat. His ears rang, and when he tried to sit up, his head whirled and his stomach heaved.

He touched flesh beneath him. An arm. An icy cold arm. He snatched his hand back in horror.

Summoning his courage, he felt around in the dark, exploring his surroundings with dread. His fingers contacted a cold face. Lifeless arms and legs.

He was trapped in utter darkness, lying on a pile of corpses.

As the ringing in his ears subsided, he heard movement. He held still and kept silent.

Light glared in his face, making him wince and turn his head.

"Here's a live one."

"Bring me the survivors." Cian recognized his uncle's voice, shouting from the top of the stairs.

Two warriors gripped Cian under the armpits and hauled him upright. Again his stomach heaved and his head whirled. Dunchad's men dragged him over the inert bodies. In the torchlight, Cian spotted the shapes of others being pulled out of the pile of corpses.

Cian was hauled up the stairs into the hall along with several others. He spotted Murchad and Cináed among them. A spark of hope flared. They were alive, though they looked no better off than he.

"Bring those two here," said Dunchad, pointing out Cian and Cináed.

The guards dragged Cian into the firelight and brought him face to face with his uncle. Pain shot though his head, and he vomited.

Dunchad chortled. "I thought I heard rats in my store room. Welcome, nephews!" Dunchad had always been a big man, now running to fat with middle age and soft living. His macabre resemblance to Cian's murdered father, features distorted by fat and greed, brought bile back up in Cian's throat. He wiped his mouth and tried to muster a fierce glare.

"Nephews, I feared I'd never see either one of you again," Dunchad boomed. "And if it isn't Lord Murchad mac Maele Duin! I am honored to host a former king of Aileach in my humble home. How far the mighty have fallen." He smirked. "Cian, you've always been a spirited lad. I'm amazed you survived the Danes. They don't tolerate defiance from their slaves." He turned his gaze to Cináed. "So good to see you, nephew. I feared you dead."

"Hoped, you mean." Cináed fixed him with an agate glare. "The dream of killing you kept me alive."

Dunchad broke the stare first. "Pardon my manners, keeping you standing there. Come, join me."

Dunchad nodded at his spearmen, who prodded them toward the benches.

"How long has it been since you've seen the inside of this hall? Last time, your father sat here." Dunchad seated himself ostentatiously in the chieftain's chair.

Cian swallowed hard and averted his gaze. He watched Cináed's fists clench so hard the knuckles turned white, though his brother's expression did not change. Only Murchad appeared at ease.

"Please, be my guests," Dunchad said, nodding to the guards, who forced the six survivors onto benches at spear point. Murchad eluded his guard and slipped into the seat reserved for the guest of honor, across the fire from his captor. Dunchad gave no sign that he had noticed.

A thud reverberated on the front door.

"What's this? More guests?" said Dunchad. "Well, let them in!"

The guards threw open the door, and Thorgeir, Einar, and four others stumbled in, pulled by the momentum of their stout log. They recovered instantly and swung the timber, taking down four of Dunchad's men. Cian heard shouts from outside, and his hopes flared.

The guards slammed the door and barred it before more attackers could force their way in. Ragnhild's húskarlar managed to mow five more men down before Dunchad's warriors overpowered them.

"Kill them all," Dunchad cried.

"WE HAVE TO SAVE THEM!" Ragnhild threw herself at the door, slamming into it with her shoulder.

Dermot said, "We can't break the door down. We'll have to think of another way."

Ragnhild turned to the Irishman in anguish. "How can we get to them? There's no time. You heard! They're going to kill them!"

She stared at the fortress. The attempt to penetrate through the souterrain had obviously failed. There was no other way in except the land bridge and the stout oak door. The place appeared impenetrable.

Murchad, Einar, and Thorgeir were inside. With a hollow

feeling in her stomach, Ragnhild realized how much she had relied on their advice.

She was on her own.

It was up to her to rescue them. But how? Ragnhild racked her brains. "We need to draw Dunchad out before he can kill them. We have enough warriors to beat him, if only he would come out. How to get him to open the door? What would make an Irish chieftain come out of his fortress?"

"He'd come out if his wealth was threatened," said Dermot. He gestured to the cleared land surrounding the fortress. "Cattle, horses, crops."

Ragnhild studied the livestock pens and neat patchwork of fields. "We need cattle bellowing in distress, horses whinnying, crops burning."

She named off a dozen warriors. "Open the cattle pens and start a stampede. Sheep and horses too. Make as much noise as possible." Counting off ten more, she ordered, "Light branches and set fire to the fields. We need smoke." They ran off to do her bidding. She turned to the Irishman who had reported from the souterrain. "What is your name?"

"Eoin," he said, standing taller.

"Eoin, you lead a party back into the tunnel and see if you can do any good there. We need someone there to help the injured and stand by to launch another attack if possible."

The Irishman squared his shoulders. "Yes, Lady. I would be proud to."

Ragnhild raised her voice to the troops. "I need a dozen volunteers to go with Eoin. You may be crawling through a narrow tunnel, so be sure you are flexible and strong. If you're willing and able, go with Eoin. The rest of you, muster to me. Stay hidden in the trees."

Ursa had barged her way to the fore. "I'm going. Cian's in there."

She and ten nimble warriors joined Eoin and headed into the forest, while the others crowded around Ragnhild.

In a short time the steading was alive with shouts as warriors opened the pens, yelling and waving their arms until they spooked the livestock into a frenzy. Their shouts were answered by the panicked whinnies of plunging horses, the frantic bleating of sheep, and bellowing of cattle. Geese and chickens squawked in alarm as they scattered before the herds.

The thunder of hooves sounded, growing until it shook the ground. Ragnhild's torch-bearing warriors set a haystack alight, then found a field of ripening wheat that burned fiercely. Soon the fields were ablaze and smoke thickened the air. The breeze carried the acrid scent of burning crops, intensifying the livestock's panic.

CIAN HEARD a rumble that shook the fortress.

"What's that noise?" Dunchad demanded.

The sentry opened the door a crack and peered outside. The thunder grew louder, and the harsh scent of smoke filtered into the roundhouse. "The livestock are stampeding," he cried. "The crops are on fire!"

Dunchad froze, mouth open, eyes wide. The warriors halted, spears pointed at the captives.

"Get out there! Save the livestock," shouted Dunchad. "Put out the fire!"

"Take cover," hissed Murchad. The twelve of them dropped to the rushes as most of their wood-be killers rushed to the door, leaving a handful of men to guard the prisoners.

Dunchad's men clogged the doorway, struggling to get through the narrow opening at once. Smoke wafted through the open door, carrying the terrified cries of horses and cattle.

"Now!" said Murchad. They sprang up and attacked their

distracted guards, wresting away their spears and turning them on their owners.

HIDDEN IN THE TREES, Ragnhild's main force waited while livestock stampeded through the clearing. Dunchad's men had eyes only for the herds as they ran after the horses and cattle, shouting and waving their hands.

"Attack!" shouted Ragnhild. Her warriors charged out of the trees and hurled spears at Dunchad's unsuspecting men. Intent on the livestock, they only saw the missiles as they struck. Several fell and were trampled by the frantic herds. Ragnhild's fighters reaped a slaughter among Dunchad's men.

As the two armies battled, the cattle and horses stormed into the forest, driven by the fire that raged across the fields. Glowing embers from the burning crops floated through the air like clouds of fireflies and lit on the thatched roof of the fortress.

Ragnhild raced to the land bridge, followed by two dozen of her best fighters.

INSIDE, the thatch began to crackle and smoke filtered into the roundhouse. Clutching his spear, Cian glanced up as cinders began to fall.

Someone shouted, "Fire!" In a panic, Dunchad's remaining folk mobbed the outside door. The prisoners stood back to back, spears couched, but no one paid them any attention.

The air above them thickened with smoke and bits of flaming thatch.

"To the store room!" Murchad whispered. "Get ready," he murmured. "Go! Stay low!" They ran, crouched, to the store room door.

Dunchad appeared out of the haze and rushed to the door. Cináed tackled him but Dunchad threw his nephew off, slamming him into Murchad, knocking them both to the floor. Coughing from the smoke, they scrambled to their feet just as Dunchad got the door open and ran inside.

They lunged for the door as it slammed behind him. A key clicked in the lock. "Farewell, nephews!" Dunchad called gaily through the door. "I'll always treasure your memory."

"We're not done yet," growled Murchad. "Follow me!" He got on all fours, low down where the air was less smoky, and began to crawl toward the front door. Everyone who had been able to had gotten out, and the doorway was now clear.

Coughing from the thickening smoke, Cian and Cináed got onto their knees and followed him. Their progress was hampered by bodies and flaming rushes, but the open door beckoned.

Cian crawled doggedly behind Murchad and Cináed, though he could barely see in the smoke, and his head was pounding. Through the haze, he glimpsed Ragnhild's and Cináed's warriors creeping along beside him. As they neared the door the air was blessedly cool, but the smoke was overwhelming Cian. He saw Murchad drop, then Cináed. Cian lay on the floor beside his brother, choking as the vast hall filled with smoke. Bits of burning thatch fell on them, and he feebly beat at the flames.

"I'm so glad I found you, brother," said Cináed.

Cian gripped his hand. "I too." Cian laid his face on the floor and knew no more.

Torch in hand, Dunchad turned to confront Eoin, Ursa, and the others, armed with spears they'd picked up from the slain who littered the floor.

They closed on the chieftain, spears pointed at him. "Kill him!" Several took up the cry.

Two men grabbed Dunchad and held him while Ursa brought her spear point to Dunchad's throat. "Where is Cian? And Cináed and Lord Murchad? Did you leave them inside?"

Dunchad did not answer, only glared as Ursa poked her spear point delicately into Dunchad's throat. A tiny drop of blood glistened on its tip.

Abruptly, Ursa slammed the butt of the spear into his head. He collapsed, unconscious. Ursa turned to the others. "Keep him under guard." She cracked the door open and smoke invaded the store room. "Cian!" she called. "Lord Cináed! Lord Murchad!"

She listened hard and heard a faint moan. "I'm going in. Close the door behind me. If I don't return soon, get out through the tunnel." She pulled up the neck of her tunic to cover her nose and dashed into the smoky hall, keeping low.

In the gloomy haze, Ursa spied the forms of several men lying inert on the floor. She stole over for a closer look and recognized Cian. Her heart stopped. It appeared he'd been trying to make it to the front door, but the smoke was too thick. The sounds of battle were loud outside.

She grabbed Cian by the ankles and pulled him to the store room, where she cracked the door open. "Help me. I found Cian. Lord Cináed and Murchad are still in there." Eoin reached through the doorway and helped her carry Cian's inert form into the store room.

They laid Cian gently on the floor. Eoin said, "Stay here with him, Lady. Six of you, come with me. Keep your noses covered. The rest of you, guard Dunchad."

A half-dozen of Cináed's men pulled their tunics over their noses and mouths and crept into the hall, closing the door behind them to keep the smoke out.

Ursa knelt beside Cian. His face was pale as milk, his breathing faint. He was alive, but he needed Unn's healing expertise.

Eoin and his men appeared in the smoke, carrying the unconscious Cináed from the blazing hall. A crack sounded as a roof timber gave way. They brought Cináed inside as flaming rafters crashed down into the hall.

Eoin slammed the door on the flames and leaned against it for a moment, coughing. He felt the door. "The hinges are getting hot. The door will catch fire soon. We've got to get out."

Ursa said, "The only way is through the tunnel."

Cian opened his eyes to Ursa's face. A cough ripped through his chest, making him wince. He searched the room and saw Cináed struggle into a sitting position. Dunchad lay on the floor beside him, unconscious. "Where is Lord Murchad?" Cian's voice rasped in painfully in his throat. "Einar and Thorgeir were in there too, and several others!"

Eoin spoke. "We saved everyone we could find before the roof collapsed. I'm sorry, there is nothing more we can do. The hall is fully engulfed in fire. We're safe for the moment, but the door is getting hot. It won't hold for long."

Cian caught movement from the corner of his eye. Faster than seemed possible, Dunchad sat up, snatched a knife from an unconscious man's belt, and lunged for Cináed.

"Look out!" Cian threw himself between his uncle and Cináed as the knife came down. Dunchad's arm hit Cian hard and drove him down on the hard stone floor. The blade plunged into Cian's abdomen. Ursa gasped and reached for him, cradling him in her arms as he sank to the ground.

"No!" Cináed reached up and gripped the blade with his bare hand. Blood dripped from his palm as he yanked the knife from Cian's stomach. He bent Dunchad's hand back on itself. A crack sounded as Dunchad's wrist broke and he lost his grip on the knife. His scream was cut short as Cináed rammed the blade into his uncle's throat.

Cináed shoved the corpse away and knelt beside Cian. "Brother!" he cried.

Cian felt strangely remote. He was somehow above the scene, able to watch as Ursa cradled his head and his brother gazed into his eyes.

"Ursa," Cian murmured faintly. "Brother."

"Hold on!" cried Ursa. "I'll get you help. First I must get you out of here."

Cináed surveyed the men who littered the store room floor, some wounded, some dead or dying. "The fire will break through that door soon. We have to get everyone out. There's no time to waste. Leave the dead, and bring the living as best you can."

Ursa gripped Cian under his arms and lifted. He cried out as pain shot through him. "Take his feet," she said to Cináed. He grabbed Cian's feet.

The pain in his abdomen forced another cry from Cian as they hoisted him off the ground. He ground his teeth to keep from screaming as they lugged him into the passage. Those who were able assisted the other wounded as best they could.

Ursa and Cináed wended through the tunnel. Though they moved carefully, pain jolted through Cian at every movement. When they came to the place where the ceiling dropped in the exit passage, it became impossible to make any progress with Cian unable to help. They tried to drag him, but the pain made him scream.

"Leave me," he gasped. "I'm not going to make it anyway."

"We're not going to leave you," said Cináed. "After all these years I can't lose you again. You have to survive. You're my only family."

Ursa gripped his shoulders and pulled while Cináed pushed. Cian bit back his cries and tried to help. At last they managed to scrape him into the narrow passage. Ursa let go of him and squirmed out of the hole. She reached in and grabbed hold of Cian under the arms and dragged him out while Cináed pushed.

The pain forced a high-pitched scream from Cian before he lost consciousness.

~

AS THE THATCHED roof became an inferno, Ragnhild rushed onto the land bridge, kicking bodies into the ditch as she ran. "Murchad!" she cried.

She peered through the door. The smoke was like a wall, so thick she could see nothing inside.

"Stop! Lady, stop!" Unn ran after her and tackled her, bringing her to the ground.

Ragnhild struggled wildly. "Murchad is in there!"

Unn held her tight. "Lady, you will do him no good if you're dead!"

Ragnhild shook her off and rushed into the flaming hall, followed by a dozen others.

"Murchad!" Ragnhild shouted, peering into the smoke. "Murchad!" She listened hard and heard groans through the crackling of fire. She pulled up the neck of her tunic to cover her nose and mouth and forged into the smoke, keeping low.

Searching through the haze, Ragnhild spied a figure lying inert on the floor. She hurried over for a closer look and recognized Murchad. "Here!" she shouted.

She dropped to the floor beside Murchad and put her ear to his mouth. He was unconscious but she could feel faint breath warm on her ear.

"Help me," Ragnhild said, grabbing Murchad's ankles and pulling him toward the door. A warrior took Murchad by the other ankle and helped her drag him through the hall to the door. More followers materialized from the haze. Gasping in a lungful of fresh air, Ragnhild jerked her head toward the remaining bodies and ordered, "See to the others. Keep your faces covered."

They turned back into the burning hall. They emerged with

the forms of Einar, Thorgeir, and the rest of their party. They dragged the unconscious men to the land bridge as the hall blazed behind them. They hurried across as the last beams of the great roof splintered and crashed.

Once out of the smoke, the unconscious men began to rouse, coughing and hacking to clear their lungs.

"Ragnhild," Murchad croaked. She cradled his head in her arms. His face and clothes were black from soot. She buried her face in his smoky tunic. "I feared you were dead!" she gasped.

He enfolded her in his arms and kissed the top of her head. "It will take more than a little fire to keep me from your side, *a chroi.*"

"Lady!" A boy broke through the crowd, out of breath. "Lady Ragnhild! I have word of the party in the tunnel."

"Report," she said, not taking her eyes from her husband.

"They're coming out. Lord Cináed is with them. Dunchad lies dead in the store room along with many of his men."

"What of Cian, and Ursa?" said Ragnhild.

The messenger bowed his head. "They have Lord Cian. He's badly wounded."

"Go, help them," said Ragnhild.

A dozen others hurried toward the souterrain. They arrived at the woodland opening to the tunnel. Men lay on the ground outside, some gasping for air, others ominously still.

Ursa and Cináed knelt at Cian's side, tears falling freely as they tried to staunch the wound in Cian's belly. "Get Unn!" she cried.

A man went running to fetch her, though Ursa feared in her heart her sister would be too late.

Cináed and Ursa stayed by Cian's side until Unn arrived. The healer knelt by the wounded man. "What happened?"

"Dunchad stabbed him in the gut. I cannot rouse him," said Ursa.

Unn put a gentle hand to feel the pulse in his throat. "It's very faint, but he lives," she murmured. She nudged Cináed aside and pulled back Cian's blood-soaked tunic. Her face blanched at the sight of the wound, but she said nothing as she pulled her medical bag close. She extracted a linen cloth, ragged but clean, poured water on it from her waterskin, and washed the wound. When she had cleaned it and staunched the blood flow, Unn dug out a linen cloth with bone needles and a coil of linen thread wrapped in it. Her hand was amazingly steady as she threaded the needle. She painstakingly stitched the gash closed, chanting a healing spell.

Blood oozed, and Ursa mopped it with the cloth while she helped Cináed hold Cian steady, but there was hardly any need. He lay still and pale, emitting an occasional faint moan.

When Unn finished sewing, she stowed the dirty linen carefully in another sack and took another fresh linen square and a small flask of mead. She poured the mead on the cloth and placed it on the wound, then bound it around his body with another length of linen.

She sat back, wiping sweat-soaked strands of hair from her forehead. "That's all I can do for now. Keep him warm and comfortable. If he rouses, call me right away."

Ursa gazed into her sister's eyes. "Will he live?"

"Sister, I don't know. I will return with leek soup. We will feed it to him when he wakes, and that may tell the tale."

Ursa nodded, unable to speak. Dread weighed on her.

She and Cináed stayed beside him in mute misery until Cian's eyes fluttered open. "Get Unn!" Ursa shouted. Cináed took off running.

Unn arrived with a warm cup of leek soup. She held it to Cian's mouth, and he sipped.

"Now we wait," she said. They all waited anxiously for the leek to make its way into Cian's guts to see if the broth leaked from the wound. If it did, then a vital organ would had been pierced, and he would soon die.

A strong odor of leek permeated the air.

Unn's eyes met Ursa's. "I'm so sorry, sister."

Cian gazed up at Ursa. "I am glad you are here," he whispered. "Hold my hand."

She took his hand in hers. "Are you holding it?" he asked.

"Yes, I'm holding it." Ursa squeezed his hand and choked back tears.

"I can't feel it…I can't feel anything."

Cian lost consciousness.

"You must save him!" Cináed clutched Unn's arm. "I can't lose him again! We've only just found each other."

Unn placed a consoling hand on his arm. "His death is certain," she said firmly. "With the mercy of the gods, it will be swift and painless. I will do what I can to prevent him from suffering. But it is beyond the skill of any healing I know of to prevent his death."

Cináed leaped to his feet. "I can't give up. I have to do something. I know a man, a holy man. He saved my life three years ago when my uncle's men stabbed me and left me in the river for dead. He healed me. I'm going to try to find him."

With that, Cináed rushed off.

Unn looked at her sister. "It's best he try to do something, even if it's too late."

CHAPTER 17

Tromøy

Åsa stared at Heid, openmouthed, then threw her arms around the völva and hugged her.

"Not so hard!" groused Heid. "I'm not carved of stone."

Åsa eased her embrace but didn't let go. "You're alive!"

"What of it? I could get no peace, so I had little choice but to rejoin you living."

"Promise me you won't leave me again."

Heid glared at her. Åsa was overjoyed by the full comprehension in the sorceress's eyes.

"I won't leave you, not this side of death." The völva did not sound happy, but at least she sounded sincere.

"I'm sorry to keep you here."

"I don't blame you. It's the Nornir who command me to stay." Heid shrugged. "The old witch is vanquished, that's all that matters."

"Victory came with a heavy price."

At Åsa's tone, a look of alarm came over Heid's face. She peered around the room. "Where is Vigdis?"

Åsa took a deep breath. The völva's look of horror made her hurry on. "Vigdis is alive, but she's unconscious and seriously injured. She was buried in the rockslide. We had to dig her out."

Stifling a groan, Heid hoisted herself out of her bed. "Take me to her." Her command was as imperious as ever.

Åsa helped the sorceress limp over to Vigdis's bed. At the sight of the völva, Sonja's eyes got wide and she hastily vacated the bedside stool. "Lady, you're awake!" Sonja and her women clustered around, murmuring in amazement.

Heid grumbled something inaudible in reply as she seated herself on the stool. She turned her attention on Vigdis. The apprentice's face was waxen and bloodless, her breathing rough. Heid took the unconscious woman's hand in hers and massaged it. "What's all this?" she said in the gentlest tone Åsa had ever heard her use. "I know you're a little banged up, but there's work to be done. You need to wake up."

Vigdis's eyelids twitched.

"That's it. Open your eyes, look at me."

The apprentice opened her eyes and met her mentor's gaze.

"That's better," Heid soothed. She stroked Vigdis's cheek. The younger woman smiled.

"I'm so glad to see you," Vigdis whispered.

"And I you," said Heid.

A tear trickled down the apprentice's cheek. "I missed you. I thought you were gone forever."

Heid brushed the teardrop away. "It's all right. You've done well, my brave girl. I'm proud of you. Rest now."

To Åsa's astonishment, the völva leaned over and kissed Vigdis on the cheek. The apprentice immediately fell into a peaceful slumber, a very different state from the stupor she'd lain in before.

Heid gazed at the sleeping woman a few moments more, then gently tucked Vigdis's hand under the covers and demanded, "What have you got to eat around here? I'm famished."

The women rushed to bring Heid a bowl of warm porridge from the pot that simmered over the fire, and a cup of ale. Heid took a few spoonfuls and sipped at the ale. "That's enough. I don't want to give it all back." She rose from the stool and looked at Sonja. "Where do you keep your herbs and salves?"

Sonja led her into a side room of the bower where herbs hung from the rafters and pots lined a workbench. In a few minutes, Heid had set her and the other women, Åsa included, to concocting potions and poultices for Vigdis. The old völva bustled about with all of her former vigor, as if she hadn't been lingering between life and death for weeks. It was astonishing.

During all this commotion Halfdan had woken, and now he joined the women, Fylgja at his side. Heid spared the boy a smile and the wolf a pat on the head. Åsa took Halfdan in her arms and rocked him as if he were a baby. He soon broke free from her embrace, and she had to content herself with watching him scamper about, getting underfoot. This woke Rognvald, who joined in the fun, setting the bower to riot. None of the women complained, so glad were they to see Halfdan safe.

Once Vigdis had been slathered with balms and force-fed potions, Heid finally agreed to rest. Exhaustion paled her face and smudged her eyes. She sipped at a cup of the brew she'd made for Vigdis, and her eyes blinked closed. Sonja caught the cup as it fell from her hand.

They tucked the völva into bed. Though Åsa longed to question Heid about what had happened back at the cave, the völva was sleeping soundly and Åsa did not want to disturb her. Time enough after the sorceress had regained her strength.

Åsa realized how exhausted she was herself. It had been more than a day since she'd slept. Pushing open the door, she stumbled outside to find it was midmorning. She made her way across the yard to the guesthouse, where her crew sat eating porridge, awake and rested.

She dispatched them to sail back to Tromøy with word that

Halfdan had been found, Vigdis injured, and Heid recovered. She herself would stay on until both Vigdis and Heid were strong enough to travel.

She staggered wearily to the private room she shared with Eyvind.

He was awake and waiting for her. As she entered the room, he rose from the bench where he'd been sitting, eyeing her anxiously. He took her in his arms and kissed her hair. "Is all well?"

She buried her head in his chest, breathing in his familiar scent of wool and the sea. "Yes, Heid was miraculously revived, and she took care of Vigdis. It seems that was what she needed—an occasion to rise to. They are both sleeping now."

"That's what we need to do," said Eyvind, drawing her toward the bed. "I've decided to stay on for a couple more days."

"Can you spare the time?" Åsa looked up at him with mingled joy and concern. This close to winter, every day counted to stay ahead of the storms.

"I can't resist an opportunity to spend time with you when you're free of responsibility," he said, kissing her upturned face.

Åsa dropped her worries and gave herself over to his embrace.

They made love, then fell into an exhausted sleep. It was late afternoon by the time Åsa woke. Eyvind was already gone. She hurriedly dressed herself and sought out the others.

She found Sonja in the great hall, organizing a feast despite her own lack of sleep. Men and women scurried hither and yon, bringing down trestles from the rafters and setting them with finest dinnerware. Tempting aromas wafted in from the yard. "We're hosting some important visitors from Gotland. I hope you and Eyvind will honor us with your presence."

Åsa looked down at her soiled tunic and breeks in dismay. "I'm sorry, Sonja, I left Tromøy in such a hurry, and I didn't bring a change of clothes."

"Don't worry, I can come up with something a bit finer for you to wear for the feast tonight." Sonja led Åsa into her bower, where she threw open a huge chest stuffed with fine fabrics and dug around. "Here, this should work nicely."

To Åsa's delight, Sonja produced a green gown of finely woven wool. She held the dress up to Åsa and eyed it critically. "You're taller than me, so we'll add some bands to the sleeves and hem." Sonja plunged back into her chest and emerged with several tablet-woven bands that shimmered with silver thread. Åsa caught her breath at their splendor. The workmanship was beyond anything she'd ever attempted.

The two queens sat together in the sun outside the hall, needles flashing as they stitched on the bands. "How did you manage to get out of that cave?" Sonja asked.

Åsa shook her head. "I'm not sure. I called on the dísir, on Heid, Vigdis too. Somehow their power came together and overcame Groa. It blasted us out of the rock. But I don't know how. I'm hoping Heid can explain it to me when she's had some rest."

Sonja looked at her with sympathy. "You've all had a long, hard journey."

Åsa sighed. For a moment, she allowed herself to think of what her life could have been, had she married Olaf when he'd asked her. She'd be living Sonja's life, one of relative peace and security compared to her own. What would it be like not to be under constant threat from enemies trying to take her kingdom? To share the responsibility rather than bear it alone? Her feelings for Olaf bubbled to the surface, and she slammed a lid firmly on that simmering cauldron. Would she really trade her independent life on Tromøy for it? Her love for Eyvind? She'd chosen the road she was on. There was no going back.

"A perfect fit," Sonja pronounced when Åsa tried the gown on. "It looks better on you than me. Perhaps I'll send it home with you. Now, let me lend you my garnet earrings and pendant."

Åsa felt a bit guilty, accepting Sonja's generosity when she harbored envious thoughts.

Though the weather was mild, the feast was held inside the hall.

"We need to make a good impression on this lady. She's a prominent merchant from Birka," Sonja murmured as she conducted Åsa to her place. As visiting royalty, Åsa sat in the guest's high seat, across the fire from her hosts. Thanks to Sonja, she looked the part. Eyvind took his place beside her.

The special guest was a woman about Åsa's age. Sonja seated her beside Eyvind. He was well acquainted with the lady from Birka from previous voyages, and they greeted each other warmly.

Sonja formally introduced Åsa. "Åsa, queen of Agder, please allow me to present Lady Astrid, from the island of Birka. She is on her way home from trading with the Danes in Haithabu."

Åsa's imagination sparked. This woman was well traveled indeed.

Astrid gazed at Åsa with interest. "My lady, I am most honored to meet you. You are the daughter of Harald Redbeard, are you not?"

"I am."

"My father told me many tales of Harald. He was a brave man and a fearless adventurer. My father was saddened to hear of his death. He sends his condolences."

Åsa nodded, a tightness in her chest. "It was a terrible loss, but I carry on. I have my son and my people to comfort me. Please send my thanks to your father. How did they meet?"

Astrid smiled. "My father met yours far across the Eastern Sea, to the east of Birka, at the trading post Aldeigja on the shores of the Volkhov River, near the great Lake Ladoga. In Aldeigja, furs and walrus ivory come down from the North, and traders take them through the river system to faraway ports. When they first met, Harald was not yet a king. He and his crew ventured farther on the Itil River than any of us have gone, past Bolghar. It is said he made it to the Sea of the Khazars, and even reached Serkland. Few have made such a journey, and fewer still returned to tell the tale."

Åsa's gaze strayed to Ulf. He sat in his corner and listened with interest, though he, who had made that legendary trip with Harald, did not join in the conversation. It was a closely guarded secret that the only Norse blacksmith who knew how to work the rare Wootz steel sat in the hall at that very moment.

The talk turned to the East, of Birka and Aldeigja. Olaf regaled the guests with tales of how he'd been kidnapped and enslaved, and made the journey on the Itil River to Bolghar. Åsa's blood was stirred by stories of traders who ventured south via the treacherous Dneipr River to the mighty city, Miklagard.

"Have you seen these places?" Åsa asked Astrid in fascination.

The trader shook her head. "I confine myself to the civilized ports—Aldeigja, the Isle of Gotland, Haithabu, and of course Skiringssal. There are many riches to be had without the risks of venturing into the wilds. But for those who dream of adventure —there is plenty to explore to the East."

The trader's words set Åsa's imagination on fire with the possibilities, and she peppered the woman with questions throughout the meal.

Åsa changed the subject to one that had been preying on her mind. "You've recently been in the land of the Danes. What news have you heard of Horik?"

Astrid snorted and shook her head. "In addition to rebuilding his hall and his fleet, Horik has other concerns that will keep him occupied for some time. The Franks, his uncle Klak Harald, his brothers in exile, all beset him. I understand that you've defeated him, and his brother before him."

"Yes, thanks to my allies." Åsa nodded toward Olaf. She was much relieved to hear this confirmation that supported her findings on her spy mission to Erritsø.

When the evening was at an end and she and Eyvind retired to their private chamber, Åsa held him close and murmured, "One day I will sail with you and see those ports for myself."

"I would love to have you by my side, to show you the world I know and love."

She fell asleep in his arms, dreaming of the sea and the exotic places it held.

In the morning, she visited the beachside market with Eyvind. Booths were set up on either side of a boardwalk that ran parallel to the shoreline. Halfdan was excused from his lessons so she could keep him by her side as long as possible. Åsa loved the bustle of the trading port, the sights and sounds almost overwhelming after Tromøy's sedate harbor. Eyvind introduced her to more travelers from Aldeigja, Birka, Haithabu, even Francia. Åsa was captivated by the fine glassware displayed in the booth of a Frankish merchant, and Eyvind bartered for a set of aqua-colored drinking glasses for her to take back to Tromøy.

She found the woman from Birka, Astrid, in a booth along the boardwalk. With her was her little daughter, a blonde girl about the same age as Halfdan.

"You take your child with you?" she said.

"Of course. I could not be parted from my Drifa." Astrid ruffled her daughter's hair affectionately. "She does very well at sea. Many children do."

Åsa was enraptured by the idea of traveling with her child as this woman did. "I can hardly keep my son off the ship. Perhaps I no longer need to."

While their mothers spoke, Halfdan and Drifa eyed each other for the briefest of moments. Without a word spoken between them, Halfdan let go of Åsa's hand and the two ran off together down the boardwalk. Åsa started to call her son back, but hesitated.

Astrid laughed. "Don't worry. Drifa knows not to go far. Come, I'll show you my ship."

Åsa followed her to the wharf, where they boarded a knarr a bit smaller than Eyvind's *Far Traveler*. It was a roomy vessel that took its main propulsion from sail rather than oars, with long sweeps for maneuvering in and out of harbors. "I carry a crew of twenty," said Astrid. "I only need half a dozen strong sailors to work the ship, but the Eastern Sea can be a dangerous place with pirates lurking. The sight of twenty armed warriors is usually enough to make them seek less challenging prey."

Eyvind also carried an armed crew larger than strictly needed, for the same reasons. He'd told many a swashbuckling tale about encounters with pirates, but his ship had never been boarded or robbed.

Four men were loading finished tools that bore Ulf's mark. It appeared that Astrid still had room in her hold. Åsa seized the opportunity. "If you are interested in a load of soapstone and whetstones, please visit me on the island of Tromøy, a day's sail to the south of here. I own the quarries." Astrid could afford to depart later than Eyvind could, because she was heading home to Birka for the winter.

"I will do that!" said Astrid. She reached into her booth and retrieved a doeskin pouch which she pressed into Åsa's hand. "A gift from me."

When Åsa opened the drawstring pouch, she caught her breath as five gleaming amber beads fell into her hand. "They are beautiful! Thank you."

Astrid winked. "I have plenty more. You can thank me by giving me a good deal on your best whetstones and soapstone."

"It's a deal!" said Åsa. The two women offered their hands and shook on it.

"I'll venture down your way before I depart for Birka," said Astrid. "It will be a week or so while I sell the rest of my cargo."

Åsa was well satisfied with the arrangement. Eyvind had loaded all his knarr could carry, but there was still plenty of stone left at Fjaere.

That evening, they feasted once more with visiting merchants in the great hall. Afterward, as they readied for bed, Eyvind said, "My love, I have treasured this time with you, but I must make ready to depart in the morning. If I don't go now, I won't make it to Aldeigja. Ulf would not forgive me if I was unable to get his Wootz steel."

"I understand. I realized this was borrowed time for us." Åsa choked on her words and could not keep the sadness from her face.

Eyvind took her in his arms and kissed her. They made love tenderly, knowing with the hazards of travel, they might never meet again. Such was the life they'd chosen.

Next morning, Åsa stood on the pier, calming the storm in her heart as she bade Eyvind good-bye. She watched *Far Traveler* row out of the harbor, comforting herself with the thought that while Eyvind was brave enough, he was no risk-taker. He would come home to her before the snow flew, and they would have the whole winter together.

Once his ship had disappeared beyond the islands, Åsa distracted herself in the smithy, watching Ulf and Knut teach the boys. She sat on a stool by the forge, listening to the two old men, just as she had when she was a girl and her brother, Gyrd, was alive. Nostalgia came over her for her childhood, her lost family. She could feel their presence, watching over her and Halfdan.

She strolled the docks, stopping to chat with Astrid while Halfdan played with Drifa, and meeting new traders. She loved to hear their tales.

She lingered a few more days while Vigdis and Heid regained their strength. Every evening traders were in and out of the hall, some noble, most not. Åsa marveled at Sonja's and Olaf's ability to entertain the constant stream of visitors from exotic ports and negotiate in a variety of languages.

Finally came the morning that Vigdis rose from her bed and

began to take her first tentative steps. Heid, too, was regaining her strength.

That night, Heid and Vigdis both appeared in the hall. Åsa decided that they were ready to make the journey home.

"I will gladly take you all to Tromøy in *Sea Dragon*," Olaf said.

"Thank you, Olaf," said Åsa. She turned to Sonja. "We are so grateful for your hospitality."

"You are always welcome here."

In the morning, Åsa held back her tears as she bade good-bye to her son and Ulf, gave Sonja and Rognvald a hug, and climbed aboard. She took delight in watching Heid grumble at Vigdis as the two women boarded the ship. Now that the apprentice was back in good health, the völva had resumed her old gruffness. Vigdis seemed happy enough to have things back to normal.

Astrid and her little daughter wandered over. "I'll be along in a few days for a load of your soapstone and whetstone."

Åsa smiled. "I'll be expecting you."

Olaf nodded to his crew, and they shoved off.

CHAPTER 18

Dún Ciannachta

As if the gods had had enough of fire, the sky opened and sent a downpour that put the flames out. Ragnhild's warband brought the wounded to shelter in the workshops and byres that had not burned.

Ursa sat beside Cian, sheltering them both beneath her cloak. When Unn came by on her rounds, she knelt by Cian and felt his pulse. A look of concern came over her face and a cold splinter of fear pierced Ursa's heart. Unn put her cheek to his mouth and closed her eyes, holding very still as she tried to sense any trace of breath.

At last Unn straightened up and opened her eyes, gazing at Ursa with sorrow. "I'm sorry, sister, he's gone."

Ursa sat motionless while an icy blade drove into her heart. Her sister grabbed her as she collapsed and held her tight while Ursa's world tumbled down around her.

Cináed arrived, drenched and downcast. "I searched for the man who saved me, but he's gone. I called his name, but after all these years, he must have moved on."

He took in the scene before him. "Cian's gone," he whispered. Unn nodded tearfully. He fell to his knees and buried his face in Cian's chest.

After the first wave of shock receded, Cináed helped Ursa ease his brother's body onto a wood plank. Together they carried him to the ruined hall.

The rain eased up, and the common folk emerged from their hiding places. They gathered in the clearing before the still-smoldering fortress. The thatched roof of the hall was a total loss and would have to be replaced, though the walls and posts within survived.

Little was said as the folk eyed their blackened crops.

"We'll stay on a few days and help you recover," Ragnhild assured Cináed. "I'll send some of my crew to find the livestock."

"Thank you, Lady. We can use the help. Now I must speak to my people." He squared his shoulders and strode to the land bridge before the ruins of the fortress, where he proclaimed in a ringing voice, "I am Cináed son of Cumuscach. You all know me —I was the elected tanist, trained to head the clan after my father. My uncle, Dunchad, told you many lies. He told you I was dead. That was obviously a lie, for here I stand before you to claim what is rightfully mine."

The people were silent. Cináed turned to Murchad, who stood at the head of the crowd. "He said this man, Murchad mac Maele Duin, was responsible for my father's death. That was another lie! The blame lies with my uncle, who murdered Cumuscach. His men tried to kill me, too, and failed. He sold my brother into slavery and has succeeded in murdering him. Now Dunchad is dead. As elected tanist, I claim the chieftainship of this place, from this day until I die. And my first act as tanist is to declare Lord Murchad innocent of my father's murder."

The people began to murmur.

"How will we eat?" one said, louder than the rest. "Our crops are burned, the livestock scattered."

"Our Norse allies have gone to recover our livestock. They've agreed to help us get started rebuilding. The wheat crop is lost, but the store room is full of grain, butter, cheese, cured meat. My uncle was hoarding food from you, but I will share with all. You will not starve."

As Cináed spoke, a great lowing of cattle and neighing of horses arose as the livestock rumbled into the clearing, driven by Ragnhild's sailors.

Thorgeir rode up, mounted on one of Dunchad's horses. "We found the cattle and sheep sheltering in the forest away from the smoke and flames, waiting patiently to be herded home. The horses had not gone far either, and they allowed themselves to be led back to their familiar corral."

The people debated among themselves. When their voices died down, Cináed spoke. "All who would swear to me, kneel. Anyone who does not give me your oath, you are free to go now, but know that you are banished from my lands."

The farmers and craft folk all knelt before Cináed. Most of the warriors who had survived the battle also swore to him, though a few ran into the forest.

As they watched the deserters go, the man who had spoken out before came forward. "Those men who fled into the forest have all committed crimes. Dunchad turned a blind eye to it. Will you do the same?"

Cináed declared, "We will hold a trial for them in absentia. I will send for a brehon judge to hear their cases, and if they are found guilty, I will declare them outlaws for their crimes."

A murmur of approval rose from the crowd.

Cináed sent a rider to summon bards from the school at Dún Geimhin to perform the funeral songs. The folk turned their attention to the wounded. Tova, Unn, Ursa, and Ylva worked side by side with the Irish healers, washing and binding wounds. Nearly all the settlement's medical supplies had burned or been used up, but the healers took to the woods and distant pastures, gathering herbs for salves and remedies. They heated a cauldron over an outdoor fire and boiled every scrap of linen they could find for clean bandages.

While the healers cared for the wounded, others turned to the fallen. The Irish stripped the dead and washed their clothes, then brought buckets of water from the river. They bathed their dead and laid them out on the ground in clean, if still damp, clothes.

Cian was placed among them with special honor. Under the watchful eye of a venerable Irishwoman, Ursa approached to wash his body. The old woman admonished her at length in Irish.

Ursa looked to Murchad for translation. "It is she who is keeper of tradition and designates when it is permitted to cry. She said you may not weep until he is properly prepared. If you cry before that, the Sidhe will hear and try to take his soul. When all is ready, the keening will guide his soul into the next world."

Ursa nodded solemnly. While she washed his body, Cian's sea chest was fetched from the ship, and she withdrew his best clothes. Choking back tears, with dry eyes Ursa dressed him in his best wool tunic and breeks, nålbound stockings with cross-gators. Last she put on his shoes. She did not know if he would have to walk the Hel road or if Christians traveled a different way in death, but she wanted him equipped for whatever awaited him in the Otherworld.

Ragnhild had lost a dozen of her Norse sailors. While the Irish mourned their dead, she and Einar supervised the building of a pyre where they would burn the bodies when night fell.

Cian was laid out on the wooden plank that served as a makeshift bier, his hands holding his harp on his chest. The Irish women brought armfuls of wild flowers, which they laid about his head. They continued on among the dead and adorned each one with flowers. When all the bodies had been properly prepared, the old woman gathered with two others and waited.

Two bards arrived on horseback from Dún Geimhin. Both women, they were regally dressed in white robes and silver torcs, and their horses outfitted with silver-gilt ornaments. The mourners parted for them, bowing in reverence. Cináed came out to greet them formally.

The elder of the two bards stepped forward and bowed. "Lord Cináed, we understand that your brother is among your dead. He was one of our most promising students, and his loss is a great one. We will mourn his passing in the old ways as custom requires. Please take us to him."

Cináed led them to his brother's corpse. The elder bard took her place at Cian's head, the other at his feet. The mourners divided into two groups and gathered around the bards, led by the three old women who had supervised the laying out.

Cináed stood at the head of Cian's bier. The mourners fell silent as he spoke. "I lost my brother three years ago. He spent three years of his life enslaved to the Danes. All that time he believed me dead, while I mourned his loss in my heart. We found each other just yesterday." Cináed's voice clogged in his throat. He took a few gulping breaths and went on. "We had only a few hours together, and now we are parted again.

"Cian mac Cumuscach longed to be a harper above all things. He did his duty and showed great courage. Against all odds, he made his way home. He was ready to give his life to avenge my death, and that of our father. If he had succeeded and survived, he vowed to take his place as chieftain of this clan, though it was the last thing he wanted."

Cináed fell silent. The bard at Cian's head struck up a tune on her harp and began to sing a sad lament. Though she could not understand all of their words, Ursa caught Cian's name several times and realized the bard was singing about him.

When the first bard finished her lament, the three old women drew a deep breath and began to wail in unearthly, broken voices, sending a shiver down Ursa's spine. The crowd joined in. Obviously the keening was well known by all. Emotion welled up in Ursa and she loosed her own voice, rough with grief.

The keeners fell silent, and the bard at Cian's feet took up the next verse. As soon as she finished, the old women initiated the keening once again. And so it went, the two groups alternating each verse.

The bards moved among the deceased, followed by the crowd, where they performed the ritual at each of the departed. This went on all day, during which time the dead were never left alone. Cináed and Ursa kept watch over Cian's body, silent now.

Suddenly the bards stopped mid-song, their eyes fixed on a newcomer who approached on foot. He wore simple white robes, and a doe walked by his side. Silence fell over the crowd as he made his way among the dead. The bards bowed as he passed.

The newcomer stopped beside each corpse, Irish and Norse, and passed a hand over their brows, whispering in their ear, then pausing, head bent, as if listening.

"Brother Brian!" Both Cináed and Murchad cried out at once. They gaped at each other.

"This is the man I sought today, the man who saved me from death," said Cináed.

"He healed me once, too," said Murchad.

"Greetings to you, my friends," said Brian. The crowd parted as he approached the bier where Cian lay. The bards followed at his side, heads bowed in reverence. "I come to you on a day of great sadness. I can do no more for your fallen. They have gone already to the Otherworld."

Brother Brian looked down at Cian. He touched the pale forehead, took the limp hand in his own. An intense expression crossed his face. "But this one is different. What is this, young lord? Why do you linger?" He turned to Ursa. "Is it because of this woman?" He looked at her kindly. "Do you not want to kiss your love good-bye?"

Trembling, Ursa leaned over and kissed Cian on the mouth. It seemed to her the afternoon sun had warmed his lips as if he still lived.

Brother Brian bent down and peered into Cian's pale face. "Do you really want to leave her? What of all the music you were to play? Young lord, everything you ever wanted is here for the taking. So why don't you get up and take it!" He gently moved Cian's hands aside from the harp and took the instrument up. Staring into the distance as if looking at something far away, he strummed the strings tentatively and tuned the harp.

Brother Brian began to play. He started with a mournful melody that brought tears to everyone's eyes, then segued into a lullaby that made eyelids droop. Suddenly the tune lightened into a merry *Geantraí* that set feet to tapping. The mourners could not help but smile as tears dried on their cheeks.

Ursa thought Cian's eyelids twitched. Her heart skipped a beat.

"Come, lad," Brian said encouragingly. "You've eluded death so many times, this should be child's play for you." He kept on playing with even more vigor. "Claim the life you deserve."

Everyone waited, scarcely daring to breathe.

Then Cian's chest heaved and he drew in a huge lungful of air. The onlookers gasped.

Cian's eyes opened and he sat up. People in the crowd screamed.

Ursa took him in her arms and kissed him again.

Everyone clustered around him, exclaiming and trying to touch him, but Ursa held him tight.

At last Cian found his voice. "Would you have anything to eat or drink? My stomach thinks my throat's been cut."

THE MOURNERS SERVED as much food and drink as could be scrounged from the ruins. The souterrain yielded up cheese, which had taken on a smoky flavor from the fire, and barrels of grain and mead and ale. Cattle and sheep had been corralled and provided fresh milk, and a few were slaughtered for the feast that would come.

After everyone had marveled over the miracle, and Cian had been plied with food and ale, the bards supervised the digging of graves to receive the Irish dead, wrapped in shrouds. They buried both Cináed's men and the warriors who had fought for Dunchad together.

"They are all my people," said Cináed. "They believed my uncle's lies. If they had lived, they might have sworn to me."

Dunchad's body had been brought out of the souterrain. He was buried in a distant field, far from the family. "Keep him out of my sight," said Cináed.

As the sun set, Ragnhild and her crew members set fire to the Norse dead. They gathered with the Irish to drink the minni cup of remembrance while they recited the feats of the dead to the sound of Cian's harp. Murchad bridged the gap between the two worlds, mourning the loss of his Norse crew members as well as the Irish.

Cian and Ursa sat side by side, holding hands. They could not be separated for any reason.

The next day, after all the dead had been properly laid to rest according to their customs, Cináed and his people began to rebuild the fortress. The Norse helped as they had promised, lending their aid to cutting thatch in the distant pastures that had not burned, and ploughing fields so that a crop of winter barley could be sown. With so many helping, soon the great hall was once again roofed.

But all was not well with Cian. He suffered from frequent headaches that left him unable to sleep and muddled his memory. "How can I ever become a master harper if I can't remember anything?" he despaired.

Brother Brian examined him. "Visit the ocean. You are strong enough to make the journey. Listen to the music of the waves, and ask Manannán mac Lir to heal you."

Cian and Ursa packed up two horses for an overnight trip and rode north through the wilderness to the ocean. They followed forest trails for most of the morning, then broke out into grasslands leading to Binevenagh Mountain. Though the horse's motion jarred Cian's head, he persevered up the steep rough road that brought them to the summit. Something in him demanded he reach the top, to cast his gaze over the entire land.

When they arrived at the summit, the skies were clear and they could see a vast distance over the Lough Feabhail. On the other side rose the hills of Innis Eoghain leading north to the sea and the distant lands of Dál Riata. Below them stretched the entire expanse of the triangular plain.

The wind on the mountain cooled Cian's face and soothed his spirit. The view calmed his mind and broadened his outlook. At his side, Ursa gazed out over the landscape, lost in her silent thoughts.

When he'd finally taken in his fill of the panoramic view, they started down the mountainside. But by the time they had descended and set out across the plain to the ocean shore, his face was pale and his head throbbed. He felt as if he was dying again. When they reached the sea, all the strength flooded out of his limbs and he began to slide from his horse. In alarm, Ursa dismounted and caught him. She helped him stumble to a driftwood log, where he slipped to the ground and leaned back, panting. Terror came over him as death reached out icy fingers to grip his heart once again.

Ursa hurried to the saddlebags and poured a cup of ale. She brought it to his lips, and as he sipped, he felt the blood return to his head and his limbs. His body warmed and the fear quieted.

He became aware of the soft, rhythmic sound of the waves surging on the beach, then gently retreating. It eased his head. His mind craved the sound. He closed his eyes and gave himself over to it, sending a prayer to Manannán mac Lir. Perhaps the old god of the sea would hear him.

As if in a trance, he heard Ursa's movements while she tended to the horses. He scented the smoke from the fire she built, heard the crackle of kindling and the trickle of water poured into a pot. With a clang she hung the pot on a tripod over the fire. He felt her presence as she took a seat on the log beside him, her breathing troubled.

The water boiled, and Ursa rose to make porridge. Cian could smell the food, and his stomach rumbled, but he could not bring himself to open his eyes or take his focus from the sound of the waves.

He had no knowledge of how long he sat there, completely submerged in the sound, entranced as if he could never get his fill. But eventually, he felt something in his head let go, and the pain flowed away like waves on the beach.

He sat still for a while longer, hardly daring to breathe for fear the agony would return.

"Ursa, I think it worked. The pain is gone," he murmured, unable to believe it.

He opened his eyes cautiously. So far, so good. He rose tentatively and strolled down the beach, still focusing on the waves as they crashed ashore and gently receded. Ursa walked by his side, her hand in his.

"It's gone," he said when he was sure. She threw her arms around him, then led him back to the fire, where she fed him porridge and more ale.

As darkness fell, they unrolled their hudfat and made love under the stars with great care. At last Cian felt he'd come fully back to life. He was a corpse no more.

In the morning, he hardly dared open his eyes, but when he did, the pain did not return. He rose and helped Ursa reheat the porridge for breakfast.

They saddled their horses and set off for the fortress. On the ride, his head still felt good. The cure had worked. Perhaps the old gods still retained their power, still listened to the prayers of mortals.

Back at the fortress, the Norse were packing up. In the morning they would sail for home. Cian and Ursa both knew this was the time for decisions. They wandered in the forest, hand in hand.

"I am not going back to Lochlainn," said Cian. "There is no future for me there. Here I can follow my dreams to complete my studies and become a master harper. My home and family are here."

"I know," said Ursa.

Cian gathered his strength from the silence of the forest. He halted and faced Ursa, gazing into her soft brown eyes that looked back at him hesitantly. What would her answer be? He gulped a breath of the rich forest air and took both of her hands in his. "Ursa, you are my family." He studied her face, trying to discern her reaction. But he could not tell.

It was now or never. He sank to one knee, still holding her hands. "Ursa, will you stay with me, become my wife? Help us rebuild? Raise children with me? I know it means giving up your home, living far from your family and friends…" His confidence began to falter.

She gazed down at him for an interminable moment. A void opened up of life without her, and he nearly tumbled in. And then she breathed, "Yes."

"Yes?" he cried. "You said yes?"

She nodded, smiling, her brown eyes dancing. "You are my home. You are my family."

He took off running, pulling her along. "We must find Brother Brian before he leaves!"

When they told Ragnhild, she said with a grin, "So, I'm to be short two more crew members on the way home?"

Cináed hugged Cian and Ursa. "Brother, that is such happy news! I've already summoned the brehon to confirm my chieftainship and pass judgement on the outlaws. She will officiate the marriage as well. I expect her to arrive today."

Cian explained to Ursa, "Brother Brian will perform our handfasting, but the brehon will advise us of the law and write our marriage contract."

"She is a law-speaker," Ragnhild explained. Ursa was very pale, and Ragnhild took her aside. "Are you sure about this? You don't have to stay. You can change your mind and come with us."

Ursa shook her head. "I'm nervous, but I want to be with Cian, and to help rebuild this place. I know enough of this land and the people to believe I will be happy here."

"Very well. But you will always have a place in my hird."

"Thank you, Lady."

Next day, the brehon arrived on horseback. She was a woman of middle years, tall and slender, who bore herself with great dignity. She wore a gown of red linen and a multicolored wool mantle, fastened at the shoulder with a fine silver brooch.

Cináed welcomed the woman with deep respect. "Lady Brigh, I welcome you."

"I understand I am to acknowledge you as chieftain of this place at your uncle's death," she said.

"Yes, I have long been the tanist here, elected to rule in my father's stead."

"This I know," the brehon acknowledged.

"My uncle falsely declared me dead and seized the chieftainship. But now all is set aright."

"Indeed," said Brigh.

"Lady, there are two other matters for which your services are needed. Some criminals have fled to escape trial and must be judged in absentia."

"Very well, you can present the cases to me tomorrow, after I have declared you chieftain. And the other matter?"

Cináed brought Cian forward. "Lady, you know my younger brother, Cian."

Cian bowed. "Greetings, Lady."

The stately woman inclined her head. "Yes, of course, I remember you when you were young. How nice to see you two boys all grown up into fine men."

Cináed laid his hand on Ursa's shoulder. "This lady, Ursa, has agreed to be my brother's wife."

The brehon gave the shield-maiden a startled glance.

Cian spoke firmly. "Lady, my wife is a *finn gaill*. We owe her people much, and I hope you will welcome her."

The brehon recovered from her surprise and took Ursa's hands in hers with a warm smile. She spoke to her in passable Norse. "Congratulations, my dear. It's quite a life-changing decision you have made, to wed an Irishman and remain in our country. I will do all I can to make you welcome here."

A bit of color returned to Ursa's face, and she managed a shy smile.

Cináed conducted Brigh to a table set out on a platform beneath the trees in the yard. The brehon was served refreshments and made comfortable after her long ride. While Brigh ate, Cináed related the events of the battle with his uncle. Several witnesses were called to substantiate his story.

When Brigh had finished her ale and cakes, she rose and quoted Cináed's heritage from memory. "I designate Cináed son of Cumuscach the lord of this place, as in the rights of tanistry. I relieve him of any guilt in the death of his uncle, Dunchad."

Cináed accepted the torc of his father as the crowd roared their approval.

When the cheering had subsided, Brigh took her seat once again. "Now it's time for a wedding, I understand."

Cian and Ursa stepped up onto the platform and faced the brehon across the table. Brigh brought out a goose quill, a small pot of dark ink, and a piece of calfskin that had been scraped smooth. The brehon sharpened her quill with a tiny knife and dipped it into the pot. She held the quill poised above the calfskin and regarded the couple before her.

"My Norse is limited. Can the bride understand our language well enough, or do we need someone to translate?" she asked.

"I can understand well enough," Ursa replied in Irish.

"Very well," said Brigh. She turned to Cian. "Cian, son of Cumuscach, please state the terms of marriage."

"It will be a marriage in the first degree," said Cian.

Brigh studied them both. "Are you of equal birth?"

"Ursa is my equal in every way," Cian declared.

The brehon nodded. With the sharp point of the quill, she wrote on the skin. "Will this be a marriage of the man contribution, the woman contribution, or of equal contribution?"

Cian said, "It will be of equal contribution. Neither the bride nor the groom have any land or cattle, nor much more than the clothes we stand up in."

Brigh inclined her head. "It will be a marriage of equal contribution. Do you agree to this, Cian son of Cumuscach?"

"I do," said Cian.

The brehon wrote some more on her calfskin, then turned her gaze on Ursa. "Lady, as you are a foreigner, I will explain your rights under this contract. You may dismiss this man as husband, and he you as wife, for the following reasons: flagrant infidelity, failure to produce a child, or bad management. To dissolve the marriage you must declare your intentions before witnesses. In such case, you are entitled to take with you all the property you brought with you, any gifts your husband has provided you with, and a share of the wealth of the marriage that your efforts entitle you to. You are responsible for your own debts and crimes, but not those of your husband. Do you understand these terms, and do you agree to them?"

Ursa gulped and nodded. "I understand, and agree."

The brehon wrote more. "Very well. I sign this as witness to your marriage contract according to the laws of Ireland." Brigh signed with a flourish and set the skin aside to dry. Then she stood and addressed the gathering. "These two people have agreed to enter into a marriage of the first degree, of equal contribution."

When the brehon had finished her speech, all the folk, Norse and Irish alike, gathered by the river to form a ring around Ursa and Cian and Brother Brian. The couple faced each other and held hands while the druid wound a tablet-woven band around their hands and tied it in a knot.

"Ursa and Cian, here in front of witnesses, by the right of handfasting, you are now bound in a trial marriage for a year and a day. When that time has passed, you will decide whether to remain together or dissolve the contract and go your separate ways. Should you decide to remain together after that time, your marriage will become permanent."

Brother Brian unbound their hands. He picked up a bejeweled chalice and offered it to Cian. He took it, brought the cup to his lips and drank. He then offered it to Ursa. When she had drunk, Brother Brian took the cup from her.

The druid raised the chalice high and said, "You are now husband and wife." The crowd roared in approval.

Cináed rose. "As ruler of this land, I award my brother and his wife the land and means to build their home."

"Thank you, brother," said Cian.

"I am so pleased to have you both here at my side," said Cináed.

A woman approached, bearing a plate of oatmeal and salt, which she presented to Cian. He dipped his hand in each and tasted them, then offered the plate to Ursa. She brought the oats and salt to her lips. The crowd cheered and congratulated the new couple.

By this time a feast had been laid out, and everyone ate and drank until they could hold no more.

The next day the brehon heard the cases against the accused outlaws, and she convicted them in absentia. Cináed put a price on each of their heads commensurate with their crimes.

After the hearings, Ragnhild wandered the riverbank. Soon she would be returning to Gausel. It was her home, her birthright. The place her son awaited her—the child who rejected her. She did not want to be tied down by the responsibility of a baby. She did not want to pretend to be content with motherhood and running the steading when she longed for the sea. How would she cope with her own restlessness? Åsa gladly gave up her liberty for the love of her son and her people. But Ragnhild was different. Without the ability to come and go as she wished, she feared she would wither away, become a bitter woman. She needed the sea, the freedom to sail to distant lands.

Yet there was no doubt she loved Herulf. She was vulnerable to him. He held the power to hurt her in his tiny hands. It already hurt her that he preferred Liv to her. Yet how could she blame him? He deserved a real mother. She was not a mother. Never would be.

All these thoughts swirled in her head as she walked.

Suddenly she stopped and looked around her, realizing the forest was unfamiliar. She had lost her way.

She scented woodsmoke and followed its trail until she spied a small hut built of branches and bracken. A deer nibbled at the foliage nearby.

A figure dressed in white emerged from the hut.

"Brother Brian! I'm surprised to find you still here."

"Ah, there you are," said the druid. "Come, rest yourself." He sat on a log and patted the spot beside him.

Ragnhild sat. "I thought you would have gone home by now."

Brother Brian smiled. "I am home. It is you who are far away."

Tears prickled at Ragnhild's eyelids. She blinked them away furiously.

He patted her hand and smiled at her. "Young Herulf awaits his mother."

Ragnhild stared at him. "How did you know my son's name?"

"Didn't you tell me?" Brother Brian said vaguely. "Something troubles you, daughter, more than the loss of your followers."

Ragnhild swallowed hard. "We sail for home tomorrow."

"And yet, you don't completely feel you are going home."

To her mortification, a tear slipped down her cheek. She blurted, "I'm not meant to be a mother. My son is better off with his nurse."

Brother Brian said gently, "A child needs his mother. There are all kinds of mothers, with many different kinds of gifts to give. Just because you are not the kind who provides coddling does not mean you have nothing to give Herulf." He gazed into the distance over her left shoulder. "Your son will need you more than you can imagine. He will need things only you can give him."

"Like what?"

"Why don't you go back to him and find out?" He touched her lightly on the top of her head.

Ragnhild felt her confusion clear and a weight lift from her shoulders. "I will. Thank you, Brother."

"You are always welcome, my lady."

She rose and easily found her way back to the steading. She went straight to Murchad and held him tight. "I can't wait to get home to Herulf."

He looked at her with pleased surprise. "Neither can I, *a chroi.*"

That night she soundly slept in Murchad's arms, filled with anticipation.

In the morning she rose and allowed herself to be caught up in the excitement of her crew as they launched her little fleet into the Lough Feabhail. She waved farewell to Cináed, Cian, and Ursa, and all the Irish folk gathered on the beach.

Ursa looked a little forlorn as she watched the ships slide into the water. "Don't worry," Ragnhild shouted. "I'll be here in a year and a day, in case you've changed your mind!"

MURCHAD WATCHED Ireland dwindle into the distance. He was not sad at their departure. He was sorry to part from Cian and Ursa, but he was glad they had found each other, and happiness. He knew he'd see them again. Unn, Tova, and Ylva sat quietly in the stern, obviously missing their sister. They had lost their eldest sister, Helga, in battle two years before, and since then the four had clung together.

Murchad was looking forward to the winter, snug in Gausel with Ragnhild and Herulf. He was glad Ragnhild felt positive about her relationship with their son. It was fine that Herulf loved his fóstra, but Murchad knew there would be room in his heart for a mother who taught him to swim, to ride and sail, to fight. Their child would learn from Ragnhild's three húskarlar as well, and they would be loyal to him as long as they lived.

Murchad would teach his son to rule wisely and well. Herulf

would learn the ways of the Norse, but also the ways of the Irish inasmuch as his father could teach him.

They sailed across the sea, taking care to give the Dál Riata a wide berth. As they neared Iona, the longing rose again in Murchad's chest to set foot on the holy isle once more.

Ragnhild caught Murchad's gaze of longing and relented. "We have time to stop for one night," she said.

The longships landed on Iona's beach, and the monks ran for the monastery walls. They cowered behind the gate until Murchad disembarked. Carrying his white shield before him, he strode up to the gate. "I am Murchad mac Maele Duin. I come to see Father Blathmac."

The gate creaked open cautiously, and a cluster of monks peered through the opening. An elderly monk came forward. "Father Blathmac is dead. I am the prior, Brother Airtri."

Though Murchad had known this would come to pass eventually, still it shocked him. "How?"

Brother Airtri bowed his head. "After the *dubh gaill* raided our island years ago, we sent all the precious objects to Kells for safety—the holy books, the treasures. We moved the scriptorium there. But Blathmac refused to send the shrine of the blessed Colm Cille to Kells. He said it belonged here, on the site that Colm Cille had founded. He believed the saint would protect it from the heathens."

Murchad waited for the inevitable end to the story.

"Blathmac was not a complete fool," Airtri continued. "In truth, we all knew he was set on martyrdom and sainthood, and we feared he would take us all with him. He realized the *dubh gaill* would come back looking for treasure, so he buried the shrine. He did so in secret, so that none of us would be able to divulge its location to the heathens, no matter what they did to us." The old prior closed his eyes and was silent for a moment. Then he took a breath and resumed his tale. "A month ago, the raiders landed and stormed the church during mass. When they found no valuables, they seized Blathmac and tortured him, trying to get him to tell where our treasure was buried. They would have done the same to the rest of us, but he managed to convince them that we knew nothing, bless him.

"The heathens burned him, they cut him, they near-drowned him. But the more the *dubh gaill* hurt our holy father, the more Blathmac became exalted. It was as if the angels were protecting him from pain. When he refused to divulge the location of the shrine, the heathens hacked him to pieces on the altar step. They searched the grounds, dug everywhere, but they did not find the shrine.

"We buried Blathmac here. And Colm Cille's holy shrine remains with us, though no living man knows where. Perhaps now the raiders will leave us in peace." The prior stared at the ground sadly. Murchad also bowed his head, and everyone observed a silence for the bold monk.

The prior looked up, seeming to remember he was receiving royalty. "Please, Lord, Lady, join us in our evening meal, and then I hope you will grace our poor guest lodgings for the night."

Murchad nodded his thanks. "Let us get our belongings, and then we will join you."

As they walked back to their ships, Murchad said to Ragnhild, "I doubt these poor monks have anything to spare. I would not want them to go hungry for our sake. Let's bring our own provisions to their table."

Ragnhild agreed. "Father Ennae was more than generous in provisioning us. I think we can even spare a little extra to tide them over."

They returned to the monastery with sacks of oats and barley, some dried meat, and fresh vegetables from the gardens of Daire Calgaich.

The prior thanked them for the provisions with tears in his eyes. As they sat down to the thin gruel and bread that was the monks' only meal of the day, Murchad admired their devotion.

After the meal, Murchad asked Prior Airtri, "When we were here before, Father Blathmac took me to the hill of angels at sundown. I have longed to visit it again and feel the holy presence once more. I wonder if you might guide me there?"

"Indeed, I go there every evening," said Airtri. "I will gladly take you with me."

"I wish to come too," said Ragnhild. Murchad looked at her in surprise.

He was even more surprised when the prior agreed to take a heathen to this holy site.

They set out as the sun was nearing the horizon. Brother Airtri led them across rocky fields to the grassy hill overlooking the shore. They climbed to the top and seated themselves on the ancient stones, still warm from the late afternoon sun. From here, they could look out over the sea to the west. They watched in silence as the sun dipped into the sea.

The prior broke the silence. "We call it the Hill of the Angels because the legend tells us that the blessed Colm Cille came here every night at sunset to pray. When the sun set, angels of light would come to him. But it is known that these beings appeared long before Colm Cille ever walked this island. They were known to the druids."

Murchad wondered if these beings were common to all lands and all beliefs. He sat silently beside the prior as the sun sank below the western horizon, far across the sea. Though he saw no angels, he let himself settle into the peace of the place.

Beside him, Ragnhild sat in silent awe. As the last rays of the sun touched them, she murmured, "It is the landvaettir."

The prior, lost in prayer, seemed to hear nothing.

When the last of the light was gone, the prior rose. He led them back to the abbey in silence, none of them willing to break the spell. Airtri left them at the guesthouse door without speaking.

"Do you think the landvaettir are the same as angels?" Ragnhild asked.

Murchad shook his head. "I don't know."

"If the druids saw these holy beings as well, could it be they are the same no matter what a person's religion might be?"

"It could be," said Murchad.

Ragnhild sighed and turned over. "Such questions are beyond my simple mind. I will tend to my seamanship and battle practice and leave them to the priests and the völur."

Murchad took her in his arms and kissed her. "I don't believe your mind is simple at all. You understand things no others perceive. I love your mind."

IN THE MORNING, the monks fed their guests gruel that had been thickened with a little of the barley the Norse had brought, and the fleet shoved off once more. Murchad felt fulfilled, as if he had accomplished all he had intended with this journey, crowned by the visit to the hill of angels. He was so happy to have shared that experience with Ragnhild. It bridged a gap between their beliefs, gave them another way to communicate.

They passed through the Southern Isles, and slipped inside the Orkneys. Then it was a straight shot across the sea to Lochlainn. Murchad was looking forward to getting back to the place he now felt was his home, and to his child.

On a sunny morning, the ships rounded the headland and entered the fjord. Murchad's heart lightened. Soon he would see his son. They would be reunited as a family again. The winter stretched before him, cozy and tranquil.

On the way in, they trolled fishing lines from the stern. Murchad got a strike, and after a rousing fight he pulled in a good-sized salmon. The ship was nearing shore as he brought the fish aboard. He killed the salmon quickly with a blow to its head and left it on deck while he hurried to assist in landing on the shore of Gausel.

Liv awaited them on the beach, Herulf in her arms. Murchad let Ragnhild clamber ashore and take the child first, while he brought his prize salmon off the boat.

"This should be a good addition to our homecoming feast," he said, holding it up.

"Yes, that's a fine fish," Ragnhild agreed, her nose buried in their son's hair. The baby started to fuss. "Liv and I will take Herulf up to the hall."

"I'll be up as soon as I clean the fish," said Murchad, bestowing a quick kiss on his wife and son.

He laid the fish on a plank and plunged his knife into the salmon's belly. The blade struck something hard, and he caught a glint deep inside. Cutting carefully, he opened the fish's innards to reveal a gleam of gold.

He cleaned it in a bucket of salt water. As the fish's blood and viscera washed away, Murchad stared in amazement at a golden object, encrusted with jewels.

The rattle that Gormlaith had given them for Herulf.

Murchad shook his head to clear it. Somehow the precious item must have fallen into the sea. He did not know how, but here it was. He put the rattle in his belt pouch and carried the fish up to the hall.

The folk of Gausel greeted him with the respect and deference due their lord. This was his rightful place.

He dropped the salmon off with the kitchen crew and made his way to the sleeping chamber he shared with Ragnhild and Herulf. Joy filled him to see his wife sitting on the bed, doting over their infant son. There was hope for a happy family yet.

He reached into his pouch and brought out the rattle. Leaning over the bed, he held the bejeweled toy above his son's face. The baby gurgled, reached out and grabbed it with both chubby fists.

Ragnhild sucked in a breath of shock and snatched the rattle away from her son. "Where did you find that?"

"It's passing strange, but it was in the belly of the salmon I caught. Somehow it got lost. Think of it, this gift must have been swallowed by the fish en route from Ireland, and then it followed us all the way here."

~

Skiringssal

THE SEAS WERE fair on the half-day's sail home to Tromøy, and Åsa relished the salt air and vast vistas of open sea. Olaf surrendered *Sea Dragon*'s helm to her, and she imagined she was already beginning a voyage to far-off places.

When Tromøy hove into view, her mind whirled with all that needed to be done. The Birka trader Astrid would arrive in a few days, so she must hurry down to Fjaere to pick up the soapstone and whetstone and bring it back. Much as she trusted the Svea trader, she was not ready to reveal the whereabouts of her quarries even to her, in case Astrid let word slip out. Fjaere was not well defended, and Åsa could not spare the warriors to protect the port. It would not do to tempt anyone with piratical leanings.

After that, the harvest must be tended to, sheep sheared of their strong summer coats, cheese put by for the winter, herbs gathered to dry in the rafters. Ships needed repair and warriors training.

They landed on Tromøy's shore, and Åsa stepped lightly onto the beach. As Olaf helped Heid off the ship, the völva said, "Careful, boy, or I'll turn your ears into cabbages."

Åsa smiled to herself. Heid was herself again.

Once up at the hall, Åsa set her folk toward making a meal for Olaf and his sailors, and ensured that the guesthouse was clean and warm. She was glad to have him at her hearth again. That evening they sat around the longfire chatting with Olvir and Dagny, easy and friendly together. Gone was the old tension that had existed between her and Olaf.

Åsa saw him off in the morning with a tasty lunch of cold meat and freshly baked flatbread. As she watched *Sea Dragon* disappear around the point, she decided now was the time to question Heid.

Striding up to the bower, she found the sorceress sitting in the yard, her face raised to the sun. "Come, Lady, let's take a walk. The exercise will do you good."

Heid hobbled along beside her dutifully, leaning hard on her staff.

When they were alone, Åsa turned to the völva and said, "Back there at the cave, was that you?"

Heid frowned, staring at the path as if it were her enemy. "Was what me?"

"Did you vanquish Groa?"

The völva shrugged. "I had a hand in it, but it was not me alone."

"Well then, who was it? My foremother, Estrid? My mother?"

Heid rolled her eyes and sighed. "It was them, yes, and me, but most of all it was you."

Åsa stared at her, mouth open in shock. "I don't have that kind of power."

"Not yet, you don't. But you are able to call on those who do, and that's what happened." Heid dragged on Åsa's arm, turning her back toward the hall.

"What do you mean?"

"You summoned the dísir to aid you, and we responded," Heid said in slow tones, as if speaking to a simpleton, guiding Åsa by the arm.

Again Åsa was dumbfounded. "We? Including…you?"

"Yes, I number among the dísir now."

"But you're alive!"

Heid scowled. "I am, and I'm not. One foot in this world and one in the next. And so I shall remain, as long as you have need of me."

Åsa was dismayed by her statement. "I'm holding you in life against your will?"

Heid shook her head, her scowl deepening. "Not you. The Nornir have doomed me to this fate."

They had reached the hall door, the same place they'd just left. "What can I do?" Åsa felt fresh guilt at keeping her mentor from what she truly desired.

Heid sighed and lowered herself gratefully onto the bench. After a moment, she spoke. "You've traveled far and dared much, bargained with the Nornir, traversed the nine worlds on Yggdrasil, bested Hel in her own hall. You've established relation- ships with those in the Otherworld, and earned the right to call on their powers in time of need. You have proven yourself coura- geous and resourceful in this world and the next. You summoned the power from the dísir. And you can do so again, if you need to."

"But I still need you," Åsa said, alarm filling her.

Heid patted her arm. "Yes, you still need me, for a while." The völva groaned. "Now I must rest."

Åsa helped Heid to her feet, and with the aid of her staff, the völva hobbled back into the bower, where she resumed her place by the fire.

Once the sorceress was settled, Åsa set off for a walk, mulling what Heid had told her. She did not feel powerful, yet she did feel confident in her ability to draw on power from others. After meeting the dísir in Hel, they'd become real to her. She'd tapped into Halfdan's abilities as well. And Heid's and Vigdis's. All these connections were her strength. Even when Heid passed on to Helheim, Åsa knew she'd be able to contact her mentor. She could make the trip to Hel again if she had to. But that day was far off. Heid had much to teach her, and Vigdis, before she was free to go.

Åsa gazed across the fields of barley that flowed like a golden ocean down the hill to the harbor, where the water sparkled under sunny skies. She was home. Those she loved were safe and restored to health. Her enemies were at bay, and her strength had grown so that, the gods willing, she could stand against them when they threatened again.

All was well in her world, for now.

AUTHOR'S NOTE

Cian mac Cumuscach is a fictitious character, though his clan, the Ard Ciannachta is real. As usual, I draw my inspiration from the terse and sometimes contradictory entries in the Annals of Ulster. A king named Cumuscach was killed in AD 822 and his murder laid at Murchad's doorstep. Confusingly, in AD 824 the Annals of Ulster mention a skirmish between Dunchad and Cumuscach, two kings of Ciannachta, in which Dunchad was the victor and Cumuscach escaped by flight. Later, a king of Ard Ciannachta named Cináed mac Cumuscach is mentioned in the Annals of Ulster as slain by Vikings in AD 828.

There was more than one clan by the name of Ciannachta. Cian's clan is Ciannachta Glinne Geimhin, or the Geimin Valley Ciannachta, not far from Daire Calgaich. There is mention of Ciannachta Glinne Geimhin having a fort in the Limavady area near the Roe River, though the name Limavady (Leim an Mhadi-adh: Leap of the Dog) was given to the place after the twelfth century, based on the legend of a faithful dog who carried a message to the chieftain warning of an enemy attack. There is also tantalizing mention of a harper school in nearby Dungiven (Dún Geimhin).

I have placed the Ard Ciannachta's Viking Age fortress in an early medieval ringfort called the Rough Fort within a mile of Limavady, and called it Dún Ciannachta for want of a better name.

Early medieval Celtic harps were strung with brass wire and plucked with long crooked fingernails. Before the triangular harp the Irish played lyres, called a cruit. The Gaelic word for a wire-strung harp is cláirseach, while instruments strung with sinew were called harps. It's not certain when the first triangular-shaped harps appeared in Ireland, though there are depictions of stringed, harp-like instruments carved on stone high crosses dating to the ninth century.

Regarding differences between bards, poets (filidh), and harpers, historical records include descriptions of harpers accompanying bards, directed by a poet, as well as singers accompanying themselves on harps. Irish Christian holy men are mentioned playing stringed instruments as early as the ninth century.

Irish keening (caoineadh or crying) has an ancient history. Its origins started with the goddess Brig, or Brigid, daughter of the Dagda and the Morrigan. Legend says that the first keening was heard in Ireland when Brigid's son was killed. Her wailing caused all who heard it to stop fighting and lay down their arms. This tale gave rise to the Ban na Sidhe, or Banshee, the faerie woman whose wailing heralds death. Traditionally, keening was performed by women who specialized in the art, and may have been led by bards. These traditional songs or chants, praising and mourning the deceased, were believed to guide the deceased soul to the next world. The practice was discouraged by Catholic priests in modern times, and has now pretty much disappeared. A few haunting recordings survive and can be heard on YouTube.

Murchad's cousin Niall did indeed marry Gormlaith ingen Dunchada, half-sister of the high king Conchobar mac Dunchada, Murchad's rival. Niall later became the high king after

Conchobar's death. Niall and Gormlaith's son, Aed Findliath mac Niall, became high king after his father's death. The troublesome necklace and the golden rattle are both fictitious.

The murder of Blathmac, leader of Iona, by Danish Vikings in AD 825 is documented in the Annals of Ulster.

I have included my interpretation of navigation in the Viking Age. Little is known of how these intrepid sailors found their way to the far reaches of the world, aside from a few tantalizing hints in the sagas. The Norse sailors used a form of navigation known as latitude sailing, mentioned in some of the old sources, such as the *Landnamabok* and the Greenland Saga. From Norway's west coast, the navigators used known points of land as departure places, from which they could sail due west to a destination of the same latitude.

Though the Vikings did not have a compass, they divided the horizon into eight directions relative to their departure point. The west coast of Norway runs north and south, and the Viking Age sailors used this to orient themselves. They recognized North, East, South, and West. Northeast was referred to as Land North and southeast as Land South, since east was the direction their homeland lay. Northwest was Out North (outbound) and Southwest was Out South.

The Norse called Polaris *leiðarstjarna*, leading star. It is the one star that is always in the north. Sailors could tell how far north or south they were (their latitude) by measuring the North Star's height above the horizon and comparing it to the star's height at a known latitude, such as their departure point.

According to the sagas, Viking Age navigators also used signs in nature, such as the behavior of birds, the direction of the ocean swell, and cloud formations to determine their proximity to land.

As for the Danes, there is evidence that Erritsø was destroyed by fire and rebuilt, though the exact timing is unknown, nor is the instigator. There are many candidates. The Danish kingdom was rife with strife, between Horik and his brothers as well as his uncle, Harald Klak, who allied himself with the powerful Franks. Horik was required to negotiate with the Franks and accept his uncle as co-ruler for part of this period. Groa and Ingebjorg are my inventions.

Skiringssal and its kaupang (trading port) was becoming a major center for trade at this time, as excavations of the site reveal. In its heyday, the port housed around one thousand people, engaged in trade and production of goods, like beads, glass, and weaving.

Álf—elf, male, often considered ancestors (plural: álfar)

Berserker—warriors said to have superhuman powers. Translates either as "bear shirt" or "bare shirt" (also berserk)

Bindrune—three or more runes drawn one over the other

Blót—sacrifice. i.e., Álfablót is sacrifice in honor of the elves, Dísablót is in honor of the dís

Bower—women's quarters, usually a separate building

Breeks—breeches

Brynja—chain-mail shirt

Dís—spirits of female ancestors (plural: dísir)

Distaff—a staff for holding unspun wool or linen fibers during the spinning process. About a meter long, usually made of wood or iron, with a bail to hold the wool. Historically associated with witchcraft.

Draugr—animated corpse

Fylgja—a guardian spirit, animal or female

Fóstra—a child's nurse (foster mother)

Flyting—a contest of insults

Galdr—spells spoken and sung

Gammelost—literally "old cheese"

Gungnir—Odin's spear

Hafvilla—lost at sea

Hamr—"skin"; the body

Hamingja—a person's luck or destiny, passed down in the family

Haugbui—mound-dwelling ghost

Haugr—mound

Hird—the warrior retinue of a noble person

Hnefatafl—also Tafl, a chess-like board game found in Viking graves

Holmgang—"isle-going"; a duel within boundaries, sometimes fought on small islets

Hudfat—sleeping bags made of sheepskin

Hugr—the soul, the mind

Húskarl—the elite household warriors of a nobleman (plural: húskarlar)

Jarl—earl, one step below a king

Jotun—giants, enemies of the gods. (plural: jotnar)

Jól—Yule midwinter feast honoring all the gods, but especially Odin

Karl—a free man, also "bonder"

Karvi—a small Viking longship

Kenning—a metaphorical expression in Old Norse poetry

Knarr—a merchant ship

Law-speaker—a learned man who knew the laws of the district by heart

Longfire—a long, narrow firepit that ran down the center of a hall

Nålebinding—an early form of knitting with a single needle

Odal land—inherited land

Ørlög—personal fate

Primstave—a flat piece of wood used as a calendar. The days of summer are carved on one side, winter on the reverse.

Runes—the Viking alphabet, said to have magical powers, also used in divination

Saeter—a summer dairy hut, usually in the mountains

Seax—long, single-edged fighting knife

Seidr—a trance to work magic

Shield-maiden—female warrior

Shield wall—a battle formation

Skáld—poet

Skagerrak—a body of water between Southeast Norway, Southwest Sweden, and Northern Denmark

Skerry—a small rocky islet

Skjaergarden—a rocky archipelago on the southern cape of Norway

Skyr—a dairy product similar to yogurt

Small beer—a beer with a low alcohol content, a common drink

Sverige, Svea—Sweden and Swedes

Swinehorn—a v-shaped battle formation

Thrall—slave

Ting, Allting—assembly at which legal matters are settled

Ulfhed—"wolf head"; another warrior like a berserker (plural: ulfhednar)

Valknut—"corpse knot," a symbol of Odin

Vardlokkur—a song to draw the spirits

Völva—a sorceress. Literally, "wand-bearer" (plural: völur)

Wergild—the value of a person's life, to be paid in wrongful death

Vaettr—a spirit of land and water, wight. (plural: vaettir)

Wootz—crucible steel manufactured in ancient India

IRISH TERMS

A chroi—my heart

A ghra—my love

A mhuirin—my darling

Ard Ri—High king

Ban na Sidhe—"banshee," a faery woman

Bard—the poet class of Irish intellectual society

Bratt—a wool wrap worn by both sexes

Brehon—a legal expert of the Irish intellectual class

Cashel—a fort with stone walls

Cenel—kindred

Cláirseach—An Irish harp with a body carved of wood and strings of brass

Crannog—an island fortress

Currach—a boat made of cowhide stretched over a framework of branches. Also Curragh

Druid—the priestly class of the Irish intellectual class

Dún—a stronghold

Filidh—the intellectual class of Irish society, predating Christianity, comprised of druids, bards, and brehons

Finn gaill—white foreigners (Norse)

Dubh gaill—dark foreigners (Danes)
Geantraí—the melody of merriment
Geis—being under a vow or curse taboo
Goiltai—the melody of sadness
Grianan—palace of the sun
Leine—a gown, worn by both men and women
Lochlainn—Norway
Ollave—the highest rank of bard (Irish: ollamh)
Rath—a fort with earthen walls
Sil—progeny
Sidhe—the faerie folk of Ireland, who dwell in the mounds and are said to be the ancient Tuatha Dé Danann
Souterrain—(French) underground rooms and passages used for escape and cold storage
Suantraí— music that will bring sleep over the listeners
Tuath—clan or tribe

CHARACTERS: NORWAY

Summer, AD 825

<u>Tromøy—an island off the east coast of Agder, Norway</u>

- Åsa, age 22, queen of Tromøy, daughter of the murdered King Harald Redbeard
- Stormrider, Åsa's peregrine falcon
- Gullfaxi, Åsa's horse
- *Ran's Lover*, Åsa's flagship
- Gudrød's Bane, Åsa's sword
- Brenna, Halfdan's nurse (fóstra)
- Olvir, head of Åsa's household guards
- Jarl Borg of Iveland, Åsa's military advisor
- Heid, a famous völva (sorceress), Åsa's mentor
- Vigdis, Heid's senior apprentice
- Other apprentices: Halla, Mor, Liv
- Cian, age 20, an Irish harper enslaved by King Horik
- Eyvind, a Svea trader, owner of *Far Traveler* and Åsa's lover, age 28
- Dagny, age 18, healer of *Far Traveler*'s crew

The Deceased

- Svartfaxi, Murchad's horse, killed in battle
- Harald Redbeard, King of East Agder, Norway, Åsa and Gyrd's father
- Gunnhild, his queen, Åsa and Gyrd's mother, a noblewoman of Lista
- Gyrd, their son, Åsa's brother
- Estrid, Åsa's ancestress, The Queen in the Mound

Vestfold

- Skiringssal, the Shining Hall of Vestfold, Norway
- Borre, another stronghold of Vestfold, north of Skiringssal
- Olaf, age 23, king of Vestfold, son of King Gudrød
- Sonja Eisteinsdottir, age 21, Olaf's wife
- Rognvald, their 3-year-old son
- Kalv, captain of Olaf's guard
- Halfdan the Black, Åsa's 6-year-old son
- Fylgja, Halfdan's blind wolf
- Ulf, blacksmith of Tromøy

The Deceased

- Gudrød, king of Vestfold, Olaf's father, formerly Åsa's husband
- Alfhild, Gudrød's first wife, Olaf's mother
- Halfdan the Mild, Gudrød's father—Olaf's grandfather
- Hrolf, Gudrød's natural son

Danes

- Horik, king of the Danes
- Rorik, deceased, one of Horik's four brothers
- Harald Klak, their uncle, brother of the murdered King Godefrid
- Groa, Horik's völva
- Ingebjorg Roriksdottir, age 17, Horik's niece

Others

- King Alfgeir, king of Vingulmark, Olaf's maternal grandfather
- Queen Gudrun—age 16, Alfgeir's queen
- Knut, a famous traveling skáld (poet and historian)
- Brother Behrt, also known as Brother Becc, Norse-born, raised in Ireland, formerly crew of *Raider Bride*, now resident at Solbakk

Gausel—a farming settlement in southwest Norway

- Ragnhild Solvisdottir, age 19, leader of Tromøy's shield-maidens, daughter of the deceased King Solvi of Solbakk
- Murchad mac Maele Duin, age 32, Ragnhild's husband, deposed king of Aileach of the Northern Ui Neill—Cenel nEoghain
- Herulf, their son, born April AD 825
- Einar, Thorgeir, Svein—warriors formerly of Solbakk, now sworn to Ragnhild
- Jofrid, headwoman of Gausel
- Thyra, Gausel's healer
- Helga, deceased, eldest of 5 sisters
- Unn, age 19, shield-maiden and healer, next eldest sister of Helga

- Ursa, age 18, Helga's younger sister, also a shield-maiden
- Tova, age 16, their younger sister
- Ylva, age 15, their younger sister

CHARACTERS: IRELAND

<u>Aileach</u>

- Niall mac Aeda, Murchad's cousin and foster brother, king of Aileach of the Northern Ui Neill—Cenel nEoghain
- Gormlaith, his queen, half-sister of the high king Conchobar
- Fiona, maidservant of Aileach
- Father Ferdia, priest of Ailcach
- Cerball, man-at-arms for Aileach
- Brunaidh, Ragnhild's pony
- Aenbarr, Murchad's horse

<u>Others</u>

- Aed, chieftain of Tullynavin
- Aine—Aed's wife
- Conchobar mac Donnchada, king of Tara, of the Southern Ui Neill, Murchad's rival, High King of Ireland

- Brother Brian, a hermit, last of the druids
- Ethne, Brian's companion, a tame deer
- Dunchad, Cian's uncle, chieftain of the Ard Ciannachta

The Deceased

- Cináed, Cian's elder brother
- Cumuscach, Cian's father, formerly chief of the Ard Ciannachta

Iona

- Blathmac, abbot of Iona
- Airtri, prior of Iona
- Colm Cille, saint of Ireland, founder of Iona (deceased ca AD 600)

Monastery of Daire Calgaich

- Abbot Ennae
- Brother Padraig, gatekeeper
- Brother Oengus

NORSE GODS AND HEROES

- Angrboda—a jotun, wife of Loki, mother of Hel, Fenrir, and Jörmandgandr
- Loki—a trickster jotun who becomes Odin's blood brother
- Hel—daughter of Loki and Angrboda, queen of the dead not killed in battle. She rules Helheim, also referred to as Hel.
- Fenrir—a giant wolf, son of Angrboda and Loki. He is bound by the magic fetter Gleipnir. He eats Odin at Ragnarok
- Jörmungandr—the Midgaard serpent, son of Angrboda and Loki. He and Thor kill each other at Ragnarok.
- Niflheim—cold and misty land of the dead, ruled by Hel
- Norn—(plural Nornir) three sisters who spin the lives of men and gods, also known as the Weird Sisters or three fates: Skuld (future), Verdandi (Present), Urdr (past)
- Ragnarok—twilight of the gods, end of the world

- Yggdrasil—"Odin's steed," the World Tree, by which Odin travels between the nine worlds
- Nidhogg—a serpent who gnaws at the roots of Yggdrasil. When he gnaws through, Ragnarok will occur

Asgaard—home of the Aesir gods

- Odin—lord of the Aesir gods, of many names
- Valhöll—Odin's hall—literally, "corpse hall"
- Einherjar—heroes slain in battle who come to Valhöll
- Gungnir—Odin's spear that marks an army as his
- Sleipnir—Odin's horse
- Baldr—Odin's son, most beautiful of gods
- Thor—Odin's son, god of thunder, preserver of mankind
- Mjölnir—Thor's hammer
- Tyr—one-handed god of war. Fenrir bit his hand off when the gods tried to fetter him.
- Freyja—originally of the Vanir gods. Goddess of love and magic. She gets first pick of the slain heroes for her hall Sessrúmnir. She owns a magic necklace, Brisingamen, and a falcon cloak.
- Freyr—Freyja's twin brother, fertility god of peace and plenty
- Idunn—goddess with the golden apples of youth
- Ran—goddess of the sea
- Njord—god of the sea, a Vanir hostage, father to Freyr & Freyja
- Skadi—a jotun shield-maiden
- Thjazi—Skadi's father, deceased
- Valkyrie—supernatural shield-maidens who choose who will live and who will die in battle. Half go to Freyja, the other half to Odin

IRISH GODS AND HEROES

- Tuatha Dé Danann—children of the goddess Danu; the Sidhe, or Fae
- Fomorians—a race of giants, enemies of the Tuatha Dé Danann
- The Dagda, father of the gods
- Uithne, the Dagda's magical harp
- Lugh of the Long Arm, sun god and god of craftsmen
- Ogma the Artificer, god of poetry and the Ogham script
- Manannán mac Lir, god of the sea

ACKNOWLEDGMENTS

I have so many people to thank in bringing this novel into being: My beloved mother who first introduced me to Åsa and the Viking world; my wonderful fellow writers at Kitsap Writers, each of whom contributed so very much and kept me going; and to critique partner DV Berkom. Thanks to my dear husband Brian who is always on my side and eager to read more, and beta readers Colleen Hogan-Taylor and Linda S., each of whom gave me priceless insights. I owe many thanks to editors Kahina Necaise and Sarah Dronfield. Any errors that exist in this book are entirely my own.

ABOUT THE AUTHOR

Like her Viking forebears, Johanna Wittenberg has sailed to the far reaches of the world. She lives on a fjord in the Pacific Northwest with her husband, whom she met on a ship bound for Antarctica.

Thank you for reading! If you enjoyed this book a review would be greatly appreciated.

If you would like updates of forthcoming titles in the Norsewomen Series, as well as blog posts on research into Viking history, visit www.JohannaWittenberg.com and join the mailing list to receive a free short story, *Mistress of Magic*, the sorceress Heid's origin story.

Join fellow author, K.S. Barton, and me on our podcast, Shieldmaidens: Women of the Norse World. Available on most platforms: https://linktr.ee/womenofthenorseworld or on YouTube: https://www.youtube.com/@WomenoftheNorseWorldPodcast

Follow me on Facebook

facebook.com/TheNorseQueen

amazon.com/stores/author/B084H88R6J

threads.net/norsewomen5

instagram.com/norsewomen5

www.ingramcontent.com/pod-product-compliance
Lightning Source LLC
Chambersburg PA
CBHW030927210726
48290CB00007B/2094